Aren't you happy for me?

and other stories

BOOKS BY RICHARD BAUSCH

Novels

Real Presence

Take Me Back

The Last Good Time

Mr. Field's Daughter

Violence

Rebel Powers

Short Stories

Spirits, And Other Stories

The Fireman's Wife, And Other Stories

Rare & Endangered Species:
A Novella & Stories

Aren't you happy for me?

and other stories

RICHARD BAUSCH

with an introduction by Richard Ford

MACMILLAN

Spirits first published 1987 by The Linden Press/Simon & Schuster
The Fireman's Wife first published 1990 by The Linden Press/Simon & Schuster
Rare & Endangered Species first published 1994 by Houghton Mifflin Company

This collection first published in this revised edition 1995 by Macmillan
an imprint of Macmillan General Books
Cavaye Place London SW10 9PG
and Basingstoke

Associated companies throughout the world

ISBN 0-333-64028-4

1 3 5 7 9 8 6 4 2

A CIP catalogue record for this book is available from
the British Library

Typeset by CentraCet Limited, Cambridge
Printed by Mackays of Chatham plc, Kent

Like all of them, for Karen

Contents

Introduction
by Richard Ford

"To think I believed you were charming. It turns out you're just a writer."

from "Spirits," by Richard Bausch

I've often mused over why certain writers get "picked up" by another country's readers and critics and given a life, while other writers either don't or experience hard times finding an audience abroad. It's a hollow chestnut of literary history, of course (one we trust at our peril), that the best writers in any age are the ones brought along, while the less great are just naturally left back. Palpable greatness *may* be a cause of endurance. But it may also simply be luck, or the intervention of a patron or the timely compulsiveness of a scholar in search of a thesis that ultimately beckons a writer—Melville, for instance, gone down to obscurity—into the canon, moves him and his work (some of it great, some of it decidedly not) from obscurity to literary sovereignty.

Where "traveling" from one contemporary reading culture to another is concerned, I have fairly well decided luck *always* plays a large part. Though so, too, must the host country's appetite for the other country's literature. Publishers and their sales projections and computer models are the sensors for this appetite, so that every generation or so a "need" is felt (or invented), and a slot opened, letting in a few new, say, American books to, say, the British bookshelves. Then quick, the slot closes, the lion's fed, and local readers go back to being interested in books by local authors.

Talent and achievement, of course, do count. Raymond Carver became a sensation with British readers because he was a greatly gifted writer, and no one had seen his like. And yet Robert Stone, one of America's most prodigiously talented and fully realized novelists, has managed only a fraction of Carver's readers. Indeed, from time to time in his distinguished thirty-year writing life, his books have even been out of print in the UK. It's the reverse of the "Jerry Lewis in France" phenomenon.

The cultural consequences of these selective oversights, errors, arbiterings are of course profound when it is excellent writers who are ignored or under-noticed. One could hardly care less if one more swarthy lawyer-novelist gets stopped at the border. But it means something if English readers see America—its moral nature, its underbelly and over-soul— through Ray Carver's eyes and words, but not Bob Stone's. Something important is lost.

Don't we then simply wonder: who else is back there writing at a high level, needing to be read, but not in view? Are Klíma and Hrabal and Kundera the only Czechs? Peter Handke the best Austrian since the war?

The American writer Richard Bausch is long overdue for British readers. Though it may be that the very soft-spoken, ruminative, subtly serious character of his stories has kept his light shaded until now—fifteen years after the flowering of the putative American short story renaissance, when Dirty Realists were riding imaginary Harleys all over Britain, gassing up at every Waterstones. At age forty-nine, Bausch has published six novels and three books of masterful stories, many of which have been anthologized, which in America means that they're read in universities and "taught" in graduate writing programs (those queer institutions Europeans and some right-wing book reviewers find so galling), yet which in turn means his stories have been taken up into our contemporary reading culture.

Introduction

Elizabeth Hardwick once wrote that it's one thing to make a living as a writer, but quite another thing to make a difference. Bausch's stories have begun making a difference in America.

In most ways stylistic, these are stories in the main stream of American realism, a stream connecting Henry James to Sherwood Anderson, Hemingway to Cheever, Eudora Welty and Jean Stafford to Carver—all of them connecting back to that old Midwesterner, Chekhov: stories that achieve their importance by supposing life-as-lived to be both fundamental and final, and that a writer using seemingly familiar but precise language can both discover and articulate essential qualities of human existence not previously recognized, while shaping narrative forms that, in their felicities, offer consolations should those very essential qualities prove somehow disturbing or discouraging.

For Bausch, in these fourteen stories selected here to form a unity, life-as-lived is indeed disturbing and disturbed. In most, the traditional family circle (Bausch's mainstay subject) has been broken by altogether traditional misfortune and bad judgment—death, divorce, boozing, wenching, free-floating unhappiness of an uncertain origin. Yet family members keep trying to fix it back, often erecting shakier, sometimes absurd replacement structures that either don't work or work much worse. Though in their failure they provide Bausch the occasion for important, provoking human drama, and us with opportunities to feel the human heart beat longingly.

In these new, unwieldy "extended" families, fresh—often bizarre—interdependencies arise free-form, break down, then disappear in short order. Unhappy adult sisters briefly consider taking nun-like refuge together for a life alone; anxious children obsess over the priesthood, while scourging their bewildered parents; a young daughter marries a teacher old enough to be her grandfather; a nostalgic, overweight boy in his twenties (not apparently gay) schemes a trip around the world with his favorite girl—mom. And there is new family lingo: love becomes "placate"; mutuality translates into "caught in the middle"; refuge signifies merely context; tenderness is nothing more than patience; understanding means *hearing*—as, "I hear you." These, of course, are vital and familiar formulations to Americans, riding usually just outside our gaze. Pleasure comes from having them moved to center-view. Bausch, the master of these contrived alliances, makes little of their comic instability, and yet by forbearing manages to make clear what's more to the point: their heartfelt earnestness, their origins in despair and hope and in the need we all feel for an existence we can think of as normal.

If I'm making it seem that these are dark stories, it's because they are. Comic in their underpinnings, but dark and very, very good. People die in them, and it isn't funny. Hippy chicks with guns stalk innocent motorists into the midnight desert and do bad things. Marriages turn grotesque. People lose their jobs, suffer spiritual dryness, then don't sober up for years. One of the few intact, semi-functioning wage-earners is a man who dresses like a clown for kids' parties, only to get schnockered, then angry, then driven off before he can make anybody happy. A wild world is just outside the frame of every Bausch story here—murder, foreboding, uncharted darkness—and all the characters sense it and wish they could help. It is, finally, the wild world that swarms us when we lose the knack of sympathizing with each other and even with ourselves and grow bemused by an enervation that passes for calm.

What causes us to lose sympathy? To lose passion? Bausch's characters speculate about it nonstop. Though Bausch is too smart to offer patent diagnoses; as though were the reasons so easily come by much less than a complex, finely tuned short story would suffice to address them.

So, it's not "the Eighties," not the decline in the church in our moral lives; not modernity. It's not the lost American paradise or the Kennedy myth going down to infamy. It's not secular humanism. It's not sex. It's not one thing that's wrong. And these stories, as a way of being curative rather than merely cautionary, mean to say that what's wrong with us (us Americans, that is) is a subject for moral meditation not problem-solving or psychoanalysis or a twelve-step program.

"Now, driving through the rainy night, he glances over at her and sees that she's simply staring out the passenger window, her hands open in her lap . . ." Here is a young couple in the throes of an argument neither can win or forgive the other for:

> He wants to be fair. He reminds himself that she's never been the sort of person who feels comfortable—or with whom one feels comfortable—at a party: something takes hold of her; she becomes objective and heavily intellectual, sees everyone as species, somehow, everything as behavior. A room full of people laughing and having a good innocent time is nevertheless a manifestation of some kind of pecking order to her: such a gathering means nothing more than a series of meaningful body languages and gestures, nothing more than the forms of competition, and, as she has told him on more than one occasion, she refuses to allow herself to be drawn in; she will not play social games. He remembers now that in their college days he considered this attitude of hers to be an element of her sharp intelligence, her wit. He had once considered that the two of them were above the winds of fashion, intellectual and otherwise; he had once been proud of this quirk of hers.
>
> It's all more complicated than that now, of course.

What both drives Richard Bausch's stories and gives them consequence is this: they are vivid moral inquiries, pleasing us with the fineness of their notice, their alarming intuition and their unstinting but never cold-eyed seriousness about human beings. No mere catalog of grotesques or typology of American woes, they are, rather, manifestations of lives lived less than perfectly that remind us to puzzle out our own more vigorously, or face bad consequences. Again and again their characters seek to understand, as if understanding (that old rationalist ghost haunting American literature) was the first step to betterment and consolation; or at the very least as if the discipline of the inquiry itself was superior to deception and nostalgia. "Life must be lived in the uncertainty of freedom of choice," a psychologist glibly advises a character in search of surcease. And yet, glib or not, isn't it just true?

If I have not made myself clear up to now, what I think you'll find in these stories is a deep seam of moral seriousness without a drop of moral arrogance, a profound instinct for humankind and full sympathy for the human condition. Richard Bausch has been biding his time, staying to his work, filling out a grave vision distinctly his own. When you read these stories, you'll see that his patience has been richly rewarded.

Aren't you happy
for me?

"*William Coombs*, with two o's," Melanie Ballinger told her father over long distance. "Pronounced just like the thing you comb your hair with. Say it."

Ballinger repeated the name.

"Say the whole name."

"I've got it, sweetheart. Why am I saying it?"

"Dad, I'm bringing him home with me. We're getting *married*."

For a moment, he couldn't speak.

"Dad? Did you hear me?"

"I'm here," he said.

"Well?"

Again, he couldn't say anything.

"Dad?"

"Yes," he said. "That's—that's some news."

"That's all you can say?"

"Well, I mean—Melanie—this is sort of quick, isn't it?" he said.

"Not that quick. How long did you and Mom wait?"

"I don't remember. Are you measuring yourself by that?"

"You waited six months, and you do too remember. And this is five months. And we're not measuring anything. William and I have known each other longer than five months, but we've been together—you know, as a couple—five months. And I'm almost twenty-three, which is two years older than Mom was. And don't tell me it was different when *you* guys did it."

"No," he heard himself say. "It's pretty much the same, I imagine."

"Well?" she said.

"Well," Ballinger said. "I'm—I'm very happy for you."

"You don't sound happy."

"I'm happy. I can't wait to meet him."

"Really? Promise? You're not just saying that?"

"It's good news, darling. I mean I'm surprised, of course. It'll take a little getting used to. The—the suddenness of it and everything. I mean, your mother and I didn't even know you were seeing anyone. But no, I'm—I'm glad. I can't wait to meet the young man."

"Well, and now there's something *else* you have to know."

"I'm ready," John Ballinger said. He was standing in the kitchen of the house she hadn't seen yet, and outside the window his wife, Mary, was weeding in the garden, wearing a red scarf and a white muslin blouse and jeans, looking young—looking, even, happy, though for a long while there had been between them, in fact, very little happiness.

"Well, this one's kind of hard," his daughter said over the thousand miles of wire. "Maybe we should talk about it later."

"No, I'm sure I can take it whatever it is," he said.

The truth was that he had news of his own to tell. Almost a week ago, he and Mary had agreed on a separation. Some time for them both to sort things out. They had decided not to say anything about it to Melanie until she arrived. But now Melanie had said that she was bringing someone with her.

She was hemming and hawing on the other end of the line: "I don't know, see, Daddy, I—God. I can't find the way to say it, really."

He waited. She was in Chicago, where they had sent her to school more than four years ago, and where after her graduation she had stayed, having landed a job with an independent newspaper in the city. In March, Ballinger and Mary had moved to this small house in the middle of Charlottesville, hoping that a change of scene might help things. It hadn't; they were falling apart after all these years.

2

"Dad," Melanie said, sounding helpless.

"Honey, I'm listening."

"Okay, look," she said. "Will you promise you won't react?"

"How can I promise a thing like that, Melanie?"

"You're going to react, then. I wish you could just promise me you wouldn't."

"Darling," he said, "I've got something to tell you, too. Promise me *you* won't react."

She said "Promise" in that way the young have of being absolutely certain what their feelings will be in some future circumstance.

"So," he said. "Now, tell me whatever it is." And a thought struck through him like a shock. "Melanie, you're not—you're not pregnant, are you?"

She said, "How did you *know*?"

He felt something sharp move under his heart. "Oh, Lord. Seriously?"

"Jeez," she said. "Wow. That's really amazing."

"You're—*pregnant*."

"Right. My God. You're positively clairvoyant, Dad."

"I really don't think it's a matter of any clairvoyance, Melanie, from the way you were talking. Are you—is it sure?"

"Of course it's sure. But—well, that isn't the really hard thing. Maybe I should just wait."

"Wait," he said. "Wait for what?"

"Until you get used to everything else."

He said nothing. She was fretting on the other end, sighing and starting to speak and then stopping herself.

"I don't know," she said finally, and abruptly he thought she was talking to someone in the room with her."

"Honey, do you want me to put your mother on?"

"No, Daddy. I wanted to talk to you about this first. I think we should get this over with."

"Get this over with? Melanie, what're we talking about here? Maybe I should put your mother on." He thought he might try a joke. "After all," he added, "I've never been pregnant."

3

"It's not about being pregnant. You *guessed* that."

He held the phone tight against his ear. Through the window, he saw his wife stand and stretch, massaging the small of her back with one gloved hand. *Oh, Mary.*

"Are you ready?" his daughter said.

"Wait," he said. "Wait a minute. Should I be sitting down? I'm sitting down." He pulled a chair from the table and settled into it. He could hear her breathing on the other end of the line, or perhaps it was the static wind he so often heard when talking on these new phones. "Okay," he said, feeling his throat begin to close. "Tell me."

"William's somewhat older than I am," she said. "There." She sounded as though she might hyperventilate.

He left a pause. "That's it?"

"Well, it's how much."

"Okay."

She seemed to be trying to collect herself. She breathed, paused. "This is even tougher than I thought it was going to be."

"You mean you're going to tell me something harder than the fact that you're pregnant?"

She was silent.

"Melanie?"

"I didn't expect you to be this way about it," she said.

"Honey, please just tell me the rest of it."

"Well, what did you mean by that, anyway?"

"Melanie, *you said* this would be hard."

Silence.

"Tell me, sweetie. Please?"

"I'm going to." She took a breath. "Dad, William's sixty—he's—he's sixty—sixty-three years old."

Ballinger stood. Out in the garden his wife had got to her knees again, pulling crabgrass out of the bed of tulips. It was a sunny near-twilight, and all along the shady street people were working in their little orderly spaces of grass and flowers.

"Did you hear me, Daddy? It's perfectly all right, too,

4

because he's really a *young* sixty-three, and *very* strong and healthy, and look at George Burns."

"George Burns," Ballinger said. "George—George Burns? Melanie, I don't understand."

"Come on, Daddy, stop it."

"No, what're you telling me?" His mind was blank.

"I said William is sixty-three."

"William who?"

"Dad. My fiancé."

"Wait, Melanie. You're saying your fiancé, the man you're going to marry, *he's* sixty-three?"

"A young sixty-three," she said.

"Melanie. Sixty-three?"

"Dad?"

"You didn't say six feet three?"

She was silent.

"Melanie?"

"Yes."

"Honey, this is a joke, right? You're playing a joke on me."

"It is not a—it's not that. God," she said. "I don't believe this."

"You don't believe—" he began. "You don't believe—"

"Dad," she said. "I told you—" Again, she seemed to be talking to someone else in the room with her. Her voice trailed off.

"Melanie," he said. "Talk into the phone."

"I know it's hard," she said. "I know it's asking you to take a lot in."

"Well, no," Ballinger said, feeling something shift inside, a quickening in his blood. "It's—it's a little more than that, Melanie, isn't it? I mean it's not a weather report, for God's sake."

"I should've known," she said.

"Forgive me for it," he said, "but I have to ask you something."

"It's all right, Daddy," she said as though reciting it for him.

5

"I know what I'm doing. I'm not really rushing into anything—"

He interrupted her. "Well, good God, somebody rushed into something, right?"

"Daddy."

"Is that what you call him? No, *I'm* Daddy. You have to call him *Grand*daddy."

"That is *not* funny," she said.

"I wasn't being funny, Melanie. And anyway, that wasn't my question." He took a breath. "Please forgive this, but I have to know."

"There's nothing you really *have* to know, Daddy. I'm an adult. I'm telling you out of family courtesy."

"I understand that. Family courtesy exactly. Exactly, Melanie, that's a good phrase. Would you please tell me, out of family courtesy, if the baby is his."

"Yes." Her voice was small now, coming from a long way off.

"I'm sorry for the question, but I have to put all this together. I mean you're asking me to take in a whole lot here, you know?"

"I said I understood how you feel."

"I don't think so. I don't think you quite understand how I feel."

"All right," she said. "I don't understand how you feel. But I think I knew how you'd react."

For a few seconds, there was just the low, sea sound of long distance.

"Melanie, have you done any of the math on this?"

"I should've bet money," she said in the tone of a person who has been proven right about something.

"Well, but Jesus," Ballinger said. "I mean he's older than *I* am, kid. He's—he's a *lot* older than I am." The number of years seemed to dawn on him as he spoke; it filled him with a strange, heart-shaking heat. "Honey, nineteen years. When he was my age, I was only two years older than you are now."

6

"I don't see what that has to do with anything," she said.

"Melanie, I'll be forty-five *all the way* in December. I'm a *young* forty-four."

"I know when your birthday is, Dad."

"Well, good God, this guy's nineteen years older than your own father."

She said, "I've grasped the numbers. Maybe you should go ahead and put Mom on."

"Melanie, you couldn't pick somebody a little closer to my age? Some snot-nosed forty-year-old?"

"Stop it," she said. "Please, Daddy. I know what I'm doing."

"Do you know how old he's going to be when your baby is ten? Do you? Have you given that any thought at all?"

She was silent.

He said, "How many children are you hoping to have?"

"I'm not thinking about that. Any of that. This is now, and I don't care about anything else."

He sat down in his kitchen and tried to think of something else to say. Outside the window, his wife, with no notion of what she was about to be hit with, looked through the patterns of shade in the blinds and, seeing him, waved. It was friendly, and even so, all their difficulty was in it, too. Ballinger waved back. "Melanie," he said, "do you mind telling me just where you happened to meet William? I mean how do you meet a person forty years older than you are. What, was there a senior citizen student mixer at the college?"

"Stop it, Daddy."

"No, I really want to know. If I'd just picked this up and read it in the newspaper, I think I'd want to know. I'd probably call the newspaper and see what I could find out."

"Put Mom on," she said.

"Just tell me how you met. You can do that, can't you?"

"Jesus Christ," she said, then paused.

Ballinger waited.

"He's a teacher, like you and Mom, only college. He was my literature teacher. He's a professor of literature. He knows

7

everything that was ever written, and he's the most brilliant man I've ever known. You have no idea how fascinating it is to talk with him."

"Yes, and I guess you understand that over the years that's what you're going to be doing a *lot* of, with him, Melanie. A lot of talking."

"I am carrying the proof that disproves *you*," she said.

He couldn't resist saying, "Did *he* teach you to talk like that?"

"I'm gonna hang up."

"You promised you'd listen to something *I* had to tell *you*."

"Okay," she said crisply. "I'm listening."

He could imagine her tapping the toe of one foot on the floor: the impatience of someone awaiting an explanation. He thought a moment. "He's a professor?"

"That's not what you wanted to tell me."

"But you said he's a professor."

"Yes, I said that."

"Don't be mad at me, Melanie. Give me a few minutes to get used to the idea. Jesus. Is he a professor emeritus?"

"If that means distinguished, yes. But I know what you're—"

"No, Melanie. It means *retired*. You went to college."

She said nothing.

"I'm sorry. But for God's sake, it's a legitimate question."

"It's a stupid, mean-spirited thing to ask." He could tell from her voice that she was fighting back tears.

"Is he there with you now?"

"Yes," she said, sniffling.

"Oh, Jesus Christ."

"Daddy, why are you being this way?"

"Do you think maybe we could've had this talk alone? What's he, listening on the other line?"

"No."

"Well, thank God for that."

8

"I'm going to hang up now."

"No, please don't hang up. Please let's just be calm and talk about this. We have some things to talk about here."

She sniffled, blew her nose. Someone held the phone for her. There was a muffled something in the line, and then she was there again. "Go ahead," she said.

"Is he still in the room with you?"

"Yes." Her voice was defiant.

"Where?"

"Oh, for God's sake," she said.

"I'm sorry, I feel the need to know. Is he sitting down?"

"I *want* him here, Daddy. We both want to be here," she said.

"And he wants to marry you."

"Yes," she said impatiently.

"Do you think I could talk to him?"

She said something he couldn't hear, and then there were several seconds of some sort of discussion, in whispers. Finally she said, "Do you promise not to yell at him?"

"Melanie, he wants me to promise not to *yell* at him?"

"Will you promise?"

"Good God, who *is* this guy?"

"Promise," she said. "Or I'll hang up."

"All right. I promise. I promise not to yell at him."

There was another small scuffing sound, and a man's voice came through the line. "Hello, sir." It was, as far as Ballinger could tell, an ordinary voice, slightly lower than baritone. He thought of cigarettes. "I realize this is a difficult—"

"Do you smoke?" Ballinger interrupted him.

"No, sir."

"Okay. Go on."

"Well, I want you to know I understand how you feel."

"Melanie says she does, too," Ballinger said. "I mean I'm certain you both *think* you do."

"It was my idea that Melanie call you about this."

"Oh, really. That speaks well of you. You probably knew I'd

9

find this a little difficult to absorb and that's why you waited until Melanie was pregnant, for Christ's sake."

The other man gave forth a small sigh of exasperation.

"So you're a professor of literature."

"Yes, sir."

"Oh, you needn't 'sir' me. After all, I mean I *am* the goddam kid here."

"There's no need for sarcasm, sir."

"Oh, I wasn't being sarcastic. That was a literal statement of this situation that obtains right here as we're speaking. And, really, Mr . . . It's Coombs, right?"

"Yes, sir."

"Coombs, like the thing you comb your hair with."

The other man was quiet.

"Just how long do you think it'll take me to get used to this? You think you might get into your seventies before I get used to this? And how long do you think it'll take my wife who's twenty-one years younger than you are to get used to this?"

Silence.

"You're too old for my *wife,* for Christ's sake."

Nothing.

"What's your first name again?"

The other man spoke through another sigh. "Perhaps we should just ring off."

"Ring off. Jesus. Ring off? Did you actually say 'ring off'? What're you, a goddam *Limey* or something?"

"I am an American. I fought in Korea."

"Not World War Two?"

The other man did not answer.

"How many other marriages have you had?" Ballinger asked him.

"That's a valid question. I'm glad you—"

"Thank you for the scholarly observation, *sir.* But I'm not sitting in a class. How many did you say?"

"If you'd give me a chance, I'd tell you."

Ballinger said nothing.

"Two, sir. I've had two marriages."

"Divorces?"

"I have been widowed twice."

"And—oh, I get it. You're trying to make sure that never happens to you again."

"This is not going well at all, and I'm afraid I—I—" The other man stammered, then stopped.

"How did you expect it to go?" Ballinger demanded.

"Cruelty is not what I'd expected. I'll tell you that."

"You thought I'd be glad my daughter is going to be getting social security before I do."

The other was silent.

"Do you have any other children?" Ballinger asked.

"Yes, I happen to have three." There was a stiffness, an over-weening tone, in the voice now.

"And how old are they, if I might ask."

"Yes, you may."

Ballinger waited. His wife walked in from outside, carrying some cuttings. She poured water in a glass vase and stood at the counter arranging the flowers, her back to him. The other man had stopped talking. "I'm sorry," Ballinger said. "My wife just walked in here and I didn't catch what you said. Could you just tell me if any of them are anywhere near my daughter's age?"

"I told you, my youngest boy is thirty-eight."

"And you realize that if *he* wanted to marry my daughter I'd be upset, the age difference there being what it is." Ballinger's wife moved to his side, drying her hands on a paper towel, her face full of puzzlement and worry.

"I told you, Mr. Ballinger, that I understood how you feel. The point is, we have a pregnant woman here and we both love her."

"No," Ballinger said. "That's not the point. The point is that you, sir, are not much more than a goddam statutory rapist. That's the point." His wife took his shoulder. He looked at her and shook his head.

11

"What?" she whispered. "Is Melanie all right?"

"Well, this isn't accomplishing anything," the voice on the other end of the line was saying.

"Just a minute," Ballinger said. "Let me ask you something else. Really now. What's the policy at that goddam university concerning teachers screwing their students?"

"Oh, my God," his wife said as the voice on the line huffed and seemed to gargle.

"I'm serious," Ballinger said.

"Melanie was not my student when we became involved."

"Is that what you call it? Involved?"

"Let me talk to Melanie," Ballinger's wife said.

"Listen," he told her. "Be quiet."

Melanie was back on the line. "Daddy? Daddy?"

"I'm here," Ballinger said, holding the phone from his wife's attempt to take it from him.

"Daddy, we're getting married and there's nothing you can do about it. Do you understand?"

"Melanie," he said, and it seemed that from somewhere far inside himself he heard that he had begun shouting at her. "Jee-zus good Christ. Your fiancé was almost *my* age *now* the day you were *born*. What the hell, kid. Are you crazy? Are you out of your mind?"

His wife was actually pushing against him to take the phone, and so he gave it to her. And stood there while she tried to talk.

"Melanie," she said. "Honey, listen—"

"Hang up," Ballinger said. "Christ. Hang it up."

"Please. Will you go in the other room and let me talk to her?"

"Tell her I've got friends. All these nice men in their forties. She can marry any one of my friends—they're babies. Forties—cradle fodder. Jesus, any one of them. Tell her."

"Jack, stop it." Then she put the phone against her chest. "Did you tell her anything about us?"

He paused. "That—no."

She turned from him. "Melanie, honey. What is this? Tell me, please."

He left her there, walked through the living room to the hall and back around to the kitchen. He was all nervous energy, crazy with it, pacing. Mary stood very still, listening, nodding slightly, holding the phone tight with both hands, her shoulders hunched as if she were out in cold weather.

"Mary," he said.

Nothing.

He went into their bedroom and closed the door. The light coming through the windows was soft gold, and the room was deepening with shadows. He moved to the bed and sat down, and in a moment he noticed that he had begun a low sort of murmuring. He took a breath and tried to be still. From the other room, his wife's voice came to him. "Yes, I quite agree with you. But I'm just unable to put this . . ."

The voice trailed off. He waited. A few minutes later, she came to the door and knocked on it lightly, then opened it and looked in.

"What," he said.

"They're serious." She stood there in the doorway.

"Come here," he said.

She stepped to his side and eased herself down, and he moved to accommodate her. He put his arm around her, and then, because it was awkward, clearly an embarrassment to her, took it away. Neither of them could speak for a time. Everything they had been through during the course of deciding about each other seemed concentrated now. Ballinger breathed his wife's presence, the odor of earth and flowers, the outdoors.

"God," she said. "I'm positively numb. I don't know what to think."

"Let's have another baby," he said suddenly. "Melanie's baby will need a younger aunt or uncle."

Mary sighed a little forlorn laugh, then was silent.

"Did you tell her about us?" he asked.

13

"No," she said. "I didn't get the chance. And I don't know that I could have."

"I don't suppose it's going to matter much to her."

"Oh, don't say that. You can't mean that."

The telephone on the bedstand rang, and startled them both. He reached for it, held the handset toward her.

"Hello," she said. Then: "Oh. Hi. Yes, well, here." She gave it back to him.

"Hello," he said.

Melanie's voice, tearful and angry: "You had something you said you had to tell *me*." She sobbed, then coughed. "Well?"

"It was nothing, honey. I don't even remember what it was."

"Well, I want you to know I would've been better than you were, Daddy, no matter how hard it was. I would've kept myself from reacting."

"Yes," he said. "I'm sure you would have."

"I'm going to hang up. And I guess I'll let you know later if we're coming at all. If it wasn't for Mom, we wouldn't be."

"We'll talk," he told her. "We'll work on it. Honey, you both have to give us a little time."

"There's nothing to work on as far as William and I are concerned."

"Of course there are things to work on. Every marriage—" His voice had caught. He took a breath. "In every marriage there are things to work on."

"I know what I know," she said.

"Well," said Ballinger. "That's—that's as it should be at your age, darling."

"Goodbye," she said. "I can't say any more."

"I understand," Ballinger said. When the line clicked, he held the handset in his lap for a moment. Mary was sitting there at his side, perfectly still.

"Well," he said. "I couldn't tell her." He put the handset back in its cradle. "God. A sixty-three-year-old son-in-law."

"It's happened before." She put her hand on his shoulder, then took it away. "I'm so frightened for her. But she says it's what she wants."

"Hell, Mary. You know what this is. The son of a bitch was her goddam teacher."

"Listen to you—what are you saying about her? Listen to what you're saying about her. That's our daughter you're talking about. You might at least try to give her the credit of assuming that she's aware of what she's doing."

They said nothing for a few moments.

"Who knows," Ballinger's wife said. "Maybe they'll be happy for a time."

He'd heard the note of sorrow in her voice, and thought he knew what she was thinking; then he was certain that he knew. He sat there remembering, like Mary, their early happiness, that ease and simplicity, and briefly he was in another house, other rooms, and he saw the toddler that Melanie had been, trailing through slanting light in a brown hallway, draped in gowns she had fashioned from her mother's clothes. He did not know why that particular image should have come to him out of the flow of years, but for a fierce minute it was uncannily near him in the breathing silence; it went over him like a palpable something on his skin, then was gone. The ache which remained stopped him for a moment. He looked at his wife, but she had averted her eyes, her hands running absently over the faded denim cloth of her lap. Finally she stood. "Well," she sighed, going away. "Work to do."

"Mary?" he said, low; but she hadn't heard him. She was already out of the doorway and into the hall, moving toward the kitchen. He reached over and turned the lamp on by the bed, and then lay down. It was so quiet here. Dark was coming to the windows. On the wall there were pictures; shadows, shapes, silently clamoring for his gaze. He shut his eyes, listened to the small sounds she made in the kitchen, arranging her flowers, running the tap. *Mary*, he had said. But he could not imagine what he might have found to say if his voice had reached her.

Tandolfo the Great

"*Tandolfo,*" he says to his own image in the mirror over the bathroom sink. "She loves you not, oh, she doesn't, you poor fool."

He's put the makeup on, packed the bag of tricks—including the rabbit, that he calls Chi-Chi, and the bird, the attention getter, that he calls Witch. He's to do a birthday party for some five-year-old on the other side of the river. A crowd of babies, and the adults waiting around for him to screw up—this is going to be one of those tough ones.

He has fortified himself, and he feels ready. He isn't particularly worried about it. But there's a little something else he has to do first. Something in the order of the embarrassingly ridiculous: he has to make a delivery.

This morning at the local bakery he picked up a big pink wedding cake, with its six tiers and scalloped edges and its miniature bride and groom on top. He'd ordered it on his own; he'd taken the initiative, planning to offer it to a young woman he worked with. He managed somehow to set the thing on the back seat of the car, and when he got home he found a note from her announcing, excited and happy, that she's engaged. The man she'd had such difficulty with has had a change of heart; he wants to get married after all. She's going off to Houston to live. She loves her dear old Tandolfo with a big kiss and a hug always, and she knows he'll have every happiness. She's so thankful for his friendship. Her magic man. Her sweet clown. She actually drove over here and, finding him gone, left the note for him, folded under the door knocker—her notepaper with the tangle of flowers at the top. She wants him to call her, come by as soon as he can, to help celebrate. *Please,* she says. *I want to give you a big hug.* He read

16

this and then walked out to stand on the sidewalk and look at the cake in its place on the back seat of the car.

"Good God," he said.

He'd thought he would put the clown outfit on, deliver the cake in person, an elaborate proposal to a girl he's never even kissed. He's a little unbalanced, and he knows it. Over the months of their working together at Bailey & Brecht department store, he's built up tremendous feelings of loyalty and yearning towards her. He thought she felt it, too. He interpreted gestures—her hand lingering on his shoulder when he made her laugh; her endearments tinged as they seemed to be with a kind of sadness, as if she were afraid of what the world might do to someone so romantic.

"You sweet clown," she said. And she said it a lot. She talked to him about her ongoing sorrows, the guy she'd been in love with who kept waffling about getting married. He wanted no commitments. Tandolfo, a.k.a. Rodney Wilbury, told her that he hated men who weren't willing to run the risks of love. Why, he personally was the type who'd always believed in marriage and children, lifelong commitments. He had caused difficulties for himself, and life was a disappointment so far, but he believed in falling in love and starting a family. She didn't hear him. It all went right through her, like white noise on the radio. For weeks he had come around to visit her, had invited her to watch him perform. She confided in him, and he thought of movies where the friend sticks around and is a good listener, and eventually gets the girl. They fall in love. He put his hope in that. He was optimistic; he'd ordered and bought the cake. Apparently the whole time, all through the listening and being noble with her, she thought of it as nothing more than friendship, accepting it from him because she was accustomed to being offered friendship.

Now he leans close to the mirror to look at his own eyes through the makeup. They look clear enough. "Loves you absolutely not. You must be crazy. You must be the Great Tandolfo."

Yes.

Twenty-six years old, out-of-luck Tandolfo. In love. With a great oversized cake in the back seat of his car. It's Sunday, a cool April day. He's a little inebriated. That's the word he prefers. It's polite; it suggests something faintly silly. Nothing could be sillier than to be dressed like this in broad daylight and to go driving across the bridge into Virginia to put on a magic show. Nothing could be sillier than to have spent all that money on a completely useless purchase—a cake six tiers high. Maybe fifteen pounds of sugar.

When he has made his last inspection of the clown face in the mirror, and checked the bag of tricks and props, he goes to his front door and looks through the screen at the architectural shadow of the cake in the back seat. The inside of the car will smell like icing for days. He'll have to keep the windows open even if it rains; he'll go to work smelling like confectionery delights. The whole thing makes him laugh. A wedding cake. He steps out of the house and makes his way in the late afternoon sun down the sidewalk to the car. As if they have been waiting for him, three boys come skating down from the top of the hill. He has the feeling that if he tried to sneak out like this at two in the morning, someone would come by and see him anyway. "Hey, Rodney," one boy says. "I mean, Tandolfo."

Tandolfo recognizes him. A neighborhood boy, a tough. Just the kind to make trouble, just the kind with no sensitivity to the suffering of others. "Leave me alone or I'll turn you into spaghetti," he says.

"Hey guys, it's Tandolfo the Great." The boy's hair is a bright blond color, and you can see through it to his scalp.

"Scram," Tandolfo says. "Really?"

"Aw, what's your hurry, man?"

"I've just set off a nuclear device," Tandolfo says with grave seriousness. "It's on a timer. Poof."

"Do a trick for us," the blond one says. "Where's that scurvy rabbit of yours?"

"I gave it the week off." Someone, last winter, poisoned the first Chi-Chi. He keeps the cage indoors now. "I'm in a hurry. No rabbit to help with the driving."

But they're interested in the cake now. "Hey, what's that in your car. Jesus, is that real?"

"Just stay back." Tandolfo gets his cases into the trunk and hurries to the driver's side door. The three boys are peering into the back seat.

"Hey man, a cake. Can we have a piece of it?"

"Back off," Tandolfo says.

The blond-haired one says, "Come on, Tandolfo."

"Hey, Tandolfo, I saw some guys looking for you, man. They said you owed them money."

He gets in, ignoring them, and starts the car.

"Sucker," one of them says.

"Hey man, who's the cake for?"

He drives away, thinks of himself leaving them in a cloud of exhaust. Riding through the green shade, he glances in the rear-view mirror and sees the clown face, the painted smile. It makes him want to laugh. He tells himself he's his own cliché—a clown with a broken heart. Looming behind him is the cake, like a passenger in the back seat. The people in the cake store had offered it to him in a box; he had made them give it to him like this, on a cardboard slab. It looks like it might melt.

He drives slow, worried that it might sag, or even fall over. He has always believed viscerally that gestures mean everything. When he moves his hands and brings about the effects that amaze little children, he feels larger than life, unforgettable. He learned the magic while in high school, as a way of making friends, and though it didn't really make him any friends, he's been practicing it ever since. It's an extra source of income, and lately income has had a way of disappearing too quickly. He's been in some travail, betting the horses, betting the sports events. He's hung over all the time. There have been several polite warnings at work. He's managed so far to tease everyone out of the serious looks, the cool study of his face. The fact is, people like him in an abstract way, the way they like distant clownish figures: the comedian whose name they can't remember. He can see it in their eyes. Even the rough characters after his loose change have a certain sense of humor about it.

He's a phenomenon, a subject of conversation.

There's traffic on Key Bridge, and he's stuck for a while. It becomes clear that he'll have to go straight to the birthday party. Sitting behind the wheel of the car with his cake behind him, he becomes aware of people in other cars noticing him. In the car to his left, a girl stares, chewing gum. She waves, rolls her window down. Two others are with her, one in the back seat. "Hey," she says. He nods, smiles inside what he knows is the clown smile. His teeth will look dark against the makeup.

"Where's the party?" she says.

But the traffic moves again. He concentrates. The snarl is on the other side of the bridge, construction of some kind. He can see the cars in a line, waiting to go up the hill into Roslyn and beyond. Time is beginning to be a consideration. In his glove box he has a flask of bourbon. More fortification. He reaches over and takes it out, looks around himself. No police anywhere. Just the idling cars and people tuning their radios or arguing or simply staring out as if at some distressing event. The smell of the cake is making him woozy. He takes a swallow of the bourbon, then puts it away. The car with the girls in it goes by in the left lane, and they are not even looking at him. He watches them go on ahead. He's in the wrong lane again; he can't remember a time when *his* lane was the only one moving. He told her once that he considered himself of the race of people who gravitate to the non-moving lanes of highways, and who cause green lights to turn to yellow merely by approaching them. She took the idea and ran with it, saying she was of the race of people who emit enzymes which instill a sense of impending doom in marriageable young men.

"No," Tandolfo/Rodney said. "I'm living proof that isn't so. I have no such fear, and I'm with you."

"But you're of the race of people who make mine relax all the enzymes."

"You're not emitting the enzymes now. I see."

"No," she said. "It's only with marriageable young men."

"I emit enzymes that prevent people like you from seeing that I'm a marriageable young man."

"I'm too relaxed to tell," she said, and touched his shoulder. A plain affectionate moment that gave him tossing nights and fever.

Because of the traffic, he's late to the birthday party. He gets out of the car and two men come down to greet him. He keeps his face turned away, remembering too late the breath mints in his pocket.

"Jesus," one of the men says, "look at this. Hey, who comes out of the cake? This is a kid's birthday party."

"The cake stays," Tandolfo says.

"What does he mean, it stays? Is that a trick?"

They're both looking at him. The one spoken to must be the birthday boy's father—he's wearing a party cap that says DAD. He has long, dirty-looking strands of brown hair jutting out from the cap, and there are streaks of sweaty grit on the sides of his face. "So you're the Great Tandolfo," he says, extending a meaty red hand. "Isn't it hot in that makeup?"

"No, sir."

"We've been playing volleyball."

"You've exerted yourselves."

They look at him. "What do you do with the cake?" the one in the DAD cap asks.

"Cake's not part of the show, actually."

"You just carry it around with you?"

The other man laughs. He's wearing a T-shirt with a smiley face on the chest. "This ought to be some show," he says.

They all make their way across the lawn, to the porch of the house. It's a big party, bunting everywhere and children gathering quickly to see the clown.

"Ladies and gentlemen," says the man in the DAD cap. "I give you Tandolfo the Great."

Tandolfo isn't ready yet. He's got his cases open, but he needs a table to put everything on. The first trick is where he releases the bird; he'll finish with the best trick, in which the rabbit appears as if from a pan of flames. This always draws a gasp, even from the adults: the fire blooms in the pan, down goes the "lid"—it's the rabbit's tight container—the latch is tripped, and the skin of the lid lifts off. Voilà! Rabbit. The fire is put out by the fireproof cage bottom. He's gotten pretty good at making the switch, and if the crowd isn't too attentive—as children often are not—he can perform certain sleight-of-hand tricks with some style. But he needs a table, and he needs time to set up.

The whole crowd of children is seated in front of their parents, on either side of the doorway into the house. Tandolfo is standing on the porch, his back to the stairs, and he's been introduced.

"Hello, boys and girls," he says, and bows. "Tandolfo needs a table."

"A table," one of the women says. The adults simply regard him. He sees light sweaters, shapely hips, and wild tresses; he sees beer cans in tight fists, heavy jowls, bright ice-blue eyes. A little row of faces, and one elderly face. He feels more inebriated than he likes, and tries to concentrate.

"Mommy, I want to touch him," one child says.

"Look at the cake," says another, who gets up and moves to the railing on Tandolfo's right and trains a new pair of shiny binoculars on the car. "Do we get some cake?"

"There's cake," says the man in the DAD cap. "But not that cake. Get down, Ethan."

"I want that cake."

"Get down. This is Teddy's birthday."

"Mommy, I want to touch him."

"I need a table, folks. I told somebody that over the telephone."

"He did say he needed a table. I'm sorry," says a woman who is probably the birthday boy's mother. She's quite pretty, leaning in the door frame with a sweater tied to her waist.

"A table," says still another woman. Tandolfo sees the birthmark on her mouth, which looks like a stain. He thinks of this woman as a child in school, with this difference from other children, and his heart goes out to her.

"I need a table," he says to her, his voice as gentle as he can make it.

"What's he going to do, perform an operation?" says DAD.

It amazes Tandolfo how easily people fall into talking about him as though he were an inanimate object or something on a television screen. "The Great Tandolfo can do nothing until he gets a table," he says with as much mysteriousness and drama as he can muster under the circumstances.

"I want that cake out there," says Ethan, still at the porch railing. The other children start talking about cake and ice cream, and the big cake Ethan has spotted; there's a lot of confusion and restlessness. One of the smaller children, a girl in a blue dress, approaches Tandolfo. "What's your name?" she says, swaying slightly, her hands behind her back.

"Go sit down," he says to her. "We have to sit down or Tandolfo can't do his magic."

In the doorway, two of the men are struggling with a folding card table. It's one of those rickety ones with the skinny legs, and it probably won't do.

"That's kind of shaky, isn't it?" says the woman with the birthmark.

"I said, Tandolfo needs a sturdy table, boys and girls."

There's more confusion. The little girl has come forward and taken hold of his pant leg. She's just standing there holding it, looking up at him. "We have to go sit down," he says, bending to her, speaking sweetly, clownlike. "We have to do what Tandolfo wants."

Her small mouth opens wide, as if she's trying to yawn, and with pale eyes quite calm and staring she emits a screech, an ear-piercing, non-human shriek that brings everything to a stop. Tandolfo/Rodney steps back, with his amazement and his inebriate heart. Everyone gathers around the girl, who continues to scream, less piercing now, her hands fisted at her sides, those pale eyes closed tight.

"What happened?" the man in the DAD cap wants to know. "Where the hell's the magic tricks?"

"I told you, all I needed is a *table*."

"What'd you say to her to make her cry?" DAD indicates the little girl, who is giving forth a series of broken, grief-stricken howls.

"I want magic tricks," the birthday boy says, loud. "Where's the magic tricks?"

"Perhaps if we moved the whole thing inside," the woman with the birthmark says, fingering her left ear and making a face.

The card table has somehow made its way to Tandolfo, through the confusion and grief. The man in the DAD cap sets it down and opens it.

"There," he says, as if his point has been made.

In the next moment, Tandolfo realizes that someone's removed the little girl. Everything's relatively quiet again, though her cries are coming through the walls of one of the rooms inside the house. There are perhaps fifteen children, mostly seated before him, and five or six men and women behind them, or kneeling with them. "OK, now," DAD says. "Tandolfo the Great."

"Hello, little boys and girls," Tandolfo says, deciding that the table will have to suffice. "I'm happy to be here. Are you glad to see me?" A general uproar commences. "Well, good," he says. "Because just look what I have in my magic bag." And with a flourish he brings out the hat that he will release Witch from. The bird is encased in a fold of shiny cloth, pulsing there. He can feel it. He rambles on, talking fast, or trying to, and when the time comes to reveal the bird, he almost flubs it. But Witch flaps his wings and makes enough of a commotion to distract even the adults, who applaud and urge the stunned

children to applaud. "Isn't that wonderful," Tandolfo hears.
"Out of nowhere."

"He had it hidden away," says the birthday boy, who has
managed to temper his astonishment. He's the type who heaps
scorn on those things he can't understand, or own.

"Now," Tandolfo says, "for my next spell, I need a helper
from the audience." He looks right at the birthday boy—round
face, short nose, freckles. Bright red hair. Little green eyes.
The whole countenance speaks of glutted appetites and sloth.
This kid could be on the Roman coins, an emperor. He's not
used to being compelled to do anything, but he seems eager for
a chance to get into the act. "How about you," Tandolfo says
to him.

The others, led by their parents, cheer.

The birthday boy gets to his feet and makes his way over the
bodies of the other children to stand with Tandolfo. In order
for the trick to work, Tandolfo must get everyone watching
the birthday boy, and there's a funny hat he keeps in the bag
for this purpose. "Now," he says to the boy, "since you're part
of the show, you have to wear a costume." He produces the
hat as if from behind the boy's ear. Another cheer goes up. He
puts the hat on the boy's head and adjusts it, crouching down.
The green eyes stare impassively at him; there's no hint of awe
or fascination in them. "There we are," he says. "What a
handsome fellow."

But the birthday boy takes the hat off.

"We have to wear the hat to be onstage."

"Ain't a stage," the boy says.

"Well, but hey," Tandolfo says for the benefit of the adults.
"Didn't you know that all the world's a stage?" He tries to put
the hat on him again, but the boy moves from under his reach
and slaps his hand away. "We have to wear the hat," Tandolfo
says, trying to control his anger. "We can't do the magic
without our magic hats." He tries once more, and the boy waits
until the hat is on, then simply removes it and holds it behind
him, shying away when Tandolfo tries to retrieve it. The noise

of the others now sounds like the crowd at a prizefight; there's a contest going on, and they're enjoying it. "Give Tandolfo the hat. We want magic, don't we?"

"Do the magic," the boy demands.

"I'll do the magic if you give me the hat."

"I won't."

Nothing. No support from the adults. Perhaps if he weren't a little tipsy; perhaps if he didn't feel ridiculous and sick at heart and forlorn, with his wedding cake and his odd mistaken romance, his loneliness, which he has always borne gracefully and with humor, and his general dismay; perhaps if he were to find it in himself to deny the sudden, overwhelming sense of the unearned affection given this lumpish, slovenly version of stupid complacent spoiled satiation standing before him—he might've simply gone on to the next trick.

Instead, at precisely that moment when everyone seems to pause, he leans down and says, "Give me the hat, you little prick."

The green eyes widen.

The quiet is heavy with disbelief. Even the small children can tell that something's happened to change everything.

"Tandolfo has another trick," Rodney says, loud, "where he makes the birthday boy pop like a balloon. Especially if he's a fat birthday boy."

A stirring among the adults.

"Especially if he's an ugly slab of gross flesh like this one here."

"Now just a minute," says DAD.

"*Pop,*" Rodney says to the birthday boy, who drops the hat and then, seeming to remember that defiance is expected, makes a face. Sticks out his tongue. Rodney/Tandolfo is quick with his hands by training, and he grabs the tongue.

"Awk," the boy says. "Aw-aw-aw."

"Abracadabra." Rodney lets go and the boy falls backward onto the lap of one of the other children. More cries. "Whoops, time to sit down," says Rodney. "Sorry you had to leave so soon."

26

Very quickly, he's being forcibly removed. They're rougher than gangsters. They lift him, punch him, tear at his costume—even the women. Someone hits him with a spoon. The whole scene boils over onto the lawn, where someone has released Chi-Chi from her case. Chi-Chi moves about wide-eyed, hopping between running children, evading them, as Tandolfo the Great cannot evade the adults. He's being pummeled, because he keeps trying to return for his rabbit. And the adults won't let him off the curb. "Okay," he says finally, collecting himself. He wants to let them know he's not like this all the time; wants to say it's circumstances, grief, personal pain hidden inside seeming brightness and cleverness. He's a man in love, humiliated, wrong about everything. He wants to tell them, but he can't speak for a moment, can't even quite catch his breath. He stands in the middle of the street, his funny clothes torn, his face bleeding, all his magic strewn everywhere. "I would at least like to collect my rabbit," he says, and is appalled at the absurd sound of it—its huge difference from what he intended to say. He straightens, pushes the grime from his face, adjusts the clown nose, and looks at them. "I would say that even though I wasn't as patient as I could've been, the adults have not comported themselves well here," he says.

"Drunk," one of the women says.

Almost everyone's chasing Chi-Chi now. One of the older boys approaches, carrying Witch's case. Witch looks out the air hole, impervious, quiet as an idea. And now one of the men, someone Rodney hasn't noticed before, an older man clearly wearing a hairpiece, brings Chi-Chi to him. "Bless you," Rodney says, staring into the man's sleepy, deploring eyes.

"I don't think we'll pay you," the man says. The others are filing back into the house, herding the children before them.

Rodney speaks to the man. "The rabbit appears out of fire."

The man nods. "Go home and sleep it off, kid."

"Right. Thank you."

He puts Chi-Chi in his compartment, stuffs everything in

its place in the trunk. Then he gets in the car and drives away. Around the corner he stops, wipes off what he can of the makeup; it's as if he's trying to remove the stain of bad opinion and disapproval. Nothing feels any different. He drives to the suburban street where she lives with her parents, and by the time he gets there it's almost dark.

The houses are set back in the trees. He sees lighted windows, hears music, the sound of children playing in the yards. He parks the car and gets out. A breezy April dusk. "I am Tandolfo the soft-hearted," he says. "Hearken to me." Then he sobs. He can't believe it. "Jeez," he says, "Lord." He opens the back door of the car, leans in to get the cake. He'd forgot how heavy it is. Staggering with it, making his way along the sidewalk, intending to leave it on her doorstep, he has an inspiration. Hesitating only for the moment it takes to make sure there are no cars coming, he goes out and sets it down in the middle of the street. Part of the top sags from having bumped his shoulder as he pulled it off the back seat. The bride and groom are almost supine, one on top of the other. He straightens them, steps back and looks at it. In the dusky light it looks blue. It sags just right, with just the right angle expressing disappointment and sorrow. Yes, he thinks. This is the place for it. The atpness of it, sitting out like this, where anyone might come by and splatter it all over creation, makes him feel a faint sense of release, as if he were at the end of a story. Everything will be all right if he can think of it that way. He's wiping his eyes, thinking of moving to another town. Failures are beginning to catch up to him, and he's still aching in love. He thinks how he has suffered the pangs of failure and misadventure, but in this painful instance there's symmetry, and he will make the one eloquent gesture—leaving a wedding cake in the middle of the road, like a sugar-icinged pylon. Yes.

He walks back to the car, gets in, pulls around, and backs into the driveway of the house across the street from hers. Leaving the engine idling, he rolls the window down and rests his arm on the sill, gazing at the incongruous shape of the cake there in the falling dark. He feels almost glad, almost, in some strange inexpressible way, vindicated. He imagines what she might do if she saw him here, imagines that she comes running from her house, calling his name, looking at the cake and admiring it. He conjures a picture of her, attacking the tiers of pink sugar, and the muscles of his abdomen tighten. But then this all gives way to something else: images of destruction, of flying dollops of icing. He's surprised to find that he wants her to stay where she is, doing whatever she's doing. He realizes that what he wants—and for the moment all he really wants— is what he now has: a perfect vantage point from which to watch oncoming cars. Turning the engine off, he waits, concentrating on the one thing. He's a man imbued with interest, almost peaceful with it—almost, in fact, happy with it—sitting there in the quiet car and patiently awaiting the results of his labor.

for Stephen & Karen & Nicholas Goodwin

The person I have
mostly become

Fridays my mother cleans at the Wiltons', and last week she said the lady, Mrs. Wilton, asked her if she knew anyone, meaning me, who can give an estimate on some remodeling work. My mother likes to tell people what I can do with a hammer and nails, so I didn't have any trouble believing this. I can hear her clear as if I'm standing there, her voice with the cigarettes in it, telling Mrs. Wilton about her carpenter son.

She came home all excited. Sure that she'd found me a job. I was sitting in my chair on the porch, and wasn't in much of a cheerful mood. She said it's not like me, which is true enough. My boy, Willy, who's almost eleven years old and ought to know better, had left his brand-new baseball glove out in the yard so the dog could get to it. Dog's not even our own, this German shepherd pup the people next door are going to start a kennel with. Thing chewed a hole in the thumb; I'd been trying to get Willy interested in baseball, and to tell the truth, Willy'd rather play soldier with plastic dolls. So I was giving him words about the baseball glove, wondering to myself if they called him sissy in school and wanting, even if I don't know exactly how to go about it, to at least be there for him— tending to him and giving a damn what happens to him—like my father never was, or did, for me. And to tell you the real truth, I was mad at him about this first baseman's mitt that I couldn't afford in the first place being left out all night, so when my mother walked up announcing that she'd got me a

30

job, this whole other area of worry came in on me—as if you could forget a thing like being out of work.

"You'd never let a little thing like that bother you, son," she said.

"Okay," I said. "But it shouldn't have happened."

"Well, things'll be better now."

Willy hung back by the door while she went on about the job. He wanted to know, too. But I was peeved at him, couldn't help this feeling that he'd begun to depend on her to smooth things over when he was being disciplined. This wasn't the first time she'd stepped between us, and Willy is smart. There's no excuse for it, but being in the kind of mess we're in doesn't leave a lot in the way of patience. Maybe she should've stepped between us a time or two. But sometimes it feels like you put so much into a child, into the raising of him, you love him so hard, there's not much left for liking him, particularly. "Get inside," I said to him, feeling low and mean, and out of control some way, watching him go on in.

"Are you listening?" my mother said.

"I'm listening, Ruth. The lady wants an estimate."

"Paint and carpentry, too. She wants a ceiling redone, and some molding put up, and wallpaper. The library needs redoing, and the whole porch has to be rebuilt and painted, and all the eaves have to be done, too. This is your job if you play your cards right."

Nothing ever stops her. She moved to the door and caught Willy, who had come back and was standing there. She put her arms around him and asked how's her little man.

"I told you to get inside," I said to him.

"Yes, sir."

He shuffled through the kitchen.

"Are you riding him again?" she said to me, but she was smiling. From the kitchen I could hear Janet rattling dishes. She'd come in from work and insisted that she would put dinner on, as she always does when things are getting her down. Lately she hasn't been very good about hiding the strain she feels with Ruth here, and there's no place for Ruth to go, not to mention the fact that Ruth is also bringing in a good part of the income. These days, she and Janet make the money, and I generally keep the house.

You have to know that I've been all over the area looking: busboy, clerk, salesman, janitor, anything. The last three houses I worked on are still empty in that big meadow south of here, and the builder—Teddy Aubrey—still owes me money. He's down to selling Oldsmobiles in Charlottesville. Went bust as a builder after the first of the year. One of the new houses that he did manage to sell he never finished, and the people who live there don't have any screens, are stuck with a dirt-and-weed patch for a lawn. No hydroseeding, because Baylor, who does hydroseeding around here, refused to do it unless Aubrey could pay him cash up front.

Which is what I should've done. I worked two months in the last one, flooring and drywall and painting, even some plumbing, and I never got paid a penny for it. I went over to the new house last week and asked the owners if I could hydroseed for them; I'd charge half what Baylor charges. Just enough above cost to pay my damn rent. Anything. But they don't have ready cash, either.

"I can't take blood from a stone." Aubrey tells me over the phone. "I'm having to bring my kids home from college. I don't know what I'm going to do."

Well, he's selling cars, is what he's doing. And he *still* drives a long cool Lincoln. I get cards from him saying, "Come on in!"

"When the big ones go down, they bring all the little ones down with them." Ruth said.

"I wouldn't characterize Teddy Aubrey as big," I told her. "Nor me as being so damn small, either." I meant it as a joke, I was always joking and kidding around before. This didn't come out sounding like any joke, though.

She said, "I was talking about the real estate companies, baby."

When I was a kid, we lived in a nice house in the country. Central air before anyone else had it. Swimming pool. Extra rooms, the whole thing. My father worked high up for the space program. Top-level executive, and he traveled all the time. Ruth had somebody in every week to help out with the housekeeping: this big Mexican lady with a partially cut-off ear, who was always blessing the house with her rosary. I wondered about that sudden place where her ear just stopped, especially after my father went off to start a new life. The ear looked like it had been snipped with scissors, a planned cut, part of some ritual or other, but then I heard my mother say it was the result of a fight between the Mexican lady and her husband, who still lived with her. Knowing this, I was always tempted to ask how it happened, but I never let on that I had noticed it.

When I say my father went off to start a new life somewhere else, I mean *as* someone else, too: a man with a new name, a new identity, in another state, or maybe even in another country, who knows? I was afraid of him a lot of the time and wasn't so sad to realize he wasn't coming back, except that we started having money problems. We wound up moving to this little place in the north end of the country, living with Ruth's older brother and his new wife, who never seemed dressed in anything but a nightgown and robe. Someone had told her once that she looked like that movie star Katharine Hepburn, and it must've gone to her head. She wore her hair in exactly the style of those old movies, and she hurried through the house with that ratty robe flowing behind her, constantly in some kind of uproar, like a person playing a scene in a movie. She loved piano music. It was always on in that house, always coming from their room during the nights, and we knew it was part of the act. But she liked to have a good laugh, too, and she didn't mind helping us out. We tolerated each other's ways, and we shared the bills, and had some fun in the evenings. By then I was working in the summers as an apprentice to Mr. Hall, who was contracting with Aubrey for almost everything. Then Mr. Hall retired and I took over, and for a while there I had a pretty steady source of income, even in the winter months. That was our life for a time. It was what I ended my growing up in. And when the changes came, they came quick.

First I got married and moved out. And we had Willy almost right away. Nobody ever talks about how scary that is, having a child. Being a father. At least nobody talked to me about it. I was plenty scared, but I loved that baby so much it hurt. Then when Willy was three, my uncle and his wife got a divorce, and while she moved to Hollywood (none of us asked why), he went north, to Boston, to live. He left the house for my mother, and she called and asked me to move back in with Janet and Willy.

"There's so much room," she said. "It's lonesome here." But we were happy where we were, though we fought a lot over dumb things, the way people do when they're finding out how to be with each other all the time.

"We'll come visit you," I told my mother.

So we'd go over for weekends. We'd play with Willy, and watch him and laugh. We'd look at old movies on TV or have a few rounds of gin rummy while he slept. I'd read something to Willy before he went to bed every night. It got so he knew the stories by heart, and then as he got older and was in school, he'd read them to me. He'd tell me how things went at school. I'd come in from being with him and the two women would be dealing cards, laughing and teasing each other. We might as well have lived over there.

But then, a couple years ago, things started to go sour for Ruth's brother up in Boston, and he had to let go of the house in Virginia. This was right before the real estate business fell through the floor around here. Anyway, Mom had to move in with us. It was supposed to be temporary. And it's a different thing when you *have* to live together.

Nobody, but nobody, thought things would dry up so suddenly. Up until two years ago, the main industry in this poor county was building houses. Now it was coming down all around, and we didn't see it coming. There had been slumps and setbacks before, but business always bounced back. This time, it got so Teddy Aubrey couldn't pay me for work I'd already done, though he kept promising he'd catch up, and I believed him because I couldn't afford not to. For a while I was doing jobs on pure spec—working for nothing in the hope of some new development. But every shift in the winds brought more bad news, and as you know, the bill collectors and the banks never have been too notable for understanding when you can't pay what you owe.

The reason I bring this up is so you'll understand what we came from, and where we had been, and maybe you'll know how much it hurt me every time I saw that woman come walking up the sidewalk with her hair tied back like that, wearing sweat clothes and no makeup, and with other people's dirt on her hands. She'd raised me; she'd never trained herself for anything else. She'd been led to believe by everybody and everything that she would never have to work outside the house if she didn't want to. She'd taken to smoking again. Her cough was back. I hated that, and so every day I was out looking for any kind of work. Even handyman stuff, which I did get now and then—forty dollars here, fifty dollars there. Enough for a couple days' worth of groceries, or for part of a payment.

Don't get me wrong. There are plenty of people worse off than we are. I'm not asking for sympathy, really. What I'm trying to do is explain.

•

The night she came home with the news about Mrs. Wilton and the remodeling job, we celebrated. We had beer in Ruth's old champagne glasses, toasting Mrs. Wilton and her big old house. Janet already had herself worked into thinking it'd last into the summer. Five thousand dollars net, at least. She hugged Willy and teased him about the baseball glove, and after dinner she asked Ruth, "How about a game of gin rummy?"

We hadn't played cards since the first days after Ruth moved in with us. Ruth looked at my wife and nodded with the best smile—a smile like the good days we'd had. It made me happy, and when I said I'd watch TV, for a second there I couldn't quite find my voice.

I went in and watched the ball game, with the sound up fairly loud, in case Willy didn't know it was on. He stayed in the kitchen with the women.

"Hey," I said. "Willy?" I was feeling good. I thought all I had to do was show him how glad I was.

He came to the doorway.

"Ball game's on," I said to him like one man talking to another.

"I heard it," he said. One thing I hate is when a man doesn't look you in the eye. When I was nine, I was playing third base in the Little League and looking straight back at people.

"Come here," I said.

"I don't want to watch the game, Dad."

I got up and turned the TV off, and when I got to the kitchen he was standing by his grandmother's chair.

"Get your mitt," I said.

"I don't want to," he said. Still not looking at me.

"Stand up straight, son."

And Janet said, "Leave him alone about it, will you?"

"I wanted to throw the ball around," I said.

"Okay," Willy said. Whining.

"No," I told them. "The hell with it."

"Go throw the ball around with your son," Ruth said.

So we went out into the yard. My heart wasn't in it. I felt wrong, and my boy looked like somebody being punished. He was scared of the ball, I could tell. No matter how easy I lobbed it. After a few minutes of this I said "Okay, I'm beat."

"Sure?" he said.

"Really."

He was a little too quick going up on the porch, and I guess he sensed it, because he stopped at the door. For that second he stood in exactly the same stance as he did when I was mad at him before. Even the same look on his face. "If you want to, we can play catch some more," he said.

"That's all right," I told him, and I patted his skinny shoulder. My boy. "You go on in," I said.

I sat on the porch and listened to them inside, Ruth and Janet playing their cards. Willy making little war sounds with his mouth, his toy men. It was a pretty twilight. The sun came through the leaves and there was a breeze stirring. I could hear the traffic way out on Route 29, and birds were singing, too. I felt sad, and it was as if I could turn around in myself and look at the feeling. I thought about how things go on, and other changes come. Hard times arrive sooner or later for everybody. Ruth's parents went through the Depression.

I was thinking about this when Ruth came out.

"What about cards?" I said.

"Janet's using the powder room. Thought I'd come out and smoke a cigarette."

Janet doesn't let her smoke in the house. She lighted up. Nobody enjoys a cigarette like my mother. "So," she said. "We'll go over to Mrs. Wilton's at nine o'clock tomorrow. That's when I told her."

"We?" I said.

"I told her I'd bring you over and introduce you."

"How bad did you brag on me, Ruth?"

"I'm not bragging." She blew smoke, then she looked down at her tennis shoes. "I need new shoes."

"Yes, ma'am," I said.

"These are comfortable, though."

"They're falling apart."

"They're like an old pair of slippers," she said, crossing one over the other. She leaned on the railing and smoked. Then she sighed, and when she started talking again there was something else in her voice: she was someone remembering a thing with pain. Except it wasn't quite that, either, because I heard no regret in it, and she didn't seem sad. "You know, I used to say that was how your father and I were, a nice old comfy worn pair of slippers. It used to make me feel good saying it. Imagine."

"I think I remember you saying it," I told her.

"It was a joke we had," she said.

I was quiet.

Then she said, "He never was much of a father to you."

"No," I said.

And she said, "I think you're doing the right thing with Willy."

"Well," I said, "I wish I knew for sure sometimes."

Inside, Janet was shuffling the cards. "Mom?" she said.

"Be right there," Ruth said. Then she flicked the cigarette out on the lawn and leaned down to kiss me on the cheek. For a second I had this funny sense of what she must've been like when she was young, a girl, before her husband took everything she had to give him and then left her. "I feel good this evening," she said to me. "I think it's going to work out fine."

Mrs. Wilton lives in those hills south of here. A big gray house with about four different entrances. I couldn't go with Ruth at nine o'clock because Willy messed around in his room and wound up missing the school bus and I had to drive him, so Ruth called Mrs. Wilton and set up a visit for later in the morning. I got Willy in the car and we headed out, neither one of us much in the mood for talk. He stared out his side. I had yelled at him for putting everything on his mother, and then Janet got miffed at me for coming down on him too hard. It was a sunny morning, and I felt like hell.

"I don't mean to be too hard on you," I said to Willy.

Nothing. It made me mad.

"You hear what I said?"

"Yes."

"Well?"

"I don't know."

I took hold of his shoulder so he looked at me, and then I pointed out the windows of the car. "That's the world out there, son. They don't care whether you make it or not. You understand? They'd just as soon walk over you as look at you. And it's my job to make you ready for it. Get you so you can walk out in it and not get knocked down." I was yelling now. But I was right. I didn't mean for him to do any daydreaming while I told him, and what I was telling him was the truth. "I need you to be tough," I said. I said, "I don't want you coming back to me when you've been out there and saying you didn't know, that I didn't tell you."

"Okay," he said. And he started to cry.

"I'm not yelling at you," I said. "I'm telling you the truth."

"Yes, sir." He was giving me this look, like a scared rabbit.

"Goddammit," I said. "Sit up straight." It was like everything I'd been through came rushing up behind my eyes, and I wanted to hit him. "Sit up," I said. "And stop blubbering. You baby."

He sat straight, looking at me out of the corner of his eye, ready to duck, as if all he ever had from me was getting hit. I have never hit him, or anyone else for that matter. I can't explain it any better than this. In my mind, I saw myself reach over and smack him. I was that close. I didn't even like him in that minute. "Quit being such a baby about it," I said. "Stop crying right now. NOW!"

"Yes, sir."

And he was trying to stop. He had wet all over his face—

39

tears, and stuff from his nose. He kept sniffling, and his hands went up to his mouth. I thought he might've gagged.

"Okay, I'm sorry," I said. "I didn't mean to yell at you."

Then I was just driving, and he was leaning over against the window, still sniffling. We went on that way for a while, and when I looked at his back, I felt something drop down inside me, like a big collapsing wall.

"They don't care about you out there," I told him when I could get my voice again. But it sounded empty now, and I knew something else had happened. I wished I had another mind, some other set of memories.

When we pulled into the school parking lot, I put my hand on his arm. "You all right now?" I said. I couldn't find any other voice to use with him; it was like I was a drill sergeant. He nodded, and I could see that all he wanted was to get away from me. I told him again, "I didn't mean to hurt your feelings. It just got me going."

"Yes, sir," he said. That little scared kid's crying voice.

"All right," I said, and let him go. He got out, dropped a book, and bent over to get it—a boy out in front of a big brick and aluminium building, going through a bad morning in his life. I watched him walk on into the school, and then I drove back to the house, so sick at heart and full of rage that I drove past it.

Ruth was waiting on the porch. "Daydreaming?" she said.

I went on up and into the kitchen, where Janet sat drinking coffee. "What," she said when I looked at her.

"Nothing," I said.

"We should go," Ruth said from the door.

"In a minute," I said.

"What happened?" Janet asked.

I have never been able to get anything past her. After we'd been married a year, I got into a little hugging-kissing thing with this woman at the end of a party I'd gone to alone, and when I got home Janet knew the whole thing. I don't mean that she saw lipstick on me or smelled the perfume or anything;

she knew from me, from the way I was with her, that something was different. Now she sat there with her coffee and waited for me to tell her.

"Maybe I'm not cut out to be a father," I said.

"Poor baby," she said.

I knew she was right about that, too. I'm not always a son of a bitch. I said, "All right."

"Did you yell at him?" she said.

I couldn't answer this.

"You did, didn't you. You got on him some more."

"I told him I was sorry," I said.

She stood and poured the rest of her coffee down the sink. "I won't have you yelling at him."

"No," I said.

"Good Lord," Ruth said from the door. "He's just like you were, baby. You could dream the year away if somebody didn't get after you and get you going."

"Ruth, please," Janet said.

"Fine. Fine. I'll be out at the end of the sidewalk."

We both watched her make her way into the sunlight. "Patience," Janet said. It was as if she had said it to herself.

I said, "I don't have any left."

"Ha," she said. "Maybe we can laugh it all off."

"I didn't mean it that way."

She got her purse and put it over her shoulder, then stood at the door, watching Ruth, who was moving Willy's bike off the sidewalk. "I hope she's got you something, I'll tell you that. Because lately I've been thinking of taking my son out of here."

"He's my son, too."

She turned, faced me, and when she spoke it was in a quick voice I didn't know. "We sound like a soap opera, don't we?"

"I love him," I said. "I love you, too."

Ruth called from the sidewalk. "We really ought to get over there."

"I'll do better," I said. I didn't want to think about what she'd do when she'd had enough of all this. "Please," I said.

41

She kissed my cheek, and then I saw that she was going to cry. "I took chicken out for dinner," she said.

"I'll make it," I told her.

"Ruth wants to make her southern fried."

We went out and joined my mother, who had opened the car door and was waiting with her hands on her hips.

"Conference over?" Ruth said.

We got in, and we took Janet to work. Nobody said much. Janet kissed me and nodded goodbye to Ruth, and we watched her walk up the steps and into the building. She likes the job, that's one lucky thing. You could see her step getting lighter the closer she got to the door.

"Okay," Ruth said as we pulled away. "So tell me."

"Nothing to tell," I said.

"She hates having me around, I know."

"It's the whole situation," I said. "It's not just you."

She said, "I don't blame her."

I didn't know what she was thinking, but I didn't want her to worry about it. "It's me," I said. "Janet's unhappy with me."

"Well, it's going to be better now," she said. "We'll have you working again. There'll be more money."

We went on south, and all the way she talked about what a nice woman Mrs. Wilton was. Not like so many people who have money. Mrs. Wilton looked right at you when she talked and never put on any airs. She had a great laugh, and she liked to tell stories on herself. She'd love me if I got to telling my stories, and all I had to do was relax and be myself. Forget everything and just be who I really was. Her husband was some sort of expert in the fitness business, and owned a few spas in the area. The house was a beautiful old Victorian. Ruth couldn't wait for me to see it.

I went the long way, so we could go past the school. "I thought I'd drive by," I said. "Wave to Willy, maybe."

There were a lot of kids out on the playground, four or five groups of them. I slowed down to look for Willy, but couldn't see him in the middle of all that running and playing, all the colors.

"I don't see him," Ruth said.

I said, "No."

And everything must have been in my voice, because she said, "It's going to be okay, son."

"I want him to know I give a damn what happens to him in life," I said. "I didn't have that when I was his age."

"Not from your father."

"That's what I meant," I said.

She didn't say anything else. She quietly directed me to the Wilton house. It was what she said it was, too, a big old gray clapboard place more than a hundred years old and, for all its nice tall rooms and big porches and balconies, needing a lot of work. Mrs. Wilton stood in her doorway as we came up the walk. I was surprised how young she was—mid-thirties, maybe. Maybe even younger than that. Pretty, with brown hair and dark eyes and a tanned look to her skin. She held the door open for us, and Ruth said my name to her. We shook hands. I noticed her hands were rough-feeling, almost like a man's. She was wearing jeans and a sweat shirt.

"So," she said. "Your mother says you're a good man with a hammer and nails."

"I do my best," I said.

"He's a real craftsman," Ruth said.

We were standing in the foyer of the house, and Mrs. Wilton turned and started through to what looked like a library.

"Why don't I just run the sweeper upstairs while you-all talk?" Ruth said.

"But you were here yesterday."

"But you had the rugs out on the porch," Ruth said. "Won't take a minute."

My shoes sounded on the hardwood floor as I followed Mrs. Wilton, and Ruth said, "Baby, you watch those big heavy shoes on my fresh-waxed floor, now."

My fresh-waxed floor.

I never felt lower, never felt smaller all my life. We went into the library and Mrs. Wilton started talking about her bookshelves and what she wanted done—the painting and the crown molding and the wiring, the track lighting, measurements and kinds of wood and designs, and I didn't hear most of it. I couldn't look her in the face, couldn't really say anything when she asked questions. I heard Ruth running the vacuum in the upstairs hall.

"Look, is something wrong?" Mrs. Wilton said.

"Yes," I said. I was utterly unable to help myself. "All sorts of things are wrong." I wanted to go on and say how my mother once had a cleaning lady of her own, and it wasn't always like this with us. But I couldn't even speak then, for what was going through me, the whole thing, the whole disaster of the last couple of years.

"Explain," she said.

I might have shrugged, I don't know.

"Is there something about all this that bothers you?"

I could see what she was thinking: what sort of lazy, ignorant type I am, maybe the sort who beats up on his children or his wife or both, a sullen, inexpressive man with dirt under his fingernails and a collection of destructive habits.

"Well?" she said. There was something wrong with the way she said this, like she could demand an answer right now.

"I want to do the work," I said. "Whatever you want me to do, I'll do." But I wasn't able to get the sullenness out of my voice.

"You don't sound like you really want anything."

"What do you expect me to do," I said, "jump up and down for you?" I couldn't help myself. It was out of me before I could stop it. This woman who was so comfortable having my mother running a vacuum in her upstairs hallway. She looked at me for a minute, then led the way out to the front porch. Ruth was at the top of the stairs as we came through the foyer. "He'll do a real good job," she called down to us.

Out on the porch, Mrs. Wilton said, "There are one or two other carpenters and contractors I'm talking to, you know. I told your mother I was. I only agreed to let you provide an estimate."

I didn't say anything.

"Do you want to continue with this?" she said.

I said, "What did I do?"

"You haven't done anything. You can take some notes down, can't you?"

I said, "Whatever you say."

"No," she said. "Well, I guess there isn't any point."

"I've got an idea what this will take," I told her. "I can write up an estimate." I couldn't look at her.

Ruth rattled the sweeper on the stairs, making her way down. Probably we were both trying to think what we would say to her, how we would break it to her.

"If you'd let me do the work," I said, "I'll do a good job."

"Well, write me an estimate," she said.

But it was clear that everything about me had scared her, and she wasn't about to go with me. She took a step back and looked me up and down. "The truth is, I've already pretty well committed to someone else."

Ruth came out then, all smiles. I wished I was dead. She took my hand and faced Mrs. Wilton. "He doesn't like to brag about himself, you know."

"You were both very nice to come out," Mrs. Wilton said.

Ruth squeezed my hand. "Yes, so. Next week then?"

"For cleaning," Mrs. Wilton said. "Oh, yes. Could you come on Tuesday?"

"Tuesday's fine," Ruth said, and she sounded a little out of breath. "Are you two finished with everything?" She looked at me and then back at Mrs. Wilton.

"Yes, I'm afraid we are," Mrs. Wilton said.

"That was fast. You-all are more efficient than I am."

Then we were quiet. It was embarrassing.

"So," Ruth said. "We won't keep you another minute." And she started down off that porch. I felt like a child being led. Ruth turned and waved. "Bye."

Mrs. Wilton waved back.

In the car, we didn't talk. I drove back out to the highway and on toward home, and the wind blew into the open windows of the car. Ruth had lighted a cigarette. Finally she said, "Boy, that was quick."

I couldn't think of anything to tell her.

"What happened?" she said.

I told her Mrs. Wilton had already taken estimates from contractors I couldn't begin to compete with; I said I would write up an estimate anyway. I said I spoke up to save the woman a lot of unnecessary inconvenience, that she appreciated my honesty, and that she promised to call me as soon as she knew for certain what she would want done. And there were other jobs, too—other jobs might come up. She'd give my name to her friends. I said, bright as I could, that things were looking up.

What would you say? I would like to know what you would find to tell her about it. Would you be able to say that hearing her talk about someone else's floor as if it was her own had set you off? That it had made you angry and sick inside, because you had once felt that you liked people and you had always wanted to be kind and you didn't have that any more, and because it reminded you of all this? Reminded you of where you were and where Ruth was, no more real to Mrs. Wilton than that poor Mexican woman with a cut ear had been to you when you were young and fortunate? That it had made you see yourself as you were now, grabbing at anything, any little hope that all this might finally somehow change for the better? That maybe you can learn to stop being this person you have ended up being—that man who makes his wife think of leaving him and frightens his own son? And if you could find a way to tell her all of this, what would you then say? If you were that man and she had asked you and you had spoken at all, you had found that you could say one thing, anything, anything at all?

All the way in
Flagstaff, Arizona

Sitting in the shaded cool quiet of St. Paul's Church in Flagstaff, Walter remembers a family picnic. This memory is two years old, but nothing ever fades from it. It takes place in a small park called Hathaway Forest, on Long Island, one Sunday afternoon in early summer. He and his wife, Irene, spread blankets on the grass next to a picnic table and a brick barbecue pit; it is a warm, clear-blue day, with a breeze. Irene has insisted that they all go, as a family, and so soccer games, trips to the movies and to the houses of friends, have been put aside. Because Walter is hung over, he tries to beg off, but she will not hear of it; she will not cater to his hangovers any more, she tells him. So they all go. He and Irene sit quietly on the blankets as, in the grass field before them, the children run—William, the oldest, hanging back a little, making a sacrifice of pretending to have a good time: he is planning for the priesthood these days, wants to be Gregory Peck in *The Keys of the Kingdom*. He saw the movie on television a year ago and now his room is full of books on China, on the lives of the saints, the missionaries, the martyrs. Every morning he goes to mass and communion. Walter feels embarrassed in his company, especially when William shows this saintly, willing face to the world.

"I wonder if it would help William to discover masturbation," Walter says. "He's at that age, isn't he? Don't boys start at fourteen? When did I start? I guess I should remember."

"I forgot the baked beans," Irene says. "I left them sitting in the middle of the kitchen counter." She has this way of not hearing him when she wants to avoid a subject; she will not talk about William. "You want some lemonade?"

"No, thanks." He makes a face; she smiles. He can always make her laugh.

The children form a ring, and begin to move in a circle. Susan, the second child, orchestrates this, calling in a kind of singing cadence as they contract and expand the ring by raising and lowering their arms. They are playing well together, cooperating; even William seems to have forgotten about heaven and hell for the moment, moving a little too fast for the youngest, the baby, Carol, to keep up with him. There is something mischievous about the way he causes the girl to falter and lose her hold on him.

"You should light the charcoal, honey," Irene says.

"Certainly," he says. He is anxious to please. He knows she will again have to ask her father for money, and she will again use the word *borrow*. There is always the hope that something will change. He stands over the brick barbecue pit and pours charcoal, while she pours more lemonade, not bothering to ask him this time if he wants any. In the car, in the space under the spare tire, hidden by a half-used roll of paper towels, is a fifth of Jim Beam. He thinks of it with something bordering on erotic anticipation, though his head feels as if it were webbed with burning wires. As he sprinkles lighter fluid on the coals, he begins to plan how he will get to the bottle without the others knowing he has done so.

"Dad."

It is William, standing a little apart from Susan and the younger children. He holds up a Nerf football, wanting to pass it.

Walter smiles. "I'm cooking. I'm the chef of the day."

William wants to get a game up, boys against the girls; he wants Irene to play. She refuses, cheerfully, and so does Susan, and the younger boys begin a desultory game of keep away from Carol, who begins to take it seriously, crying and demanding that she be given a chance to throw and catch the ball. William and Susan walk off toward the far edge of the woods, talking, William pausing now and then to pick up and throw a stone or a piece of wood. Irene sits reading a magazine, with a pad and pencil on her lap. She likes to write down the recipes she finds, and keeps the pad for this purpose. In fact, she doesn't read these magazines as much as she ransacks them, looking for things to save. She's a frugal woman; she's had to be. She controls the money now, what there is of it. Since the last hitch in the Army, Walter has worked seven different jobs; now, at forty-six, he's night clerk in a 7-Eleven store.

"That's enough," Irene calls to the two younger boys, Brad and James, who have tormented Carol to the point of a tantrum. Carol is lying on her stomach, beating her fists into the grass, while they toss the ball above her head, keeping it just out of reach. "Brad! Bra-a-a-d! James!"

The two boys stop, finally, walk away scuffing the ground. In a moment they are running across the field, and Carol has come crying to her mother. Because she is the youngest and the smallest, she has learned to be feisty and short-tempered; she seems somehow always dogged, face into the wind, daunt-less. "Don't pay any attention to them," Irene is saying.

Walter lights the fire, stands watching it.

"You go on, now, and play," Irene says, and Carol whines that she doesn't want to, she wants to stay here. "No—now, go on. Go have fun. I don't want you hanging back all afternoon. Go on—go."

Carol wanders over to a little play area near the car; it is, in fact, too near: it will be hard for Walter to get anything out of the trunk if she stays where she is, riding a sea dragon on a corkscrew-like metal spring.

"I don't like her being over there by herself," Walter says.

"She's fine," says Irene. "Let her alone."

He sits down, rubs his hands; he wants a drink.

"You want to put the hot dogs on sticks?" Irene asks.

"That tire's low," he says.

"No, it's not."

"It is—look. Look at it. It's low. I better change it."

"You're in no shape to change a tire."

49

He gets up. "I think it's low."

"Walter."

"I'm just going to look at it."

"Hi, Daddy," Carol says as he approaches.

"Go and see your mother."

"I'm riding the dragon."

"Your mother wants you."

"I don't wanna."

"Come on," he says, "I have to look at this tire." He lifts her from the dragon, puts her down on her feet, or tries to: she raises her legs, so that he comes close to falling forward; he lifts again, tries again to set her down, and it's as if they dance. "Stop it," he says, "stand up." She laughs, and he sets her suddenly, with a bump, down on her rear end. "Now you can sit there," he says. She begins to cry. He walks over to the car and stands gazing at the right rear tire, which is not low enough. Even so, he opens the trunk, glances back at Irene, who is lying on the blanket like a sunbather now, her arms straight at her sides, her eyes closed. Carol still whines and cries, sitting in the dust in the foreground.

"Go on," Walter says, "you're not hurt."

"Carol," Irene calls without moving, "come here."

Walter is already reaching into the little well beneath the spare. The Beam is wrapped in a paper bag, and carefully he removes it, leaning into the hot space. In almost the same motion, he has broken the seal on the bottle and held the lip of it to his mouth, swallowing. He caps it, peers out at Irene and Carol, who are frozen for him in a sort of tableau: Carol beginning to move toward her mother, and Irene lying face up to the sun. He leans in, takes another swallow, caps the bottle again and sets it down, rattles the jack, stands back slowly, and puts his hands on his hips.

"Walter."

"It's okay," he calls. "I guess it'll have to do—the spare's no better." He looks at Irene, sees that Carol has reached her, that she is involved with Carol, who wants her to fix and bow her hair. So he leans into the trunk again, swallows more of the whiskey. Then he recaps the bottle one more time, puts it back in its place, retrieves it almost immediately, and takes still another swallow. He closes the trunk hard, walks steadily across to the blanket, where Irene and Carol are busy trying to get Carol's hair braided and bowed. He sits down, looks at the flames licking low along the whitening coals. When Carol asks him to look at how pretty her hair is, he tells her she is the most beautiful little girl he ever saw. He reaches for her, pulls her to him, and hugs her. "You are my sweet sweet sweet sweet thing," he says, "You are my sweetie-pie. My little baby love darling boost-a-booter."

"I love you, Daddy."

She removes herself from him, dances, for his benefit, in a circle around the blanket. Then she runs off to meet William and Susan, who are coming across the crest of the field.

"It could be like this all the time," Irene says.

He says, "Yeah." He gets up, stands over the fire. "The coals are almost ready."

"What's the mat—" she begins.

He has swayed only slightly; he pretends to have simply lost his balance on an unevenness in the ground, looks at his feet, lifts one leg, puts it down. It is a beautiful blurred world, and he believes he can do anything.

"It's brave of you to come out today," she says.

"I wanted to."

"You know, Walter, I am going to leave you."

"Right now?"

She ignores this. "I don't want to. I love you. But I really am. You don't believe me, Walter, because you've never believed me. But this time you're wrong. In a while, very soon, I'm going to take the children and go."

"But don't you see?" he says. "I'm going to quit. I'm never touching the stuff again."

"No," she says.

"Come on, kid," he says.

"Let me tell you, dear, what you were thinking all the way here, and what you finally got your hands on a few minutes ago. You were thinking all the time, weren't you, about the bottle of booze you had stashed in the trunk of the car."

"What bottle of booze?"

"I believe it was Jim Beam?" she looks at him.

He wonders if she can see the color changing in his face and neck, the blood rushing there. "Jim Beam," he says. "Jim Beam."

"It won't work, Walter."

"You think that's it? You think I've been—you think that's what I've been doing, huh." He is nodding, looking away from her, trying to control his voice. "You think—on a beautiful day like this, when I'm with my family—some—a bottle of booze in the trunk—"

"Forget it," she says.

"I didn't know—I didn't even know if there was a bottle of booze in the goddam spare-tire well."

"Please," she says.

"You think I've been thinking about a goddam bottle of booze in the trunk of the car."

"All right, then."

"That's what you think of me. I mean—we've come that far—that you'd think I could be standing here on this nice day thinking about sneaking drinks like there's some—like there's a problem or something—"

"Walter," she says.

"I mean like it wasn't just—you know, a drink in the afternoon or something—"

"Don't say any more," she tells him.

"Just something I found and—you think I haven't been sick at heart for what I've done, Irene." He has never meant anything more. "I didn't even think anything about it, honey—you think I'd do anything to hurt you or the kids—

something—some bottle or something that's supposed to be hidden or something. Like I planned it or something. I swear I just remembered it was there—I didn't—didn't want to worry you, Irene—Irene—"

"The sad thing," Irene says, "is that I could've stopped you today—just now. I knew what you were doing—after all, Walter, you've become a bit sloppy in your various deceptions and ruses. They've become pretty transparent. I could've stopped you, only I just—I just didn't have the energy."

"I don't know what you're talking about," he says. He looks at his children, all of them coming now from the crest; they seem somehow not together, though they come in a group, no more than five feet apart.

"I wish I could feel anything but this exhaustion," Irene says.

"It's not anything like I'm drunk or anything," Walter says. "I just need to get calmed down, honey."

"No," she says.

"You know me, Irene. I always—haven't I always come through?"

She looks at him. "I think—now—that you think you have."

"I just need a little time," he says.

"Walter."

"That's all, honey. Just let me get straight a little." He doesn't want to talk any more. He drops down at her side. "I'm nervous, kid. I get real bad nervous—and—and I'm not going to drink any more. I'm simply—absolutely done with it. Forever, Renie. Okay? I'm going to pull it together this time." As he gazes out at the field, at his children returning, he is full of resolve, and courage. Irene sighs, pats his shoulder, and then takes his hand into her own. "Poor Walter," she says, "so sick."

"I'll be all right," he says. "I just need to be calm."

The children are there now, and the picnic is made ready: William puts hot dogs on the grill, and Susan dishes out potato salad, Jell-O, bread, pickles. There is a lot of vying for attention, a lot of energy and noise. It all rises around Walter and his wife, who do not look at each other.

Anyone walking into St. Paul's at this hour will see a man sitting in the last pew, hands folded neatly in his lap. He sits very straight, with dignity, though his clothes are soiled and disheveled. In his mind are the voices of two years ago, the quality of light on that day, and how the breezes blew, fragrant and warm. He can hear the voices.

"Oh," William says, shortly before they start to eat. "We forgot to say grace."

"It's too late now," Susan says.

"It's not too late. It can't ever be too late."

"It's too late."

"It's not too late—that's just silly, Susan."

"Daddy, isn't it too late?"

"It's not too late," Irene says. "William, go ahead."

"Bless us, O Lord, and these Thy gifts which we are about to receive from Thy bounty, through Christ our Lord, amen."

"I still say it was too late," Susan says.

Irene says, "Susan."

"I've decided I'm going to be a nun," Susan says.

"Susan—that's nothing to joke about."

"It's not a joke. I'm going to be a nun and wear icky black clothes and have my hair cut off at the roots and sit in church with my hands open in my lap and sing off tune like Sister Marie does."

"That's a sacrilege," William says.

"What's a sacrilege?" Brad asks.

"It's when you talk like Susan," says William.

"A sacrilege," says Susan, "is when you take Holy Communion with a mortal sin on your soul."

"And when you say you're going to be a nun when you're not," William says.

"Come on now, kids," Walter says, "let's get off each other a little. Let's talk about something nice."

"I know," says Brad, "let's talk about Pac-Man."

"Who wants to talk about *that,*" says Carol.

"All I said was I was going to be a nun," Susan says, "and everybody gets crazy. Mostly Saint William. You should've heard Saint William a little while ago, planning his martyrdom in China—shot by the Commies. Right, William?"

"That's enough," Walter says. "Let him alone. Let's everybody let everybody else alone. Jesus."

"Have mercy on us," William mutters.

"Oh, look," Walter says, "don't do that. Don't pray when I talk."

Irene says, "Let's just eat quietly, all right?"

"Well, he keeps praying around me. Jesus, I *hate* that."

"Have mercy on us," says William.

"When're you leaving for China, son?"

"You don't have to make fun of me."

"Okay, look—let's all start over. Jesus." Walter spins around, to catch William moving his lips. "Jesus Jesus Jesus Jesus Jesus," he says.

William crosses himself.

"Amazing. The kid's amazing."

"Let's all please just stop it and eat. Can we please just do that?"

Susan says, "I've changed my mind about being a nun. I'm going to be a priest."

"Oh," William says, "that *is* a sacrilege."

"William," says Walter, "will you please pronounce the excommunications so we can all go to hell in peace?"

"I don't even like this family," the boy mutters.

"Perhaps you should've asked your Father in heaven to have chosen another family for you to be raised in on your trek to the cross."

"Have mercy."

"I don't believe I used any profanity that last time."

"Have mercy on us," William mutters.

"All right!" Irene shouts. "We're going to eat and stop all this arguing and bickering. Please, Walter."

"You might address your displeasure to the Christ, here. Or is it the Vicar of Christ?"

"Have mercy on us."

"I'll be the first lady priest in the Catholic Church," Susan says, "and then I'll get married."

Walter says, "Don't pay any attention to her, William. Think of her as a cross to bear."

"Walter," Irene says.

He stands. "Okay. Truce. No more teasing and no more bickering. We are a family, right? We have to stick together and tolerate each other sometimes."

They are looking at him. He touches his own face, where his mouth, his lips are numb. His eyes feel swollen.

"And then," Susan says, "after I'm married, I'll become Pope."

Walter bursts into laughter as William turns to Susan and says, "You are committing a mortal sin."

"Susan!" Irene says.

Walter says, "Judge not, lest ye be judged, William, my boy."

"I know what a mortal sin is," Brad says.

"Everybody knows that," says James.

"Look for the mote, William. When you see the gleam, look for the mote," Walter is saying.

William mutters, "I don't even know what that means."

"Walter, sit down," Irene says. "Let him alone. All of you let him alone."

"Let's all leave each other alone, that's right," Walter says. He sits down. They eat quietly for a while, and he watches them. Irene wipes mustard from Carol's mouth, from the front of her dress. William's eyes are glazed, and he eats furiously, not looking at anyone. He has been caught out in his pride, Walter thinks, has been shown to himself as less perfect than the glorious dream of a movie he wants to live. It dawns on Walter that his son probably prays for him, since he does not go to church. He wonders, now, what they all think of that, of the fact that he is, by every tenet of their religion, bound for hell. This makes him laugh.

"What?" Irene says. "Tell me."

"Nothing. I was—" He thinks for a moment. "I was thinking about this one," pointing to Susan, "planning to be a married lady priest."

Susan beams under his gaze.

And then he looks at William, feels sorry. "It's okay, William," he says, "it's all in fun."

The boy continues to eat.

"William."

Irene touches Walter's wrist.

"No," Walter says, "the kid can accept somebody's—a gesture—can't he? My God."

William crosses himself again.

Walter stands. "That's the last time."

"Father Boyer, at church," William says almost defiantly, "he told us to do it whenever someone used the Lord's name—"

Walter interrupts him. "I don't care what Father Boyer said. I'm bigger than Father Boyer. I can beat the *shit* out of Father Boyer."

"Not another word from anyone!" Irene shouts.

For a moment no one says anything.

"Well," Walter says, "aren't we a happy bunch?"

James says, "What do you expect?"

"Why don't you explain that one, James?"

The boy shrugs. He is always saying these mysteriously adult things that seem to refer slyly to other things, and then shrugging them off as if he is too tired to bother explaining them. Last year, at the age of eight, he announced to Irene that he did not believe in God. It was a crisis; Irene feared that something serious was wrong. James has since revised himself:

57

he will grant the existence. Those are the words he used. Walter looks upon him with more than a little trepidation, because James is the one who most resembles him. More even than William, who, now, with his heart in the lap of God, is hard to place. Even Irene, for all her devoutness, finds William irritating at times.

"I am going to be a priest," Susan says now. "All I have to do is get them to change the rules."

"You," says Walter, "are the saint of persistence. You know what a wolverine is?"

"Some kind of wolf?"

"The wolverine kills its prey by sheer persistence. I mean, if it decided it wanted you for dinner, you could take a plane to Seattle, the wolverine would meet you at the airport, bib on, knife and fork ready, licking his chops. Salt and pepper by the plate, oregano, parsley, a beer . . ."

Susan laughs.

"Daddy's funny," Carol says.

"When I'm the first lady priest and married Pope, I'll buy a wolverine and keep it as a pet," Susan says.

"Have mercy on us," says William.

"All right," Walter says, "let's drop it, please, William. No more prayers, please. We're all right. God will forgive us, I'm sure, if we all just shut the fuck up for a while."

"Walter!"

"I'm sorry, I'm sorry," he says.

They are quiet, then, for a long time. The youngest ones, Brad and James and Carol, look at him with something like amazement. He makes two more trips to the trunk of the car, not even hiding it now, and in the end he gets Carol and James to laugh at him by making faces, miming someone sliding off a bench, pretending to be terrified of his food. Susan and William laugh too, now, as he does a man unable to get a hot dog into his mouth.

"You clown," Irene says, but she smiles.

They all laugh and talk now; the afternoon wanes that way:

Walter tosses the football with William, and Brad and James chase a Frisbee with Susan and Carol. Irene sits on the picnic table, sipping her lemonade. It grows cooler, and others come to the field, and finally it's time to leave. They all work together, gathering the debris of the afternoon, and Walter packs the trunk. He's bold enough to take the bottle of Beam out of its place and drink from it—small sips, he tells Irene, offering her some. She refuses as she has always refused, but she does so with, he is sure, a smile. It strikes him that there is nothing to worry about, not a thing in the world, and he clowns with his children, makes them laugh, all the way home, Irene driving. He calls to people out the window of the car, funny things, and they are all almost hysterical with laughter. They arrive; there is the slow unwinding, getting out of the car and stretching legs and arms, and Walter begins to wrestle with Carol, bending over her, tickling her upper legs, swinging her through his own as she wriggles and laughs. Brad jumps on his back, then, and he pretends to be pulled down, rolls in the grass with the boy, and then chases him, bent over, arms dangling, like an ape's. He is hearing the delightful keening sound of his children's laughter in the shadows. It is getting dark. He chases Brad and James around to the back yard, and they are hiding there, just beyond the square lighter shape of Irene's garden. He crouches in the shadow of the house and makes an ape sound, *whoo-hooo, whooo-hooo hah-hah-hah-hah.* He can hear them talking low and he thinks, Why this is easy, this is fun. Carefully he works his way closer, seeing William and Susan running along the back fence, their silhouettes in the dusky light. *Whoo-hoo, whoo-hoo.* And now he makes his run at them, changes direction, follows Brad, while the others scatter. When he catches Brad, he carries him under his arm, kicking and struggling, to the house, the screened-in back porch, where the others have gathered and are huddling, laughing in the dark. He comes stumbling up onto the porch and he has them, they are trapped with him. He puts Brad down in the mass of struggling arms and legs; he engulfs them, kneeling; he has them all in the wide embrace of his arms; he's tickling a leg here, pinching or squeezing an arm there, roaring, gorilla-like. He catches one of them trying to get away, then turns and grabs another. He's got them all again, and they are yelling and laughing, there is light on them now, a swath of yellow light, and he looks up to see Irene's shape in the doorway, everything speeding up again, until there is a long shout, a scream.

And he stops. He stands, sees that they are cringing against the base of the porch wall, to the left of the door, cringing there and shaking, their eyes enormous, filled with tears.

"Kids?" he says.

They are sobbing, and he steps back, nearly tumbles backward out of the screen door and down the stairs. "Kids?" he says.

Nobody moves.

"H-hey. Kids?"

Irene steps down, bends to help William rise. They all get up slowly, looking at him with the tremendous wariness of animals at bay.

"H-hey—it's me," he says, holding out one hand. "Kids?"

"Come on," Irene is saying, "don't be silly. Your daddy would never hurt you." She makes each of them kiss him, then ushers them inside. "Susan, will you start the bathwater?" The door closes on them. Walter looks at his hands and says, "God. Oh my God." He doesn't really hear himself. And in a moment Irene opens the door and steps out lightly, closing it behind her. All around, now, the insects are starting up. Irene's voice begins softly: "We've been through so much, Walter, so much together—and I simply can't do it any more. I don't know what to say or do any more. I love you, but I can't make it be enough any more." She kisses him on the side of the face, turns, and is gone.

Yet it takes more than a year for her finally to leave him. She gives him every chance. She waits for him to put it together as he keeps saying he will. He tries for a while, in fact: he goes to a doctor, a psychologist specializing in family counselling, who tells him he has not broken with his father, and instructs him to find some ritual way of making the break. So he goes back to Alabama to stand over his father's grave. At first, nothing happens. He feels anger, but it is only what he expected to feel. And then there is a kind of sorrow, almost sweet, welling up in him. It makes him wince, actually take a step back from the grave as if something had moved there. When he was seven years old his father took him outside of the house in Montgomery and made him urinate on his mother's roses. He tells himself, standing over the grave in Montgomery, that children have been through worse; indeed, he himself has. Yet it takes all the moisture from his mouth, remembering it. Perhaps it is the fact that it was done to him not for himself but to get at his mother—there is something so terrifying about being used that way, merely as an instrument of wounding. In any case, it has haunted him, and now at the gravesite he spits, he rages, he tears the grass. It all seems simply ordained. It is a role he plays, watching himself play it. It exorcizes nothing.

He returns from Alabama with a sense of doom riding him like a spirit, a weight on his neck, the back of his shoulders. He visits the psychologist, who seems slightly alarmed at the effect of the journey on him. He is determined, vibrant with will, and hopelessly afraid. The psychologist wants to know what his exact thought was the first time he ever picked up a drink. Walter can't remember that. His father never drank. He believes he wanted at first to show his freedom, like other boys. He says finally he wanted it to relax and be kind, to relieve some of the tensions that build in him. And so the psychologist begins to try to explore, with him, those tensions. They are many, but they all have the same root, and there is no use talking about childhood trauma and dreams: Walter is versed in the canon; his hopes are for something else. He can tell the psychologist the whole thing in a single sentence: he has always been paralyzed by the fear that he will repeat, with his own children, the pattern of his father's brutality. What he wants is for the psychologist to guarantee him that this won't happen, tell him categorically that there will be no such repetition, and of course this can't be done. Life must be lived in the uncertainty of freedom of choice, the psychologist says. The problem is that Walter is afraid to take responsibility for himself. It is all talk, and it is all true. Walter's father had a thing he liked to call "night dances," in which, for the benefit of Walter, for his correction and edification, Walter's father became a sort of dark gibbet that Walter danced beneath, held by the wrist within the small circumference, the range, of a singing swung belt whose large buckle was embossed with the head of a longhorn steer. This all took place in the basement of the house in Montgomery, before Walter was ten years old. There was no light at all in the basement, and so it was necessary for the boy to dodge blindly, and to keep from crying too loudly, so he could hear the *whoosh-whoosh* of the belt. Walter trembles to think of that. He tells the psychologist how his father would swing the belt calmly, without passion, like a machine, quiet in the dark. He shakes, telling it. He talks about the ancient story: the man who, in the act of trying to avoid some evil in himself, embraces it, creates it.

The visits end. He is dry for about two weeks, but falters, and Irene finally does leave him.

This is what has happened to him. He is in Flagstaff, Arizona. He sits gazing at the small stained-glass windows on either side of the church, where in a few minutes he will probably be talking to a priest. God, he thinks, Flagstaff, Arizona. There is no reason for it. Perhaps he will go somewhere else, too. There is no telling where he might wind up. Irene and the children are all the way in Atlanta, Georgia, with Irene's parents. He has not had anything to drink today, and his hands shake, so he looks at them. He wonders if he should wait to talk to a priest, if he should tell a priest anything, or just ask for some food, maybe. He wonders if maybe he shouldn't tell the priest about the day of the picnic

that he has been remembering so vividly, when Irene came out
on the porch and told him she couldn't make it be enough any
more. He wonders if he should talk about it: how he walked
out to the very edge of the lawn and turned to look upon the
lighted windows of the house, thinking of the people inside,
whom he had named and loved and called sons, daughters,
wife. How he had stood there trembling, shaking as from a
terrific chill, while the dark, the night, came.

Ancient history

In the car on the way south, after hours of quiet between them, of only the rattle and static of the radio, she began to talk about growing up so close to Washington: how it was to have all the shrines of Democracy as a part of one's daily idea of home; she had taken it all for granted, of course. "But your father was always a tourist in his own city," she said. "It really excited him. That's why we spent our honeymoon there. Everybody thought we'd got tickets to travel, and we weren't fifteen minutes from home. We checked into the Lafayette Hotel, right across from the White House. The nicest old hotel. I was eighteen years old, and all my heroes were folk singers. Jack Kennedy was President. Lord, it seems so much closer than it is." She was watching the country glide past the window, so Charles couldn't see her face. He was driving. The road was wet, probably icy in places. On either side were brown, snowpatched hills, and the sky seemed to move like a smoke along the crests. "My God. Charles, I was exactly your age now. Isn't that amazing. Well, I don't suppose you find it so amazing."

"It's amazing, Mom." He smiled at her.

"Yes, well, you wait. Wait till you're my age. You'll see."

A little later, she said, "All the times you and your father and I have been down here, and I still feel like it's been a thousand years."

"It's strange to be coming through when the trees are all bare," said Charles. Aunt Lois had asked them to come. She didn't want to be alone on Christmas, and she didn't want to travel any more; she had come north to visit every Christmas for fifteen years, and now that Lawrence was gone she didn't feel there was any reason to put herself through the journey again, certainly not to sit in that house with Charles's mother and pine for some other Christmas. She was going to stay put, and if people wanted to see her, they could come south. "Meaning us," Charles's mother said. And Aunt Lois said, "That's exactly what I meant, Marie. I'm glad you're still quick on the uptake." They were talking on the telephone, but Aunt Lois's voice was so clear and resonant that Charles, sitting across the room from his mother, could hear every word. His mother held the receiver an inch from her ear and looked at him and smiled. They'd go. Aunt Lois was not about to budge. "We do want to see her," Charles's mother said, "and I guess we don't really want to be here for Christmas, do we?"

Charles shook his head no.

"I guess we don't want Christmas to come at all," she said into the phone. Charles heard Aunt Lois say that it was coming anyway, and nothing would stop it. When his mother had hung up, he said, "I don't think I want to go through it anywhere," meaning Christmas.

She said, "We could just stay here and not celebrate it or something. Or we could have a bunch of people over, like we did on Thanksgiving."

"No," Charles said, "let's go."

"I know one thing," she said. "Your father wouldn't want us moping around on his favorite holiday."

"I'm not moping," Charles said.

"Good. Dad wouldn't like it."

It had been four months, and she had weathered her grief, had shown him how strong she was, yet sometimes such a bewildered look came into her eyes. He saw in it something of his own bewilderment: his father had been young and vigorous, his heart had been judged to be strong—and now life seemed so frail and precarious.

Driving south, Charles looked over at his mother and wondered how he would ever be able to let her out of his sight. "Mom," he said, "let's travel somewhere."

"I thought we were doing just that," she said.

"Let's close the house up and go to Europe or someplace."

"We don't have that kind of money; are you kidding? There's money for you to go to school, and that's about it. And you know it, Charles."

"It wouldn't cost that much to go somewhere for a while. There's all kinds of package deals—discounts and special fares—it wouldn't cost that much."

"Why don't *you* go?"

"By myself?"

"Isn't there a friend you'd like to go with—somebody with the money to go?"

"I thought *we'd* go."

"Don't you think I'd get in your way a little? A young man like you, in one of those touring groups with his mother?"

"I thought it might be a good thing," he muttered.

She turned a little on the seat, to face him. "Don't mope, Charles."

"I'm not. I just thought it might be fun to travel together."

"We travel everywhere together these days," she said.

He stared ahead at the road.

"You know," she said after a moment, "I think Aunt Lois was a little surprised that we took her up on her invitation."

"Wouldn't *you* like traveling together?" Charles said.

"I think you should go with somebody else if you go. I'm glad we're taking *this* trip together. I really am. But for me to go on a long trip like that with you—well, it just seems, I don't know, uncalled for."

"Why uncalled for?" he asked.

"Let's take one trip at a time," she said.

"Yes, but why uncalled for?"

"We'll talk about it later." This was her way of curtailing a discussion; she would say, very calmly, as if there were all the time in the world, "We'll talk about it later," and of course her intention was that the issue, whatever its present importance, would be forgotten, the subject would be closed. If it was broached again, she was likely to show impatience and, often, a kind of dismay, as if one had shown very bad manners calling up so much old-hat, so much ancient history.

"I'm not doing anything out of duty," Charles said.

"Who said anything about duty?"

"I just wanted you to know."

"What an odd thing to say."

"Well, you said that about it being uncalled for."

"I just meant it's not necessary, Charles. Besides, don't you think it's time for you to get on with the business of your own life?"

"I don't see how traveling together is stopping me," he said.

"All right, but I don't want to talk about it now."

"Okay, then."

"Aren't you going a little fast?"

He slowed down.

A few moments later, she said, "You're driving. I guess I shouldn't have said anything."

"I *was* going too fast," he said.

"I'm kind of jumpy, too."

They lapsed into silence. It had begun to rain a little, and Charles turned the windshield wipers on. Other cars, coming by them, threw a muddy spray up from the road.

"Of all things," his mother said, "I really am nervous all of a sudden."

Aunt Lois's house was a little three-bedroom rambler in a row of three-bedroom ramblers just off the interstate. At the end of her block was an overpass sixty feet high, which at the same time each clear winter afternoon blotted out the sun; a wide band of shade stretched across the lawn and the house, and the sidewalk often stayed frozen longer than the rest of the street. Aunt Lois kept a five-pound bag of rock salt in a child's wagon on her small front porch, and in the evenings she would stand there and throw handfuls of it on the walk. Charles's father would tease her about it, as he teased her about everything: her chain-smoking, her love of country music—which she denied vehemently—her fear of growing fat, and her various disasters with men, about which she was apt to hold forth at great length and with very sharp humor, with herself as the butt of the jokes, the bumbling central character.

She stood in the light of her doorway, arms folded tight, and called to them to be careful of ice patches on the walk. There was so much rock salt it crackled under their feet, and Charles thought of the gravel walk they had all traversed following his father's body in the funeral procession, the last time he had seen Aunt Lois. He shivered as he looked at her now, outlined in the light.

"I swear," she was saying, "I can't believe you actually decided to come."

"Whoops," Charles's mother said, losing her balance slightly. She leaned on his arm as they came up onto the porch. Aunt Lois stood back from the door. Charles couldn't shake the feeling of the long funeral walk, that procession in his mind. He held tight to his mother's elbow as they stepped up through Aunt Lois's door. Her living room was warm, and smelled of cake. There was a fire in the fireplace. The lounge chair his father always sat in was on the other side of the room. Aunt Lois had moved it. Charles saw that the imprint of its legs was still in the nap of the carpet. Aunt Lois was looking at him.

"Well," she said, smiling and glancing away. She had put pine cones and sprigs of pine along the mantel. On the sofa the Sunday papers lay scattered. "I was beginning to worry," she said, closing the door. "It's been such a nasty day for driving." She took their coats and hung them in the closet by the front door. She was busying herself, bustling around the room. "Sometimes I think I'd rather drive in snow than rain like this." Finally she looked at Charles. "Don't I get a hug?"

He put his arms around her, felt the thinness of her shoulders. One of the things his father used to say to her was that she couldn't get fat if it was required, and the word *required* had had some other significance for them both, for all the adults. Charles had never fully understood it; it had something to do with when they were all at school. He said, "Aunt Lois, you couldn't get fat if it was required."

"Don't," she said, waving a hand in front of her face and blinking. "Lord, boy, you even sound like him."

He said, "We had a smooth trip." There wasn't anything else he could think of. She had moved out of his arms and was embracing his mother. The two women stood there holding tight, and his mother sniffled.

"I'm so glad you're here," Aunt Lois said. "I feel like you've come home."

Charles's mother said, "What smells so good?" and wiped her eyes with the backs of her hands.

"I made spice cake. Or I *tried* spice cake. I burned it, of course."

"It smells good," Charles said.

"It does," said his mother.

Aunt Lois said, "I hope you like it *very* brown." And then they were at a loss for something else to say. Charles looked at the empty lounge chair, and Aunt Lois turned and busied herself with the clutter of newspapers on the sofa. "I'll just get this out of the way," she said.

"I've got to get the suitcases out of the trunk," Charles said.

They hadn't heard him. Aunt Lois was stacking the newspapers, and his mother strolled about the room like a daydreaming tourist in a museum. He let himself out and walked to the car, feeling the cold, and the aches and stiffnesses of having driven all day. It was misting now, and a wind was blowing. Cars and trucks rumbled by on the overpass, their headlights fanning out into the fog. He stood and watched them go by, and quite suddenly he did not want to be here. In the house, in the warm light of the window, his mother and Aunt Lois moved, already arranging things, already settling themselves for what would be the pattern of the next few days; and

Charles, fumbling with the car keys in the dark, feeling the mist on the back of his neck, had the disquieting sense that he had come to the wrong place. The other houses, shrouded in darkness, with only one winking blue light in the window of the farthest one, seemed alien and unfriendly somehow. "Aw, Dad," he said under his breath.

As he got the trunk open, Aunt Lois came out and made her way to him, moving very slowly, her arms out for balance. She had put on an outlandish pair of floppy yellow boots, and her flannel bathrobe collar jutted above the collar of her raincoat. "Marie seems none the worse for wear," she said to him. "How are you two getting along?"

"We had a smooth trip," Charles said.

"I didn't mean the trip."

"We're okay, Aunt Lois."

"She says you want to go to Europe with her."

"It didn't take her long," Charles said, "did it. I just suggested it in the car on the way here. It was just an idea."

"Let me take one of those bags, honey. I don't want her to think I came out here just to jabber with you, although that's exactly why I did come out."

Charles handed her his own small suitcase.

"You like my boots?" she said. "I figured I could attract a handsome fireman with them." She modeled them for him, turning.

"They're a little big for you, Aunt Lois."

"You're no fun."

He was struggling with his mother's suitcases.

"I guess you noticed that I moved the chair. You looked a little surprised. But when I got back here after the funeral I walked in there and—well, there it was, right where he always was whenever you all visited. I used to tease him about sleeping in it all day—you remember. We all used to tease him about it. Well, I didn't want you to walk in and see it that way—"

Charles closed the trunk of the car and hefted the suitcases, facing her.

"You want to go home, don't you?" she said.

It seemed to him that she had always had a way of reading him. "I want everything to be back the way it was," he said.

"I know," Aunt Lois said.

He followed her back to the house. On the porch she turned and gave him a sad look and then forced a smile. "You're an intelligent young man, and a very good one, too. So serious and sweet—a very dear, sweet boy."

He might have mumbled a thank-you, he didn't really know. He was embarrassed and confused and sick at heart; he had thought he wanted this visit. Aunt Lois kissed him on the cheek, then stood back and sighed. "I'm going to need your help about something. Boy, am I ever."

"What's the matter?" he said.

"It's nothing. It's just a situation." She sighed again. She wasn't looking at him now. "I don't know why, but I find it—well, reassuring, somehow, that we—we—leave such a gaping hole in everything when we go."

He just stood there, weighted down with the bags.

"Well," she said, and opened the door for him.

Charles's mother said she wanted to sit up and talk, but she kept nodding off. Finally she was asleep. When Aunt Lois began gently to wake her, to walk her in to her bed, Charles excused himself and made his way to his own bed. A few moments later he heard Aunt Lois in the kitchen. As had always been her custom, she would drink one last cup of coffee before retiring. He lay awake, hearing the soft tink of her cup against the saucer, and at last he began to drift. But in a little while he was fully awake again. Aunt Lois was moving through the house turning the lights off, and soon she too was down for the night. Charles stared through the shadows of the doorway to what he knew was the entrance to the living room, and listened to the house settle into itself. Outside, there were the hum and whoosh of traffic on the overpass, and the occasional sighing rush of rain at the window, like surf. Yet he knew he wouldn't sleep. He was thinking of summer nights in a cottage on Cape Cod, when his family was happy, and he lay with the sun burning in his skin and listened to the adults talking and laughing out on the screened porch, the sound of the bay rushing like this rain at this window. He couldn't sleep. Turning in the bed, he cupped his hands over his face.

A year ago, two years—at some time and in some way that was beyond him—his parents had grown quiet with each other, a change had started, and he could remember waking up one morning near the end of his last school year with a deep sense that something somewhere would go so wrong, was already so wrong that there would be no coming back from it. There was a change in the chemistry of the household that sapped his will, that took the breath out of him and left him in an exhaustion so profound that even the small energy necessary for speech seemed unavailable to him. This past summer, the first summer out of high school, he had done nothing with himself; he had found nothing he wanted to do, nothing he could feel anything at all about. He looked for a job because his parents insisted that he do so; it was an ordeal of walking, of managing to talk, to fill out applications, and in the end he found nothing. The summer wore on and his father grew angry and sullen with him. Charles was a disappointment and knew it; he was overweight, and seemed lazy, and he couldn't find a way to explain himself. His mother thought there might be something physically wrong, and so then there were doctors, and medical examinations to endure. What he wanted was to stay in the house and have his parents be the people that they once were—happy, fortunate people with interest in each other and warmth and humor between them. And then one day in September his father keeled over on the sidewalk outside a restaurant in New York, and Charles had begun to be this person he now was, someone hurting in this irremediable way, lying awake in his aunt's house in the middle of a cold

December night, wishing with all his heart it were some other time, some other place.

In the morning, after breakfast, Aunt Lois began to talk about how good it would be to have people at her table for dinner on Christmas Eve. She had opened the draperies wide, to watch the snow fall outside. The snow had started before sunrise, but nothing had accumulated yet; it was melting as it hit the ground. Aunt Lois talked about how Christmasy it felt, and about getting a tree to put up, about making a big turkey dinner. "I don't think anybody should be alone on Christmas," he said. "Do you, Marie?"

"Not unless they want to," Marie said.

"Right, and who wants to be alone on Christmas?"

"Lois, I suppose you're going to come to the point soon."

"Well," Aunt Lois said, "I guess I am driving at something. I've invited someone over to dinner on Christmas Eve."

"Who."

"It's someone you know."

"Lois, please."

"I ran into him on jury duty last June," Aunt Lois said. "Can you imagine? After all these years—and we've become very good friends again. I mean I'd court him if I thought I had a chance."

"Lois, who are we talking about?"

"Well," Aunt Lois said, "it's Bill Downs."

Marie stood. "You're not serious."

"It has nothing to do with anything," Lois said. "To tell you the truth, I invited them before I knew you were coming."

"Them?"

"He has a cousin visiting. I told him they could both come."

"Who's Bill Downs?" Charles asked.

"He's nobody," said his mother.

"He's somebody from a long time ago," Aunt Lois said. They had spoken almost in unison. Aunt Lois went on: "His cousin

73

just lost his wife. Well—last year. Bill didn't want him to be alone. He says he's a very interesting man—"

"Lois, I don't care if he's the King of England."

"I didn't mean anything by it," Aunt Lois said. "Don't make it into something it isn't. Look at us, anyway—look how depleted we are. I want people here. I don't want it just the three of us on Christmas. You have Charles; I'm the last one in this family, Marie. And this—this isn't just *your* grief. Lawrence was my brother. I didn't want to be alone—do you want me to spell it out for you?"

Marie now seemed too confused to speak. She only glanced at Charles, then turned and left the room. Her door closed quietly. Aunt Lois sat back against the cushions of the sofa and shut her eyes for a moment.

"Who's Bill Downs?" Charles said.

When she opened her eyes it was as if she had just noticed him there. "The whole thing is just silly. We were all kids together. It was a million years ago."

Charles said nothing. In the fireplace a single charred log hissed. Aunt Lois sat forward and took a cigarette from her pack and lighted it. "I wonder what you're thinking."

"I don't know."

"Do you have a steady girl, Charles?"

He nodded. The truth was that he was too shy, too aware of his girth and the floridness of his complexion, too nervous and clumsy to be more than the clownish, kindly friend he was to the girls he knew.

"Do you think you'll go on and marry her?"

"Who?" he said.

"Your girl."

"Oh," he said, "probably not."

"Some people do, of course. And some don't. Some people go on and meet other people. Do you see? When I met your mother, your father was away at college."

"I think I had this figured out already, Aunt Lois."

"Well—then that's who Bill Downs is." She got to her feet,

with some effort, then stood gazing down at him. "This just isn't the way it looks, though. And everybody will just have to believe me about it."

"I believe you," Charles said.

"She doesn't," said Aunt Lois, "and now she's probably going to start lobbying to go home."

Charles shook his head.

"I hope you won't let her talk you into it."

"Nobody's going anywhere," Marie said, coming into the room. She sat down on the sofa and opened the morning paper, and when she spoke now it was as if she were not even attentive to her own words. "Though it would serve you right if everybody deserted you out of embarrassment."

"You might think about *me* a little, Marie. You might think how *I* feel in all this."

Marie put the newspaper down on her lap and looked at her. "I am thinking of you. If I wasn't thinking of you I'd be in the car this minute, heading north, whether Charles would come or not."

"Well, fine," Aunt Lois said, and stormed out of the room.

A little later, Charles and Marie went into the city. They parked the car in a garage on H Street and walked over to Lafayette Square. It was still snowing, but the ground was too warm; it wouldn't stick. Charles said, "Might as well be raining," and realized that neither of them had spoken since they had pulled away from Aunt Lois's house.

"Charles," his mother said, and then seemed to stop herself. "Never mind."

"What?" he said.

"Nothing. It's easy to forget that you're only eighteen. I forget sometimes, that's all."

Charles sensed that this wasn't what she had started to say, but kept silent. They crossed the square and entered a sandwich shop on Seventeenth Street, to warm themselves with a cup of coffee. They sat at a table by the window and looked out at the street, the people walking by—shoppers mostly, burdened with packages.

"Where's the Lafayette Hotel from here?" Charles asked.

"Oh, honey, they tore that down a long time ago."

"Where was it?"

"You can't see it from here." She took a handkerchief out of her purse and touched the corners of her eyes with it. "The cold makes my eyes sting. How about you?"

"It's the wind," Charles said.

She looked at him. "My ministering angel."

"Mom," he said.

Now she looked out the window. "Your father would be proud of you now." She bowed her head slightly, fumbling with her purse, and then she was crying. She held the handkerchief to her nose, and the tears dropped down over her hand.

"Mom," he said, reaching for her wrist.

She withdrew from him a little. "No, you don't understand."

"Let's go," Charles said.

"I don't think I could stand to be home now, Charles. Not on Christmas. Not this Christmas."

Charles paid the check and then went back to the table to help her into her coat. "Goddam Lois," she said, pulling the furry collar up to cover her ears.

"Tell me about your girlfriend," Aunt Lois said.

He shrugged this off.

They were sitting in the kitchen, breaking up bread for the dressing, while Marie napped on the sofa in the living room. Aunt Lois had brought the turkey out and set it on the counter. The meat deep in its breast still had to thaw, she told Charles. She was talking just to talk. Things had been very cool since the morning, and Charles was someone to talk to.

"Won't even tell me her name?"

76

"I'm not really going with anybody," he said.

"A handsome boy like you."

"Aunt Lois, could we talk about something else?"

She said, "All right. Tell me what you did all fall."

"I took care of the house."

"Did you read any good books or see any movies or take anybody out besides your mother?"

"Sure," he said.

"Okay, tell me about it."

"What do you want to know?"

"I want to know what you did all fall."

"What is this?" Charles said.

She spoke quickly. "I apologize for prying. I won't say another word."

"Look," he said, "Aunt Lois, I'm not keeping myself from anything right now. I couldn't have concentrated in school in September."

"I know," she said, "I know."

There was a long silence.

"I wonder if it's too late for me to get married and have a bunch of babies," she said suddenly. "I think I'd like the noise they'd make."

That night, they watched Christmas specials. Charles dozed in the lounge chair by the fireplace, a magazine on his lap, and the women sat on the sofa. No one spoke. On television, celebrities sang old Christmas songs, and during the commercials other celebrities appealed to the various yearnings for cheer and happiness and possessions, and the thrill of giving. In a two-hour cartoon with music and production numbers, Scrooge made his night-long journey to wisdom and love; the Cratchits were portrayed as church mice. Aunt Lois remarked that this was cute, and no one answered her. Charles feigned sleep. When the news came on, Aunt Lois turned the television off, and they said good night. Charles kissed them both on the cheek, and went to his room. For a long while after he lay down, he heard them talking low. They had gone to Aunt Lois's room. He couldn't distinguish words, but the tones were chilly and serious. He rolled over on his side and punched the pillow into shape and stared at the faint outline of trees outside the window, trying not to hear. The voices continued, and he heard his mother's voice rising, so that he could almost make out words now. His mother said something about last summer, and then both women were silent. A few moments later, Aunt Lois came marching down the hall past his door, on into the kitchen, where she opened cabinets and slammed them, and ran water. She was going to make coffee, she said, when Marie called to her. If she wanted a cup of coffee in her own house at any hour of the night she'd have a coffee.

Charles waited a minute or so, then got up, put his robe on, and went in to her. She sat at the table, arms folded, waiting for the water to boil.

"It's sixty dollars for a good Christmas tree," she said. "A ridiculous amount of money."

Charles sat down across from her.

"You're just like your father," she said, "you placate. And I think he placated your mother too much—that's what I think."

He said, "Come on, Aunt Lois."

"Well, she makes me so mad, I can't help it. She doesn't want to go home and she doesn't want to stay here and she won't listen to the slightest suggestion about you or the way you've been nursemaiding her for four months. And she's just going to stay mad at me all week. Now, you tell me."

"I just wish everybody would calm down," Charles said.

She stood and turned her back to him and set about making her coffee.

According to the medical report, Charles's father had suffered a massive coronary occlusion, and death was almost instantaneous; it could not have been attended with much pain.

Perhaps there had been a second's recognition, but little more than that. The doctor wanted Charles and his mother to know that the speed with which an attack like that kills is a blessing. In his sleep, Charles heard the doctor's voice saying this, and then he was watching his father fall down on the sidewalk outside the restaurant; people walked by and stared, and Charles looked at their faces, the faces of strangers.

He woke trembling in the dark, the only one awake on Christmas Eve morning. He lay on his side, facing the window, and watched the dawn arrive, and at last someone was up, moving around in the kitchen.

It was his mother. She was making coffee. "You're up early," she said.

"I dreamed about Dad."

"I dream about him too," she said. She opened the refrigerator. "Good God, there's a leg of lamb in here. Where did this come from? What in the world is that woman thinking of? The turkey's big enough for eight people."

"Maybe it's for tomorrow."

"And don't always defend her, either, Charles. She's not infallible, you know."

"I never said she was."

"None of them—your father wasn't. I mean—" She closed the refrigerator and took a breath. "He wouldn't want you to put him on a pedestal."

"I didn't," Charles said.

"People are people," she said. "They don't always add up."

This didn't seem to require a response.

"And I've known Lois since she was seventeen years old. I know how she thinks."

"I'm not defending anybody," he said, "I'm just the one in between everything here. I wish you'd both just leave me out of it."

"Go get dressed," she said. "Nobody's putting you in between anybody."

"Mom."

"No—you're right. I won't involve you. Now really, go get dressed." She looked as though she might begin to cry again. She patted him on the wrist and then went back to the refrigerator. "I wanted something in here," she said, opening it. There were dark blue veins forking over her ankles. She looked old and thin and afraid and lonely, and he turned his eyes away.

The three of them went to shop for a tree. Charles drove. They looked in three places and couldn't agree on anything, and when it began to rain Aunt Lois took matters into her own hands. She made them wait in the car while she picked out the tree she wanted for what was, after all, her living room. They got the tree home, and had to saw off part of the trunk to get it up, but when it was finished, ornamented and wound with popcorn and tinsel, they all agreed that it was a handsome tree—a round, long-needled pine that looked like a jolly rotund elf, with its sawed-off trunk and its top listing slightly to the left under the weight of a tinfoil star. They turned its lights on and stood admiring it, and for a while there was something of the warmth of other Christmases in the air. Work on the decorations, and all the cooperation required to get everything accomplished, seemed to have created a kind of peace between the two women. They spent the early part of the evening wrapping presents for the morning, each in his own room with his gifts for the others, and then Aunt Lois put the television on, and went about her business, getting the dinner ready. She wanted no help from anyone, she said, but Marie began to help anyway, and Aunt Lois did nothing to stop her. Charles sat in the lounge chair and watched a parade. It was the halftime of a football game, but he was not interested in it, and soon he had begun to doze again. He sank deep, and there were no dreams, and then Aunt Lois was telling him to wake up. "Charles," she said, "they're here." He sat forward in the chair, a little startled, and Aunt Lois laughed. "Wake up, son," she said. Charles saw a man standing by the Christmas tree, smiling at him. Another man sat on the sofa, his legs spread a little to make room for his stomach; he looked blown up, his neck bulging over the collar of his shirt.

"Charles," Aunt Lois said, indicating the man on the sofa, "this is Mr. Rainy."

Mr. Rainy was smiling in an almost imbecilic way, not really looking at anyone.

"This is Charles," Aunt Lois said to him.

They shook hands. "Nice to meet you," Mr. Rainy said. He had a soft, high-pitched voice.

"And this is Mr. Downs."

Charles looked at him, took the handshake he offered. Bill Downs was tall and a little stooped, and he seemed very uneasy. He looked around the room, and his hands went into his pockets and then flew up to his hair, which was wild-looking and very sparse.

"Marie will be out any time, I'm sure," Aunt Lois said in a voice that, to Charles at least, sounded anything but sure. "In the meantime, can I get anybody a drink?"

No one wanted anything right away. Mr. Rainy had brought two bottles of champagne, which Aunt Lois took from him and put on ice in the kitchen. The two men sat on the sofa across from Charles, and the football game provided them with something to look at. Charles caught himself watching Bill Downs, and thinking about how his mother had once felt something for him. It was hard to picture them together, as it was hard not to stare at the man, at his skinny hands, never still in the long-legged lap, and the nervous way he looked around the room. He did not look past forty years old, except for the thinning hair.

"You boys get your football watching before dinner," Aunt Lois said, coming back into the room. "I won't have it after we begin to eat."

"I'm not much of a football fan," Bill Downs said.

Charles almost blurted out that his father had loved football.

He kept silent. In the next moment, Marie made her entrance. It struck Charles exactly that way: that it was an entrance, thoroughly dramatic and calculated to have an effect. It was vivacious in a nervous, almost automatic way. She crossed the room to kiss him on the forehead and then she turned to face the two men on the sofa. "Bill, you haven't changed a bit."

Downs was clambering over himself to get to his feet. "You either, Marie."

"Merry Christmas," Mr. Rainy said, also trying to rise.

"Oh, don't get up," Marie was saying.

Charles sat in his chair and watched them make their way through the introductions and the polite talk before dinner. He watched his mother, mostly. He knew exactly what she was feeling, understood the embarrassment and the nervousness out of which every gesture and word came, and yet something in him hated her for it, felt betrayed by it. When she went with the two men into the kitchen to open one of the bottles of champagne, he got out of the chair and faced Aunt Lois, whose expression seemed to be saying "Well?" as if this were only what one should have expected. He shook his head, and she said, "Come on."

They went into the kitchen. Marie was leaning against the counter with a glass of champagne in her hand. Charles decided that he couldn't look at her. She and Bill Downs were talking about the delicious smell of the turkey.

"I didn't have Thanksgiving dinner this year," Mr. Rainy was saying. "You know, I lost my wife. I just didn't feel like anything, you know."

"This is a hard time of year," Aunt Lois said.

"I simply don't know how to act any more," Mr. Rainy said.

Charles backed quietly away from them. He took himself to the living room and the television, where everyone seemed to know everyone else. They were all celebrating Christmas on television, and then the football game was on again. Charles got into his coat and stepped out onto the porch, intending at first just to take a few deep breaths, to shake if he could this feeling of betrayal and anger that had risen in him. It was already dark. The rain had turned to mist again. When the wind blew, cold drops splattered on the eaves of the porch. The cars and trucks racing by on the overpass at the end of the block seemed to traverse a part of the sky. Charles moved to the steps of the porch, and behind him the door opened. He turned to see his mother, who came out after glancing into the house, apparently wanting to be sure they would be alone. She wasn't wearing her coat, and he started to say something about the chill she would get when the expression on her face stopped him.

"What do you expect from me, Charles?"

He couldn't speak for a moment.

She advanced across the porch, already shivering. "What am I supposed to do?"

"I don't know what you're talking about."

"Oh, God." She paced back and forth in front of him, her arms wrapped around herself. Somewhere off in the misty dark, a group of people were singing carols. The voices came in on a gust of wind, and when the wind died they were gone. "God," she said again. Then she muttered, "Christmas."

"I wish it was two years ago," Charles said suddenly.

She had stopped pacing. "It won't ever be two years ago, and you'd better get used to that right now."

Charles was silent.

"You're turning what you remember into a paradise," she said, "and I've helped you get a good start on it."

"I'm not," Charles said, "I'm not doing that at all. I remember the way it was last summer when I wasn't—when I couldn't do anything and he couldn't make me do anything, and you and he were so different with each other—" He halted. He wasn't looking at her.

"Go on," she said.

He said, "Nothing."

"What went on between your father and me is nobody's business."

"I didn't say it was."

"It had nothing to do with you, Charles."

"All right," he said.

She was shivering so hard now that her voice quavered when she spoke. "I wish I could *make* it all right, but I can't."

Charles reached for her, put his arms around her, and she cried into the hollow of his shoulder. They stood that way for a while, and the wind blew and again there was the sound of the carolers.

"Mom," Charles said, "he was going to leave us, wasn't he."

She removed herself, produced a handkerchief from somewhere in her skirt, and touched it to her nose, still trembling, staring down. Then she breathed out as if something had given way inside her, and Charles could see that she was gathering herself, trying not to show whatever it was that had just gone through her. When she raised her eyes she gave him the softest, the kindest look. "Not you," she said. Then: "Don't think such things." She turned from him, stepped up into the doorway, and the light there made a willowy shadow of her. "Don't stay out here too long, son. Don't be rude."

When she had closed the door, he walked down the street to the overpass and stood below it, his hands deep in his coat pockets. It wasn't extremely cold out yet, but he was cold. He was cold, and he shook, and above him the traffic whooshed by. He turned and faced the house, beginning to cry now, and a sound came out of him that he put his hands to his mouth to stop. When a car came along the road he ducked back into the deeper shadow of the overpass, but he had been seen. The car pulled toward him, and a policeman shined a light on him.

"What're you doing there, feller?"

"Nothing," Charles said. "My father died."

The policeman kept the light on him for a few seconds, then turned it off. He said, "Go on home, son," and drove away.

Charles watched until the taillights disappeared in the mist. It was quiet; even the traffic on the overpass had ceased for a moment. The police car came back, slowing as it passed him, then going on, and once more it was quiet. He turned and looked at the house with its Christmas tree shimmering in the window, and in that instant it seemed to contain only the light and tangle of adulthood; it was their world, so far from him. He wiped his eyes with the backs of his hands, beginning to cry again. No, it wasn't so far. It wasn't so far at all. Up the street, Aunt Lois opened her door and called his name. But she couldn't see him, and he didn't answer her.

What feels like
the world

Very early in the morning, too early, he hears her trying to jump rope out on the sidewalk below his bedroom window. He wakes to the sound of her shoes on the concrete, her breathless counting as she jumps—never more than three times in succession—and fails again to find the right rhythm, the proper spring in her legs to achieve the thing, to be a girl jumping rope. He gets up and moves to the window and, parting the curtain only slightly, peers out at her. For some reason he feels he must be stealthy, must not let her see him gazing at her from this window. He thinks of the heartless way children tease the imperfect among them, and then he closes the curtain.

She is his only granddaughter, the unfortunate inheritor of his big-boned genes, his tendency toward bulk, and she is on a self-induced program of exercise and dieting, to lose weight. This is in preparation for the last meeting of the PTA, during which children from the fifth and sixth grades will put on a gymnastics demonstration. There will be a vaulting horse and a mini-trampoline, and everyone is to participate. She wants to be able to do at least as well as the other children in her class, and so she has been trying exercises to improve her coordination and lose the weight that keeps her rooted to the ground. For the past two weeks she has been eating only one meal a day, usually lunch, since that's the meal she eats at school, and swallowing cans of juice at other mealtimes. He's afraid of anorexia but trusts her calm determination to get ready for the event. There seems no desperation, none of the classic symptoms of the disease. Indeed, this project she's set for herself seems quite sane: to lose ten pounds, and to be able to get over the vaulting horse—in fact, she hopes that she'll be able to do a handstand on it and, curling her head and shoulders, flip over to stand upright on the other side. This, she has told him, is the outside hope. And in two weeks of very grown-up discipline and single-minded effort, that hope has mostly disappeared; she's still the only child in the fifth grade who has not even been able to propel herself over the horse, and this is the day of the event. She will have one last chance to practice at school today, and so she's up this early, out on the lawn, straining, pushing herself.

He dresses quickly and heads downstairs. The ritual in the mornings is simplified by the fact that neither of them is eating breakfast. He makes the orange juice, puts vitamins on a saucer for them both. When he glances out the living-room window, he sees that she is now doing somersaults in the dewy grass. She does three of them while he watches, and he isn't stealthy this time but stands in the window with what he hopes is an approving, unworried look on his face. After each somersault she pulls her sweat shirt down, takes a deep breath, and begins again, the arms coming down slowly, the head ducking slowly under; it's as if she falls on her back, sits up, and then stands up. Her cheeks are ruddy with effort. The moistness of the grass is on the sweat suit, and in the ends of her hair. It will rain this morning—there's thunder beyond the trees at the end of the street. He taps on the window, gestures, smiling, for her to come in. She waves at him, indicates that she wants him to watch her, so he watches her. He applauds when she's finished—three hard, slow tumbles. She claps her hands together as if to remove dust from them and comes trotting to the door. As she moves by him, he tells her she's asking for a bad cold, letting herself get wet so early in the morning. It's his place to nag. Her glance at him acknowledges this.

"I can't get the rest of me to follow my head," she says about the somersaults.

They go into the kitchen, and she sits down, pops a vitamin into her mouth, and takes a swallow of the orange juice. "I guess I'm not going to make it over that vaulting horse after all," she says suddenly.

"Sure you will."

"I don't care." She seems to pout. This is the first sign of true discouragement she's shown.

He's been waiting for it. "Brenda—honey, sometimes people aren't good at these things. I mean, I was never any good at it."

"I bet you were," she says. "I bet you're just saying that to make me feel better."

"No," he says, "really."

He's been keeping to the diet with her, though there have been times during the day when he's cheated. He no longer has a job, and the days are long; he's hungry all the time. He pretends to her that he's still going on to work in the mornings after he walks her to school, because he wants to keep her sense of the daily balance of things, of a predictable and orderly routine, intact. He believes this is the best way to deal with grief—simply to go on with things, to keep them as much as possible as they have always been. Being out of work doesn't worry him, really; he has enough money in savings to last awhile. At sixty-one, he's almost eligible for Social Security, and he gets monthly checks from the girl's father, who lives with another woman, and other children, in Oregon. The father has been very good about keeping up the payments, though he never visits or calls. Probably he thinks the money buys him the privilege of remaining aloof, now that Brenda's mother is gone. Brenda's mother used to say he was the type of man who learned early that there was nothing of substance anywhere in his soul, and spent the rest of his life trying to hide this fact from himself. No one was more upright, she would say, no one more honorable, and God help you if you ever had to live with him. Brenda's father was the subject of bitter sarcasm and scorn. And yet, perhaps not so surprisingly,

Brenda's mother would call him in those months just after the divorce, when Brenda was still only a toddler, and she would try to get the baby to say things to him over the phone. And she would sit there with Brenda on her lap and cry after she had hung up.

"I had a doughnut yesterday at school," Brenda says now.

"That's lunch. You're supposed to eat lunch."

"I had spaghetti, too. And three pieces of garlic bread. And pie. And a big salad."

"What's one doughnut?"

"Well, and I didn't eat anything the rest of the day."

"I know," her grandfather says. "See?"

They sit quiet for a little while. Sometimes they're shy with each other—more so lately. They're used to the absence of her mother by now—it's been almost a year—but they still find themselves missing a beat now and then, like a heart with a valve almost closed. She swallows the last of her juice and then gets up and moves to the living room, to stand gazing out at the yard. Big drops have begun to fall. It's a storm, with rising wind and, now, very loud thunder. Lightning branches across the sky, and the trees in the yard disappear in sheets of rain. He has come to her side, and he pretends an interest in the details of the weather, remarking on the heaviness of the rain, the strength of the wind. "Some storm," he says finally. "I'm glad we're not out in it." He wishes he could tell what she's thinking, where the pain is; he wishes he could be certain of the harmlessness of his every word. "Honey," he ventures, "we could play hooky today. If you want to."

"Don't you think I can do it?" she says.

"I know you can."

She stares at him a moment and then looks away, out at the storm.

"It's terrible out there, isn't it?" he says. "Look at that lightning."

"You don't think I can do it," she says.

"No. I know you can. Really."

"Well, I probably can't."

"Even if you can't. Lots of people—lots of people never do anything like that."

"I'm the only one who can't that *I* know."

"Well, there's lots of people. The whole thing is silly, Brenda. A year from now it won't mean anything at all—you'll see."

She says nothing.

"Is there some pressure at school to do it?"

"No." Her tone is simple, matter-of-fact, and she looks directly at him.

"You're sure."

She's sure. And of course, he realizes, there *is* pressure; there's the pressure of being one among other children, and being the only one among them who can't do a thing.

"Honey," he says lamely, "it's not that important."

When she looks at him this time, he sees something scarily unchildlike in her expression, some perplexity that she seems to pull down into herself. "It is too important," she says.

He drives her to school. The rain is still being blown along the street and above the low roofs of the houses. By the time they arrive, no more than five minutes from the house, it has begun to let up.

"If it's completely stopped after school," she says, "can we walk home?"

"Of course," he says. "Why shouldn't we?"

She gives him a quick wet kiss on the cheek. "Bye, Pops."

He knows she doesn't like it when he waits for her to get inside, and still he hesitates. There's always the apprehension that he'll look away or drive off just as she thinks of something she needs from him, or that she'll wave to him and he won't see her. So he sits here with the car engine idling, and she walks quickly up the sidewalk and into the building. In the few seconds before the door swings shut, she turns and gives him a wave, and he waves back. The door is closed now. Slowly he lets the car glide forward, still watching the door. Then he's down the driveway, and he heads back to the house.

It's hard to decide what to do with his time. Mostly he stays in the house, watches television, reads the newspapers. There are household tasks, but he can't do anything she might notice, since he's supposed to be at work during these hours. Sometimes, just to please himself, he drives over to the bank and visits with his old co-workers, though there doesn't seem to be much to talk about any more and he senses that he makes them all uneasy. Today he lies down on the sofa in the living room and rests awhile. At the windows the sun begins to show, and he thinks of driving into town, perhaps stopping somewhere to eat a light breakfast. He accuses himself with the thought and then gets up and turns on the television. There isn't anything of interest to watch, but he watches anyway. The sun is bright now out on the lawn, and the wind is the same, gusting and shaking the window frames. On television he sees feasts of incredible sumptuousness, almost nauseating in the impossible brightness and succulence of the food: advertisements from cheese companies, dairy associations, the makers of cookies and pizza, the sellers of seafood and steaks. He's angry with himself for wanting to cheat on the diet. He thinks of Brenda at school, thinks of crowds of children, and it comes to him more painfully than ever that he can't protect her. Not any more than he could ever protect her mother.

He goes outside and walks up the drying sidewalk to the end of the block. The sun has already dried most of the morning's rain, and the wind is warm. In the sky are great stormy Matterhorns of cumulus and wide patches of the deepest blue. It's a beautiful day, and he decides to walk over to the school. Nothing in him voices this decision; he simply begins to walk. He knows without having to think about it that he can't allow her to see him, yet he feels compelled to take the risk that she might; he feels a helpless wish to watch over her, and, beyond this, he entertains the vague notion that by seeing her in her world he might be better able to be what she needs in his.

So he walks the four blocks to the school and stands just beyond the playground, in a group of shading maples that whisper and sigh in the wind. The playground is empty. A bell rings somewhere in the building, but no one comes out. It's not even eleven o'clock in the morning. He's too late for morning recess and too early for the afternoon one. He feels as though she watches him make his way back down the street.

His neighbor, Mrs. Eberhard, comes over for lunch. It's a thing they planned, and he's forgotten about it. She knocks on the door, and when he opens it she smiles and says, "I knew you'd forget." She's on a diet too, and is carrying what they'll eat: two apples, some celery and carrots. It's all in a clear plastic bag, and she holds it toward him in the palms of her hands as though it were piping hot from an oven. Jane Eberhard is relatively new in the neighborhood. When Brenda's mother died, Jane offered to cook meals and regulate things, and for a while she was like another member of the family. She's moved into their lives now, and sometimes they all forget the circumstances under which the friendship began. She's a solid, large-hipped woman of fifty-eight, with clear, young blue eyes and gray hair. The thing she's good at is sympathy; there's something oddly unspecific about it, as if it were a beam she simply radiates.

"You look so worried," she says now, "I think you should be proud of her."

They're sitting in the living room, with the plastic bag on the coffee table before them. She's eating a stick of celery.

"I've never seen a child that age put such demands on herself," she says.

"I don't know what it's going to do to her if she doesn't make it over the damn thing," he says.

"It'll disappoint her. But she'll get over it."

"I don't guess you can make it tonight."

"Can't," she says. "Really. I promised my mother I'd take her to the ocean this weekend. I have to go pick her up tonight."

"I walked over to the school a little while ago."

"Are you sure you're not putting more into this than she is?"

"She was up at dawn this morning, Jane. Didn't you see her?"

Mrs. Eberhard nods. "I saw her."

"Well?" he says.

She pats his wrist. "I'm sure it won't matter a month from now."

"No," he says, "that is not true. I mean, I wish I could believe you. But I've never seen a kid work so hard."

"Maybe she'll make it."

"Yes," he says. "Maybe."

Mrs. Eberhard sits considering for a moment, tapping the stick of celery against her lower lip. "You think it's tied to the accident in some way, don't you?"

"I don't know," he says, standing, moving across the room. "I can't get through somehow. It's been all this time and I still don't know. She keeps it all to herself—all of it. All I can do is try to be there when she wants me to be there. I don't know—I don't even know what to say to her."

"You're doing all you can do, then."

"Her mother and I . . ." he begins. "She—we never got along that well."

"You can't worry about that now."

Mrs. Eberhard's advice is always the kind of practical good advice that's impossible to follow.

He comes back to the sofa and tries to eat one of the apples, but his appetite is gone. This seems ironic to him. "I'm not hungry now," he says.

"Sometimes worry is the best thing for a diet."

"I've always worried. It never did me any good, but I worried."

"I'll tell you," Mrs. Eberhard says. "It's a terrific misfortune to have to be raised by a human being."

He doesn't feel like listening to this sort of thing, so he asks her about her husband, who is with the government in some capacity that requires him to be both secretive and mobile. He's always off to one country or another, and this week he's in India. It's strange to think of someone traveling as much as he does without getting hurt or killed. Mrs. Eberhard says she's so used to his being gone all the time that next year, when he retires, it'll take a while to get used to having him underfoot. In fact, he's not a very likable man; there's something murky and unpleasant about him. The one time Mrs. Eberhard brought him to visit, he sat in the living room and seemed to regard everyone with detached curiosity, as if they were all specimens on a dish under a lens. Brenda's grandfather had invited some old friends over from the bank—everyone was being careful not to let on that he wasn't still going there every day. It was an awkward two hours, and Mrs. Eberhard's husband sat with his hands folded over his rounded belly, his eyebrows arched. When he spoke, his voice was cultivated and quiet, full of self-satisfaction and haughtiness. They had been speaking in low tones about how Jane Eberhard had moved in to take over after the accident, and Mrs. Eberhard's husband cleared his throat, held his fist gingerly to his mouth, pursed his lips, and began a soft-spoken, lecture-like monologue about his belief that there's no such thing as an accident. His considered opinion was that there are subconscious explanations for everything. Apparently, he thought he was entertaining everyone. He sat with one leg crossed over the other and held forth in his calm, magisterial voice, explaining how everything can be reduced to a matter of conscious or subconscious will. Finally his wife asked him to let it alone, please, drop the subject.

"For example," he went on, "there are many collisions on the highway in which no one appears to have applied brakes before impact, as if something in the victims had decided on death. And of course there are the well-known cases of people stopped on railroad tracks, with plenty of time to get off, who simply do not move. Perhaps it isn't being frozen by the perception of one's fate but a matter of decision making, of will. The victim decides on his fate."

"I think we've had enough, now," Jane Eberhard said.

The inappropriateness of what he had said seemed to dawn on him then. He shifted in his seat and grew very quiet, and when the evening was over he took Brenda's grandfather by the elbow and apologized. But even in the apology there seemed to be a species of condescension, as if he were really only sorry for the harsh truth of what he had wrongly deemed it necessary to say. When everyone was gone, Brenda said, "I don't like that man."

"Is it because of what he said about accidents?" her grand-father asked.

She shook her head. "I just don't like him."

"It's not true, what he said, honey. An accident is an accident."

She said, "I know." But she would not return his gaze.

"Your mother wasn't very happy here, but she didn't want to leave us. Not even—you know, without . . . without knowing it or anything."

"He wears perfume," she said, still not looking at him.

"It's cologne. Yes, he does—too much of it."

"It smells," she said.

In the afternoon he walks over to the school. The sidewalks are crowded with children, and they all seem to recognize him. They carry their books and papers and their hair is windblown and they run and wrestle with each other in the yards. The sun's high and very hot, and most of the clouds have broken apart and scattered. There's still a fairly steady wind, but it's gentler now, and there's no coolness in it.

Brenda is standing at the first crossing street down the hill from the school. She's surrounded by other children yet seems separate from them somehow. She sees him and smiles. He waits on his side of the intersection for her to cross, and when she reaches him he's careful not to show any obvious affection, knowing it embarrasses her.

"How was your day?" he begins.

"Mr. Clayton tried to make me quit today."

He waits.

"I didn't get over," she says. "I didn't even get close."

"What did Mr. Clayton say?"

"Oh—you know. That it's not important. That kind of stuff."

"Well," he says gently, "*is* it so important?"

"I don't know." She kicks at something in the grass along the edge of the sidewalk—a piece of a pencil someone else had discarded. She bends, picks it up, examines it, and then drops it. This is exactly the kind of slow, daydreaming behavior that used to make him angry and impatient with her mother. They walk on. She's concentrating on the sidewalk before them, and they walk almost in step.

"I'm sure I could never do a thing like going over a vaulting horse when I was in school," he says.

"Did they have that when you were in school?"

He smiles. "It was hard getting everything into the caves. But sure, we had that sort of thing. We were an advanced tribe. We had fire, too."

"Okay," she's saying, "okay, okay."

"Actually, with me, it was pull-ups. We all had to do pull-ups. And I just couldn't do them. I don't think I ever accomplished a single one in my life."

"I can't do pull-ups," she says.

"They're hard to do."

"Everybody in the fifth and sixth grades can get over the vaulting horse," she says.

.

How much she reminds him of her mother. There's a certain mobility in her face, a certain willingness to assert herself in the smallest gesture of the eyes and mouth. She has her mother's green eyes, and now he tells her this. He's decided to try this. He's standing, quite shy, in her doorway, feeling like an intruder. She's sitting on the floor, one leg outstretched, the other bent at the knee. She tries to touch her forehead to the knee of the outstretched leg, straining, and he looks away.

"You know?" he says. "They're just the same color—just that shade of green."

"What was my grandmother like?" she asks, still straining.

"She was a lot like your mother."

"I'm never going to get married."

"Of course you will. Well, I mean—if you want to, you will."

"How come you didn't ever get married again?"

"Oh," he says, "I had a daughter to raise, you know."

She changes position, tries to touch her forehead to the other knee.

"I'll tell you, that mother of yours was enough to keep me busy. I mean, I called her double trouble, you know, because I always said she was double the trouble a son would have been. That was a regular joke around here."

"Mom was skinny and pretty."

He says nothing.

"Am I double trouble?"

"No," he says.

"Is that really why you never got married again?"

"Well, no one would have me, either."

"Mom said you liked it."

"Liked what?"

"Being a widow."

"Yes, well," he says.

"Did you?"

"All these questions," he says.

"Do you think about Grandmom a lot?"

97

"Yes," he says. "That's—you know, we remember our loved ones."

She stands and tries to touch her toes without bending her legs. "Sometimes I dream that Mom's yelling at you and you're yelling back."

"Oh, well," he says, hearing himself say it, feeling himself back down from something. "That's—that's just a dream. You know, it's nothing to think about at all. People who love each other don't agree sometimes—it's—it's nothing. And I'll bet these exercises are going to do the trick."

"I'm very smart, aren't I?"

He feels sick, very deep down. "You're the smartest little girl I ever saw."

"You don't have to come tonight if you don't want to," she says. "You can drop me off if you want, and come get me when it's over."

"Why would I do that?"

She mutters. *"I would."*

"Then why don't we skip it?"

"Lot of good *that* would do," she says.

For dinner they drink apple juice, and he gets her to eat two slices of dry toast. The apple juice is for energy. She drinks it slowly and then goes into her room to lie down, to conserve her strength. She uses the word *conserve*, and he tells her he's so proud of her vocabulary. She thanks him. While she rests, he does a few household chores, trying really just to keep busy. The week's newspapers have been piling up on the coffee table in the living room, the carpets need to be vacuumed, and the whole house needs dusting. None of it takes long enough; none of it quite distracts him. For a while he sits in the living room with a newspaper in his lap and pretends to be reading it. She's restless too. She comes back through to the kitchen, drinks another glass of apple juice, and then joins him in the living room, turns the television on. The news is full of traffic deaths, and she turns to one of the local stations that shows reruns of old situaton comedies. They both watch M*A*S*H without really taking it in. She bites the cuticles of her nails, and her gaze wanders around the room. It comes to him that he could speak to her now, could make his way through to her grief— and yet he knows that he will do no such thing; he can't even bring himself to speak at all. There are regions of his own sorrow that he simply lacks the strength to explore, and so he sits there watching her restlessness, and at last it's time to go over to the school. Jane Eberhard makes a surprise visit, bearing a handsome good-luck card she's fashioned herself. She kisses Brenda, behaves exactly as if Brenda were going off to some dangerous, faraway place. She stands in the street and waves at them as they pull away, and Brenda leans out the window to shout goodbye. A moment later, sitting back and staring out at the dusky light, she says she feels a surge of energy, and he tells her she's way ahead of all the others in her class, knowing words like *conserve* and *surge*.

"I've always known them," she says.

It's beginning to rain again. Clouds have been rolling in from the east, and the wind shakes the trees. Lightning flickers on the other side of the clouds. Everything seems threatening, relentless. He slows down. There are many cars parked along both sides of the street. "Quite a turnout," he manages.

"Don't worry," she tells him brightly. "I still feel my surge of energy."

It begins to rain as they get out of the car, and he holds his sport coat like a cape to shield her from it. By the time they get to the open front doors, it's raining very hard. People are crowding into the cafeteria, which has been transformed into an arena for the event—chairs set up on four sides of the room as though for a wrestling match. In the center, at the end of the long, bright-red mat, are the vaulting horse and the mini-trampoline. The physical-education teacher, Mr. Clayton, stands at the entrance. He's tall, thin, scraggly looking, a boy really, no older than twenty-five.

"There's Mr. Clayton," Brenda says.

"I see him."

"Hello, Mr. Clayton."

Mr. Clayton is quite distracted, and he nods quickly, leans toward Brenda, and points to a doorway across the hall. "Go on ahead," he says. Then he nods at her grandfather.

"This is it," Brenda says.

Her grandfather squeezes her shoulder, means to find the best thing to tell her, but in the next confusing minute he's lost her; she's gone among the others and he's being swept along with the crowd entering the cafeteria. He makes his way along the walls behind the chairs, where a few other people have already gathered and are standing. At the other end of the room a man is speaking from a lectern about old business, new officers for the fall. Brenda's grandfather recognizes some of the people in the crowd. A woman looks at him and nods, a familiar face, he can't quite place. She turns to look at the speaker. She's holding a baby, and the baby's staring at him over her shoulder. A moment later, she steps back to stand beside him, hefting the baby higher and patting its bottom.

"What a crowd," she says.

He nods.

"It's not usually this crowded."

Again, he nods.

The baby protests, and he touches the miniature fingers of one hand—just a baby, he thinks, and everything still to go through.

"How is—um . . . Brenda?" she says.

"Oh," he says, "fine." And he remembers that she was Brenda's kindergarden teacher. She's heavier than she was then, and her hair is darker. She has a baby now.

"I don't remember all my students," she says, shifting the baby to the other shoulder. "I've been home now for eighteen months, and I'll tell you, it's being at the PTA meeting that makes me see how much I *don't* miss teaching."

He smiles at her and nods again. He's beginning to feel

awkward. The man is still speaking from the lectern, a meeting is going on, and this woman's voice is carrying beyond them, though she says everything out of the side of her mouth.

"I remember the way you used to walk Brenda to school every morning. Do you still walk her to school?"

"Yes."

"That's so nice."

He pretends an interest in what the speaker is saying.

"I always thought it was so nice to see how you two got along together—I mean these days it's really rare for the kids even to know who their grandparents *are*, much less have one to walk them to school in the morning. I always thought it was really something." She seems to watch the lectern for a moment, and then speaks to him again, this time in a near whisper. "I hope you won't take this the wrong way or anything, but I just wanted to say how sorry I was about your daughter. I saw it in the paper when Brenda's mother . . . Well. You know, I just wanted to tell you how sorry. When I saw it in the paper, I thought of Brenda, and how you used to walk her to school. I lost my sister in an automobile accident, so I know how you feel—it's a terrible thing. Terrible. An awful thing to have happen. I mean it's much too sudden and final and everything. I'm afraid now every time I get into a car." She pauses, pats the baby's back, then takes something off its ear. "Anyway, I just wanted to say how sorry I was."

"You're very kind," he says.

"It seems so senseless," she murmurs. "There's something so senseless about it when it happens. My sister went through a stop sign. She just didn't see it, I guess. But it wasn't a busy road or anything. If she'd come along one second later or sooner nothing would've happened. So senseless. Two people driving two different cars coming along on two roads on a sunny afternoon and they come together like that. I mean— what're the chances, really?"

He doesn't say anything.

"How's Brenda handling it?"

"She's strong," he says.

"I would've said that," the woman tells him. "Sometimes I think the children take these things better than the adults do. I remember when she first came to my class. She told everyone in the first minute that she'd come from Oregon. That she was living with her grandfather, and her mother was divorced."

"She was a baby when the divorce—when she moved here from Oregon."

This seems to surprise the woman. "Really," she says, low. "I got the impression it was recent for her. I mean, you know, that she had just come from it all. It was all very vivid for her, I remember that."

"She was a baby," he says. It's almost as if he were insisting on it. He's heard this in his voice, and he wonders if she has, too.

"Well," she says, "I always had a special place for Brenda. I always thought she was very special. A very special little girl."

The PTA meeting is over, and Mr. Clayton is now standing at the far door with the first of his charges. They're all lining up outside the door, and Mr. Clayton walks to the microphone to announce the program. The demonstration will commence with the mini-trampoline and the vaulting horse: a performance by the fifth- and sixth-graders. There will also be a break-dancing demonstration by the fourth-grade class.

"Here we go," the woman says. "My nephew's afraid of the mini-tramp."

"They shouldn't make them do these things," Brenda's grandfather says, with a passion that surprises him. He draws in a breath. "It's too hard," he says, loudly. He can't believe himself. "They shouldn't have to go through a thing like this."

"I don't know," she says vaguely, turning from him a little. He has drawn attention to himself. Others in the crowd are regarding him now—one, a man with a sparse red beard and wild red hair, looking at him with something he takes for agreement.

"It's too much," he says, still louder. "Too much to put on a child. There's just so much a child can take."

Someone asks gently for quiet.

The first child is running down the long mat to the mini-trampoline; it's a girl, and she times her jump perfectly, soars over the horse. One by one, other children follow. Mr. Clayton and another man stand on either side of the horse and help those who go over on their hands. Two or three go over without any assistance at all, with remarkable effortlessness and grace.

"Well," Brenda's kindergarden teacher says, "there's my nephew."

The boy hits the mini-tramp and does a perfect forward flip in the air over the horse, landing upright and then rolling forward in a somersault.

"Yea, Jack!" she cheers. "No sweat! Yea, Jackie boy!"

The boy trots to the other end of the room and stands with the others; the crowd is applauding. The last of the sixth-graders goes over the horse, and Mr. Clayton says into the microphone that the fifth-graders are next. It's Brenda who's next. She stands in the doorway, her cheeks flushed, her legs looking too heavy in the tights. She's rocking back and forth on the balls of her feet, getting ready. It grows quiet. Her arms swing slightly, back and forth, and now, just for a moment, she's looking at the crowd, her face hiding whatever she's feeling. It's as if she were merely curious as to who is out there, but he knows she's looking for him, searching the crowd for her grandfather, who stands on his toes, unseen against the far wall, stands there thinking his heart might break, lifting his hand to wave.

The man who knew
Belle Starr

MCrae *picked up a hitcher* on his way west, a young woman, carrying a paper bag and a leather purse, wearing jeans and a shawl—which she didn't take off, though it was more than ninety degrees out, and MCrae had no air conditioning. He was driving an old Dodge Charger with a bad exhaust system, and one long crack in the wraparound windshield. He pulled over for her and she got right in, put the leather purse on the seat between them, and settled herself with the paper bag on her lap between her hands. He had just crossed into Texas.

"Where you headed," he said.

She said, "What about you?"

"Nevada, maybe."

"Why maybe?"

And that fast he was answering *her* questions. "I just got out of the Air Force," he told her, though this wasn't exactly true. The Air Force had put him out with a dishonorable discharge after four years at Leavenworth for assaulting a staff sergeant. He was a bad character. He had a bad temper that had got him into a load of trouble already and he just wanted to get out west, out to the wide-open spaces. Just to see it, really. He had the feeling people didn't require as much from a person way out where there was that kind of room. He didn't have any family now. He had five thousand dollars from his father's insurance policy, and he was going to make the money last him awhile. He said, "I'm sort of undecided about a lot of things."

"Not me," she said.

"You figured out where you were going," he said.

"You could say that."

"So where might that be."

She made a fist and then extended her thumb, and turned it over. "Under," she said. "Down."

"Excuse me?"

"Does the radio work?" she asked, reaching for it.

"It's on the blink," he said.

She turned the knob anyway, then sat back and folded her arms over the paper bag.

He took a glance at her. She was skinny and long necked, and her hair was the color of water in a metal pail. She looked just old enough for high school.

"What's in the bag?" he said.

She sat up a little. "Nothing. Another blouse."

"Well, so what did you mean back there?"

"Back where?"

"Look," he said, "we don't have to do any talking if you don't want to."

"Then what will we do?"

"Anything you want," he said.

"What if I just want to sit here and let you drive me all the way to Nevada?"

"That's fine," he said. "That's just fine."

"Well, I won't do that. We can talk."

"Are *you* going to Nevada?" he asked.

She gave a little shrug of her shoulders. "Why not?"

"All right," he said, and for some reason he offered her his hand. She looked at it, and then smiled at him, and he put his hand back on the wheel.

It got a little awkward almost right away. The heat was awful, and she sat there sweating, not saying much. He never thought he was very smooth or anything, and he had been in prison: it

105

had been a long time since he had found himself in the company of a woman. Finally she fell asleep, and for a few miles he could look at her without worrying about anything but staying on the road. He decided that she was kind of good looking around the eyes and mouth. If she ever filled out, she might be something. He caught himself wondering what might happen, thinking of sex. A girl who traveled alone like this was probably pretty loose. Without quite realizing it, he began to daydream about her, and when he got aroused by the daydream he tried to concentrate on figuring his chances, playing his cards right, not messing up any opportunities—but being gentlemanly, too. He was not the sort of person who forced himself on young women. She slept very quietly, not breathing loudly or sighing or moving much; and then she simply sat up and folded her arms over the bag again and stared out at the road.

"God," she said, "I went out."

"You hungry?" he asked.

"No."

"What's your name?" he said. "I never got your name."

"Belle Starr," she said, and, winking at him, she made a clicking sound out of the side of her mouth.

"Belle Starr," he said.

"Don't you know who Belle Starr was?"

All he knew was that it was a familiar-sounding name. "Belle Starr."

She put her index finger to the side of his head and said, "Bang."

"Belle Starr," he said.

"Come on," she said. "Annie Oakley. Wild Bill Hickok."

"Oh," MCrae said. "Okay."

"That's me," she said, sliding down in the seat. "Belle Starr."

"That's not your real name."

"It's the only one I go by these days."

They rode on in silence for a time.

"What's *your* name?" she said.

He told her.

"Irish?"

"I never thought about it."

"Where you from, MCrae?"

"Washington, DC."

"Long way from home."

"I haven't been there in years."

"Where *have* you been?"

"Prison," he said. He hadn't known he would say it, and now that he had, he kept his eyes on the road. He might as well have been posing for her; he had an image of himself as he must look from the side, and he shifted his weight a little, sucked in his belly. When he stole a glance at her he saw that she was simply gazing out at the Panhandle, one hand up like a visor to shade her eyes.

"What about you?" he said, and felt like somebody in a movie—two people with a past come together on the open road. He wondered how he could get the talk around to the subject of love.

"What *about* me?"

"Where're you from?"

"I don't want to bore you with all the facts," she said.

"I don't mind," MCrae said. "I got nothing else to do."

"I'm from way up north."

"Okay," he said, "you want me to guess?"

"Maine," she said. "Land of Moose and Lobster."

He said, "Maine. Well, now."

"See?" she said. "The facts are just a lot of things that don't change."

"Unless you change them," MCrae said.

She reached down and, with elaborate care, as if it were fragile, put the paper bag on the floor. Then she leaned back and put her feet upon the dash. She was wearing low-cut tennis shoes.

"You going to sleep?" he asked.

107

"Just relaxing," she said.

But a moment later, when he asked if she wanted to stop and eat, she didn't answer, and he looked over to see that she was sound asleep.

His father had died while he was at Leavenworth. The last time MCrae saw him, he was lying on a gurney in one of the bays of DC General's emergency ward, a plastic tube in his mouth, an IV set into an ugly yellow-blue bruise on his wrist. MCrae had come home on leave from the Air Force—which he had joined at the order of a juvenile judge—to find his father on the floor in the living room, in a pile of old newspapers and bottles, wearing his good suit, with no socks or shoes and no shirt. It looked as if he were dead. But the ambulance drivers found a pulse, and rushed him off to the hospital. MCrae cleaned the house up a little, and then followed in the Charger. The old man had been steadily going downhill from the time MCrae was a boy, and so this latest trouble wasn't new. In the hospital, they got the tube into his mouth and hooked him to the IV, and then left him there on the gurney. MCrae stood at his side, still in uniform, and when the old man opened his eyes and looked at him it was clear that he didn't know who it was. The old man blinked, stared, and then sat up, took the tube out of his mouth, and spat something terrible looking into a small metal dish which was suspended from the complicated apparatus of the room, and which made a continual water-dropping sound like a leaking sink. He looked at MCrae again, and then he looked at the tube. "Jesus Christ," he said.

"Hey," MCrae said.

"What."

"It's me."

The old man put the tube back into his mouth and looked away.

"Pops," MCrae said. He didn't feel anything.

The tube came out. "Don't look at me, boy. You got yourself into it. Getting into trouble, stealing and running around. You got yourself into it."

"I don't mind it, Pops. It's three meals and a place to sleep."

"Yeah," the old man said, and then seemed to gargle something. He spit into the little metal dish again.

"I got thirty days of leave, Pops."

"Eh?"

"I don't have to go back for a month."

"Where you going?"

"Around," MCrae said.

The truth was that he hated the Air Force, and he was thinking of taking the Charger and driving to Canada or someplace like that, and hiding out the rest of his life—the Air Force felt like punishment, it *was* punishment, and he had already been in trouble for his quick temper and his attitude. That afternoon, he'd left his father to whatever would happen, got into the Charger, and started north. But he hadn't made it. He'd lost heart a few miles south of New York City, and he turned around and came back. The old man had been moved to a room in the alcoholic ward, but MCrae didn't go to see him. He stayed in the house, watching television and drinking beer, and when old high school buddies came by he went around with them a little. Mostly he stayed home, though, and at the end of his leave he locked the place and drove back to Chanute, in Illinois, where he was stationed. He wasn't there two months before the staff sergeant caught him drinking beer in the dayroom of one of the training barracks, and asked for his name. MCrae walked over to him, and said, "My name is trouble," and at the word *trouble*, struck the other man in the face. He'd had a lot of beer, and he had been sitting there in the dark, drinking the last of it, going over everything in his mind, and the staff sergeant, a baby-faced man with a spare tire of flesh around his waist and an attitude about the stripes on his sleeves, had just walked into it. MCrae didn't even know him. Yet he stood over the sergeant where he had fallen, and then started kicking him. It took two other men to get him off the poor man, who wound up in the hospital with a broken jaw (the first punch had done it), a few cracked ribs, and multiple lacerations and bruises. The court-martial was swift. The sentence was four years at hard labor, along with the dishonorable discharge. He'd had less than a month to go on the sentence when he got the news about his father. He felt no surprise, nor, really, any grief; yet there was a little thrill of something like fear; he was in his cell, and for an instant some part of him actually wanted to remain there, inside walls, where things were certain, and there weren't any decisions to make. A week later, he learned of the money from the insurance, which would have been more than the five thousand except that his father had been a few months behind on the rent, and on other payments. MCrae settled what he had to of those things, and kept the rest. He had started to feel like a happy man out of Leavenworth and the Air Force, and now he was on his way to Nevada, or someplace like that—and he had picked up a girl.

He drove on until dusk, stopping only for gas, and the girl slept right through. Just past the line into New Mexico, he pulled off the interstate and went north for a mile or so, looking for some place other than a chain restaurant to eat. She sat up straight, pushed the hair back away from her face. "Where are we?"

"New Mexico," he said. "I'm looking for a place to eat."

"I'm not hungry."

"Well," he said, "*you* might be able to go all day without anything to eat, but I got a three-meal-a-day habit to support."

She bought the paper bag up from the floor and held it in her lap.

"You got food in there?" he asked.

"No."

"You're very pretty—child-like, sort of—when you sleep."

"I didn't snore?"

"You were quiet as a mouse."

"And you think I'm pretty."

"I guess you know a thing like that. I hope I didn't offend you."

"I don't like dirty remarks," she said. "But I don't guess you meant to be dirty."

"Dirty."

"Sometimes people can say a thing like that and mean it very dirty, but I could tell you didn't."

He pulled in at a roadside diner and turned off the ignition. "Well?" he said.

She sat there with the bag on her lap. "I don't think I'll go in with you."

"You can have a cold drink or something," he said.

"You go in. I'll wait out here."

"Come on in there with me and have a cold drink," MCrae said. "I'll buy it for you. I'll buy you dinner if you want."

"I don't want to," she said.

He got out and started for the entance, and before he reached it he heard her door open and close, and turned to watch her come toward him, thin and waif-like in the shawl, which hid her arms and hands.

The diner was empty. There was a long, low bar, with soda fountains on the other side of it, and glass cases in which pies and cakes were set. There were booths along one wall. Everything seemed in order, except that no one was around. MCrae and the girl stood in the doorway for a moment and waited, and finally she stepped in and took a seat in the first booth. "I guess we're supposed to seat ourselves," she said.

"This is weird," said MCrae.

"Hey," she said, rising, "there's a jukebox." She strode over to it and leaned on it, crossing one leg behind the other at the ankle, her hair falling down to hide her face.

"Hello?" MCrae said. "Anybody here?"

"Got any change?" asked the girl.

He gave her a quarter, and then sat at the bar. The door at the far end swung in, and a big, red-faced man entered, wearing a white cook's apron over a sweat-stained baby-blue shirt, whose sleeves he had rolled up past the meaty curve of his elbows. "Yeah?" he said.

"You open?" MCrae asked.

"That juekbox don't work honey," the man said.

"You open?" MCrae said, as the girl came and sat down beside him.

"Sure, why not?"

"Place is kind of empty."

"What do you want to eat?"

"You got a menu?"

"You want a menu?"

"Sure," MCrae said, "why not?"

"Truth is," the big man said, "I'm selling this place. I don't have menus any more. I make hamburgers and breakfast stuff. Some french fries and cold drinks. A hot dog maybe. I'm not keeping track."

"Let's go somewhere else," the girl said.

"Yeah," said the big man, "why don't you do that."

"Look," said MCrae, "what's the story here?"

The other man shrugged. "You came in at the end of the run, you know what I mean? I'm going out of business. Sit down and I'll make you a hamburger on the house."

MCrae looked at the girl.

"Okay," she said, in a tone which made it clear that she would've been happier to leave.

The big man put his hands on the bar and leaned toward her. "Miss, if I were you I wouldn't look a gift horse in the mouth."

"I don't like hamburger," she said.

"You don't want a hot dog?" the man said. "I got a hot dog for you. Guaranteed to please."

"I'll have some french fries," she said.

The big man turned to the grill and opened the metal drawer

under it. He was very wide at the hips, and his legs were like trunks. "I get out of the Army after twenty years," he said, "and I got a little money put aside. The wife and I decide we want to get into the restaurant business. The government's going to be paying me a nice pension and we got the savings, so we sink it all in this goddam diner. Six and a half miles from the interstate. You get the picture? The guy's selling us this diner at a great price, you know? A terrific price. For a song, I'm in the restaurant business. The wife will cook the food, and I'll wait tables, you know, until we start to make a little extra, and then we'll hire somebody—a high school kid or somebody like that. We might even open another restaurant if the going gets good enough. But of course, this is New Mexico. This is six and a half miles from the interstate. There's nothing here any more because there's nothing up the road. You know what's up the road? Nothing." He had put the hamburger on, and a basket of frozen french fries. "Now the wife decides she's had enough of life on the border, and off she goes to Seattle to sit in the rain with her mother and here I am trying to sell a place nobody else is dumb enough to buy. You know what I mean?"

"That's rough," MCrae said.

"You're the second customer I've had all *week*, bub."

The girl said, "I guess that cash register's empty then, huh."

"It ain't full, honey."

She got up and wandered across the room. For a while she stood gazing out the windows over the booths, her hands invisible under the woolen shawl. When she came back to sit next to MCrae again, the hamburger and french fries were ready.

"On the house," the big man said.

And the girl brought a gun out of the shawl—a pistol that looked like a toy. "Suppose you open up that register, Mr Poormouth," she said.

The big man looked at her, then at MCrae, who had taken a large bite of his hamburger, and had it bulging in his cheeks.

"This thing is loaded, and I'll use it."

"Well for Christ's sake," the big man said.

MCrae started to get off the stool. "Hold on a minute," he said to them both, his words garbled by the mouthful of food, and then everything started happening all at once. The girl aimed the pistol. There was a popping sound—a single, small pop, not much louder than the sound of a cap gun—and the big man took a step back, against the counter, into the dishes and pans there. He stared at the girl, wide eyed, for what seemed a long time, then went down, pulling dishes with him in a tremendous shattering.

"Jesus Christ," MCrae said, swallowing, standing back from her, raising his hands.

She put the pistol back in her jeans under the shawl, and then went around the counter and opened the cash register. "Damn," she said.

MCrae said, low, "Jesus Christ."

And now she looked at him; it was as if she had forgotten he was there. "What're you standing there with your hands up like that?"

"God," he said. "Oh, God."

"Stop it," she said. "Put your hands down."

He did so.

"Cash register's empty." She sat down on one of the stools and gazed over at the body of the man where it had fallen. "Damn."

"Look," MCrae said, "take my car. You—you can have my car."

She seemed puzzled. "I don't want your car. What do I want your.car for?"

"You—" he said. He couldn't talk, couldn't focus clearly, or think. He looked at the man, who lay very still, and then he began to cry.

"Will you stop it?" she said, coming off the stool, reaching under the shawl and bringing out the pistol again.

"Jesus," he said. "Good Jesus."

114

She pointed the pistol at his forehead. "Bang," she said. "What's my name?"

"Your—name?"

"My name."

"Belle—" he managed.

"Come on," she said. "The whole thing—you remember."

"Belle—Belle Starr."

"Right." She let the gun hand drop to her side, into one of the folds of the shawl. "I like that so much better than Annie Oakley."

"Please," MCrae said.

She took a few steps away from him and then whirled and aimed the gun. "I think we better get out of here, what do you think?"

"Take the car," he said, almost with exasperation; it frightened him to hear it in his own voice.

"I can't drive," she said simply. "Never learned."

"Jesus," he said. It went out of him like a sigh.

"God," she said, gesturing with the pistol for him to move to the door, "it's hard to believe you were ever in *prison*."

The road went on into the dark, beyond the fan of the headlights; he lost track of miles, road signs, other traffic, time; trucks came by and surprised him, and other cars seemed to materialize as they started the lane change that would bring them over in front of him. He watched their taillights grow small in the distance, and all the while the girl sat watching him, her hands somewhere under the shawl. For a long time there was just the sound of the rushing night air at the windows, and then she moved a little, shifted her weight, bringing one leg up on the seat.

"What were you in prison for, anyway?"

Her voice startled him, and for a moment he couldn't think to answer.

"Come on," she said, "I'm getting bored with all this quiet. What were you in prison for?"

"I—beat up a guy."

"That's all?"

"Yes, that's all." He couldn't keep the irritation out of his voice.

"Tell me about it."

"It was just—I just beat up a guy. It wasn't anything."

"I didn't shoot that man for money, you know."

MCrae said nothing.

"I shot him because he made a nasty remark to me about the hot dogs."

"I didn't hear any nasty remark."

"He shouldn't have said it or else he'd still be alive."

MCrae held tight to the wheel.

"Don't you wish it was the Wild West?" she said.

"Wild West," he said, "yeah." He could barely speak for the dryness in his mouth and the deep ache of his own breathing.

"You know," she said, "I'm not really from Maine."

He nodded.

"I'm from Florida."

"Florida," he managed.

"Yes, only I don't have a Southern accent, so people think I'm not from there. Do you hear any trace of a Southern accent at all when I talk?"

"No," he said.

"Now you—you've got an accent. A definite Southern accent."

He was silent.

"Talk to me," she said.

"What do you want me to say?" he said. "Jesus."

"You could ask me things."

"Ask you things—"

"Ask me what my name is."

"Ask me what my name is."

Without hesitating, MCrae said, "What's your name?"

"You know."

"No, really," he said, trying to play along.

"It's Belle Starr."

"Belle Starr," he said.

"Nobody *but*," she said.

"Good," he said.

"And I don't care about money, either," she said. "That's not what I'm after."

"No," MCrae said.

"What I'm after is adventure."

"Right," said MCrae.

"Fast living."

"Fast living, right."

"A good time."

"Good," he said.

"I'm going to live a ton before I die."

"A ton, yes."

"What about you?" she said.

"Yes," he said. "Me too."

"Want to join up with me?"

"Join up," he said. "Right." He was watching the road.

She leaned toward him a little. "Do you think I'm lying about my name?"

"No."

"Good," she said.

He had begun to feel as though he might start throwing up what he'd had of the hamburger. His stomach was cramping on him, and he was dizzy. He might even be having a heart attack.

"Your eyes are big as saucers," she said.

He tried to narrow them a little. His whole body was shaking now.

"You know how old I am, MCrae? I'm nineteen."

He nodded, glanced at her and then at the road again.

"How old are you?"

"Twenty-three."

"Do you believe people go to heaven when they die?"

"Oh, God," he said.

"Look, I'm not going to shoot you while you're driving the car. We'd crash if I did that."

"Oh," he said. "Oh, Jesus, please—look. I never saw anybody shot before—"

"Will you *stop it?*"

He put one hand to his mouth. He was soaked; he felt the sweat on his upper lip, and then felt the dampness all through his clothes.

She said, "I don't kill everybody I meet, you know."

"No," he said. "Of course not." The absurdity of this exchange almost brought a laugh up out of him. It was astonishing that such a thing as a laugh could be anywhere in him at such a time, but here it was, rising up in his throat like some loosened part of his anatomy. He held on with his whole mind, and it was a moment before he realized that *she* was laughing.

"Actually," she said, "I haven't killed all that many people."

"How—" he began. Then he had to stop to breathe. "How many?"

"Take a guess."

"I don't have any idea," he said.

"Well," she said, "you'll just have to guess. And you'll notice that I haven't spent any time in prison."

He was quiet.

"*Guess*," she said.

MCrae said, "Ten?"

"No."

He waited.

"Come on, keep guessing."

"More than ten?"

"Maybe."

"More than ten," he said.

"Well, all right. Less than ten."

"Less than ten," he said.

"Guess," she said.

"Nine."

"No."

"Eight."

"No, not eight."

"Six?"

"Not six."

"Five?"

"Five and a half people," she said. "You almost hit it right on the button."

"Five and a half people," said MCrae.

"Right. A kid who was hitchhiking, like me; a guy at a gas station; a dog that must've got lost—I count him as the half—another guy at a gas station; a guy that took me to a motel and made an obscene gesture to me; and the guy at the diner. That makes five and a half."

"Five and a half," MCrae said.

"You keep repeating everything I say. I wish you'd quit that."

He wiped his hand across his mouth and then feigned a cough to keep from having to speak.

"Five and a half people," she said, turning a little in the seat, putting her knees up on the dash. "Have you ever met anybody like me? Tell the truth."

"No," MCrae said, "nobody."

"Just think about it, MCrae. You can say you rode with Belle Starr. You can tell your grandchildren."

He was afraid to say anything to this, for fear of changing the delicate balance of the thought. Yet he knew the worst mistake would be to say nothing at all. He was beginning to feel something of the cunning that he would need to survive, even as he knew the slightest miscalculation would mean the end of him. He said, with fake wonder, "I knew Belle Starr."

She said, "Think of it."

"Something," he said.

And she sat further down in the seat. "Amazing."

•

119

He kept to fifty-five miles an hour, and everyone else was speeding. The girl sat straight up now, nearly facing him on the seat. For long periods she had been quiet, simply watching him drive, and soon they were going to need gas. There was now less than half a tank.

"Look at these people speeding," she said. "We're the only ones obeying the speed limit. Look at them."

"Do you want me to speed up?" he asked.

"I think they ought to get tickets for speeding, that's what I think. Sometimes I wish I was a policeman."

"Look," MCrae said, "we're going to need gas pretty soon."

"No, let's just run it until it quits. We can always hitch a ride with somebody."

"This car's got a great engine," MCrae said. "We might have to outrun the police, and I wouldn't want to do that in any other car."

"This old thing? It's got a crack in the windshield. The radio doesn't work."

"Right. But it's a fast car. It'll outrun a police car."

She put one arm over the seat back and looked out the rear window. "You really think the police are chasing us?"

"They might be," he said.

She stared at him a moment. "No. There's no reason. Nobody saw us."

"But if somebody did—this car, I mean, it'll go like crazy."

"I'm afraid of speeding, though," she said. "Besides, you know what I found out? If you run slow enough the cops go right past you. Right on past you looking for somebody who's in a hurry. No, I think it's best if we just let it run until it quits and then get out and hitch."

MCrae thought he knew what might happen when the gas ran out: she would make him push the car to the side of the road, and then she would walk him back into the cactus and brush there, and when they were far enough from the road, she would shoot him. He knew this as if she had spelled it all out,

120

and he began again to try for the cunning he would need. "Belle," he said. "Why don't we lay low for a few days in Albuquerque?"

"Is that an obscene gesture?" she said.

"No!" he said, almost shouted. "No! That's—it's outlaw talk. You know. Hide out from the cops—lay low. It's—it's prison talk."

"Well, I've never been in prison."

"That's all I meant."

"You want to hide out."

"Right," he said.

"You and me?"

"You—you asked if I wanted to join up with you."

"Did I?" She seemed puzzled by this.

"Yes," he said, feeling himself press it a little. "Don't you remember?"

"I guess I do."

"You did," he said.

"I don't know."

"Belle Starr had a gang," he said.

"She did."

"I could be the first member of your gang."

She sat there thinking this over. MCrae's blood moved at the thought that she was deciding whether or not he would live. "Well," she said, "maybe."

"You've got to have a gang, Belle."

"We'll see," she said.

A moment later, she said, "How much money do you have?"

"I have enough to start a gang."

"It takes money to start a gang?"

"Well—" He was at a loss.

"How much do you have?"

He said, "A few hundred."

"Really?" she said. "That much?"

"Just enough to—just enough to get to Nevada."

"Can I have it?"

He said, "Sure." He was holding the wheel and looking out into the night.

"And we'll be a gang?"

"Right," he said.

"I like the idea. Belle Starr and her gang."

MCrae started talking about what the gang could do, making it up as he went along, trying to sound like all the gangster movies he'd seen. He heard himself talking about things like robbery and getaway and staying out of prison, and then, as she sat there staring at him, he started talking about being at Leavenworth, what it was like. He went on about it, the hours of forced work, and the time alone; the harsh day-to-day routines, the bad food. Before he was through, feeling the necessity of deepening her sense of him as her new accomplice—and feeling strangely as though in some way he had indeed become exactly that—he was telling her everything, all the bad times he'd had: his father's alcoholism, and growing up wanting to hit something for the anger that was in him; the years of getting into trouble; the fighting and the kicking and what it had got him. He embellished it all, made it sound worse than it really was because she seemed to be going for it, and because, telling it to her, he felt oddly sorry for himself; a version of this story of pain and neglect and lonely rage was true. He had been through a lot. And as he finished, describing for her the scene at the hospital the last time he saw his father, he was almost certain that he had struck a chord in her. He thought he saw it in the rapt expression on her face.

"Anyway," he said, and smiled at her.

"MCrae?" she said.

"Yeah?"

"Can you pull over?"

"Well," he said, his voice shaking, "why don't we wait until it runs out of gas?"

She was silent.

"We'll be that much further down the road," he said.

"I don't really want a gang," she said. "I don't like dealing with other people that much. I mean I don't think I'm a leader."

"Oh, yes," MCrae said. "No—you're a leader. You're definitely a leader. I was in the Air Force and I know leaders and you are definitely what I'd call a leader."

"Really?"

"Absolutely. You are leadership material all the way."

"I wouldn't have thought so."

"Definitely," he said, "definitely a leader."

"But I don't really like people around, you know."

"That's a leadership quality. Not wanting people around. It is definitely a leadership quality."

"Boy," she said, "the things you learn."

He waited. If he could only think himself through to the way out. If he could get her to trust him, get the car stopped—be there when she turned her back.

"You want to be in my gang, huh?"

"I sure do," he said.

"Well, I guess I'll have to think about it."

"I'm surprised nobody's mentioned it to you before."

"You're just saying that."

"No, really."

"Were you ever married?" she asked.

"Married?" he said, and then stammered over the answer. "Ah—uh, no."

"You ever been in a gang before?"

"A couple of times, but—but they never had good leadership."

"You're giving me a line, huh."

"No," he said, "it's true. No good leadership. It was always a problem."

"I'm tired," she said, shifting toward him a little. "I'm tired of talking."

The steering wheel was hurting the insides of his hands. He held tight, looking at the coming-on of the white stripes in the road. There were no other cars now, and not a glimmer of light anywhere beyond the headlights.

"Don't you get tired of talking, sometimes?"

"I never was much of a talker," he said.

"I guess I don't mind talking as much as I mind listening," she said.

He made a sound in his throat that he hoped she took for agreement.

"That's just when I'm tired, though."

"Why don't you take a nap," he said.

She leaned back against the door and regarded him. "There's plenty of time for that later."

"So," he wanted to say, "you're not going to kill me—we're a gang?"

They had gone for a long time without speaking, a nerve-wrecking hour of minutes, during which the gas gauge had sunk to just above empty; and finally she had begun talking about herself, mostly in the third person. It was hard to make sense of most of it. Yet he listened as if to instructions concerning how to extricate himself. She talked about growing up in Florida, in the country, and owning a horse; she remembered when she was taught to swim by somebody she called Bill, as if MCrae would know who that was; and then she told him how when her father ran away with her mother's sister, her mother started having men friends over all the time. "There was a lot of obscene goings-on," she said, and her voice tightened a little.

"Some people don't care what happens to their kids," said MCrae.

"Isn't it the truth?" she said. Then she took the pistol out of the shawl. "Take this exit."

He pulled onto the ramp and up an incline to a two-lane road that went off through the desert, toward a glow that burned on the horizon. For perhaps five miles the road was straight as a plumb line, and then it curved into long, low undulations of sand and mesquite and cactus.

"My mother's men friends used to do whatever they wanted to me," she said. "It went on all the time. All sorts of obscene goings-on."

MCrae said, "I'm sorry that happened to you, Belle." And for an instant he was surrounded by the sincerity of his feeling: it was as if he couldn't feel sorry enough. Yet it was genuine: it all had to do with his own unhappy story. The whole world seemed very, very sad to him. "I'm really very sorry," he said.

She was quiet a moment, as if thinking about this. Then she said, "Let's pull over now. I'm tired of riding."

"It's almost out of gas," he said.

"I know, but pull it over anyway."

"You sure you want to do that?"

"See?" she said. "That's what I mean. I wouldn't like being told what I should do all the time, or asked if I was sure of what I wanted or not."

He pulled the car over and slowed to a stop. "You're right," he said, "See? Leadership. I'm just not used to somebody with leadership qualities."

She held the gun a little toward him. He was looking at the small, dark, perfect circle of the end of the barrel. "I guess we should get out, huh," she said.

"I guess so." He hadn't even heard himself.

"Do you have any relatives left anywhere?" she said.

"No."

"Your folks are both dead?"

"Right, yes."

"Which one died first?"

"I told you," he said, "didn't I? My mother. My mother died first."

"Do you feel like an orphan?"

He sighed. "Sometimes." The whole thing was slipping away from him.

"I guess I do, too." She reached back and opened her door.

"Let's get out now." And when he opened his door she aimed the gun at his head. "Get out slow."

"Aw, Jesus," he said. "Look, you're not going to do this, are you? I mean I thought we were friends and all."

"Just get out real slow, like I said to."

"Okay," he said. "I'm getting out." He opened his door, and the ceiling light surprised and frightened him. Some wordless part of himself understood that this was it, and all his talk had come to nothing; all the questions she had asked him, and everything he had told her—it was all completely useless. This was going to happen to him, and it wouldn't mean anything; it would just be what happened.

"Real slow," she said. "Come on."

"Why are you doing this?" he said. "You've got to tell me that before you do it."

"Will you please get out of the car now?"

He just stared at her.

"All right, I'll shoot you where you sit."

"Okay," he said, "don't shoot."

She said in an irritable voice, as though she were talking to a recalcitrant child, "You're just putting it off."

He was backing himself out, keeping his eyes on the little barrel of the gun, and he could hear something coming, seemed to notice it in the same instant that she said, "Wait." He stood half in and half out of the car, doing as she said, and a truck came over the hill ahead of them, a tractor-trailer, all white light and roaring.

"Stay still," she said, crouching, aiming the gun at him.

The truck came fast, was only fifty yards away, and without having to decide about it, without even knowing that he would do it, MCrae bolted into the road. He was running: there was the exhausted sound of his own breath, the truck horn blaring, coming on, louder, the thing bearing down on him, something buzzing past his head. Time slowed. His legs faltered under him, were heavy, all the nerves gone out of them. In the light of the oncoming truck, he saw his own white hands outstretched as if to grasp something in the air before him, and then the truck was past him, the blast of air from it propelling him over the side of the road and down an embankment in high, dry grass, which pricked his skin and crackled like hay.

He was alive. He lay very still. Above him was the long shape of the road, curving off in the distance, the light of the truck going on. The noise faded and was nothing. A little wind stirred. He heard the car door close. Carefully, he got to all fours, and crawled a few yards away from where he had fallen. He couldn't be sure of which direction—he only knew he couldn't stay where he was. Then he heard what he thought were her footsteps in the road, and he froze. He lay on his side, facing the embankment. When she appeared there, he almost cried out.

"MCrae? Did I get you?" She was looking right at where he was in the dark, and he stopped breathing. "MCrae?"

He watched her move along the edge of the embankment.

"MCrae?" She put one hand over her eyes, and stared at a place a few feet over from him; then she turned and went back out of sight. He heard the car door again, and again he began to crawl farther away. The ground was cold and rough, and there was a lot of sand.

He heard her put the key in the trunk, and he stood up, began to run, he was getting away, but something went wrong in his leg, something sent him sprawling, and a sound came out of him that seemed to echo, to stay on the air, as if to call her to him. He tried to be perfectly still, tried not to breathe, hearing now the small pop of the gun. He counted the reports: one, two, three. She was just standing there at the edge of the road, firing into the dark, toward where she must have thought she heard the sound. Then she was rattling the paper bag, reloading. He could hear the click of the gun. He tried to get up, and couldn't. He had sprained his ankle, had done something very bad to it. Now he was crawling wildly, blindly through the tall grass, hearing again the small report of the pistol. At last he rolled into a shallow gully, and lay there with his face down, breathing the dust, his own voice leaving him in a whimpering animal-like sound that he couldn't stop, even as he held both shaking hands over his mouth.

"MCrae?" She sounded so close. "Hey," she said. "MCrae?"

He didn't move. He lay there, perfectly still, trying to stop himself from crying. He was sorry for everything he had ever done. He didn't care about the money, or the car or going out west or anything. When he lifted his head to peer over the lip of the gully, and saw that she had started down the embankment with his flashlight, moving like someone with time and the patience to use it, he lost his sense of himself as MCrae: he was just something crippled and breathing in the dark, lying flat in a little winding gully of weeds and sand. MCrae was gone, was someone far, far away, from ages ago—a man fresh out of prison, with the whole country to wander in, and insurance money in his pocket, who had headed west with the idea that maybe his luck, at long last, had changed.

Spirits

I

I met Brooker at one of those parties for new faculty. I was
just out of graduate school, after a stint in the Army, and I had
arrived, that July, to get myself ready for the fall semester.
Brooker was the most distinguished member of the faculty, and
I think I must've been surprised to see him. When I had come
through on my campus interview in the spring, the people who
squired me from place to place gave me the impression that he
was notoriously aloof; there were bets among them as to who
would next catch a glimpse of the creature.

But then, I was a fiction writer, the first ever hired to teach
at this small, rather conservative teachers' college, and he
wanted to get a look at me. He told me this in the first minute
of our acquaintance, as if he wanted me to know he wasn't a
regular at such gatherings: he really had come specifically to
meet me. He had seen my stories in the magazines; he knew I
had a book coming out, and he liked everything of mine that
he'd seen. I was, of course, immediately and wholeheartedly in
thrall. Remember that I was only twenty-six, and I suppose I
offer this as an explanation, if not as an excuse; it could never
have occurred to me then that he was merely flattering me.

The party took place on the lawn of the president's house,
which was a two-hundred-year-old Colonial mansion with walls
two feet thick and new polished tile floors that shone unnatu-
rally and made me think of carcinogens, for some reason. The
president was a small, frail-looking old man with a single tuft
of cottony white hair at the crown of his head, and twin tufts
above his ears. His name was Keller, and he was a retired

military officer with a Ph.D. in modern political history, Brooker told me. Dr. Keller was clearly delighted that Brooker had decided to attend his party. He stood in the open door to his house, the hallway shining behind him in a long perspective toward other open doors, and offered me his hand. "Come right through and get something else to drink, young man," he said. We had all been filing toward him from the lawn, which was dry and burned where there was no shade, and lush green under the willows and oaks and sycamores that surrounded the house.

"This is our writer," Brooker said to him.

"Well, and what do you write?"

"He writes stories, Dr. Keller."

"Oh. What kind of stories?"

Brooker left me to answer this, and I stammered something about seriousness that I'm sure Dr. Keller took as evidence of the folly of the English Department in having hired me in the first place.

"Are you tenure-track?"

"Yes, I am."

He nodded, and then he had turned to Brooker. They stood there exchanging comments about the turnout, the weather, the long spell without rain that had killed the grass, and I took this opportunity to study Brooker. For a man of nearly sixty, he was remarkably youthful-looking. His hair was gray, but thick, and his face still had the firm look of the face in the photographs of Brooker with Jack Kennedy before he ran for the presidency, or with Robert Kennedy near the end, or, later, with Lyndon Johnson. I remembered reading that Brooker had become disaffected with public service after the riots in Chicago, and had joined the faculty of a small private college in Virginia, and I was a little pie-eyed about the fact that I too was joining the faculty of that college. Life was roomy and full of possibility and promise; and I was for the moment quite simple and happy.

"So," Brooker said to me, entering the hall where I stood, "you have met our fine old president in his fine old house."

"Very nice," I said, gazing at the walls, the paintings there, which were of Virginia country scenes of a century ago.

"Have you found a place to live yet?"

I was paying a weekly rate at the Sweeney Motel off the interstate. I had paid the first month's deposit to rent a house that wouldn't be ready until the first week in September, and I was using the advance money on my book to make it until then. My wife had remained behind at the large Midwestern school where I had taken my degree; she would make her way here as soon as things were settled. I told him all this, feeling a little silly as I went on but finding myself unable to stop; it was information he seemed glad to have, and yet I wondered what could possibly interest him in it. I wound up talking about Mrs. Sweeney, who, because I was the same age as her son, had given me the single-room rate for a double, and kept stopping by to see me in the evenings, as if to give to the general pool of the world's kindness in the hope that somewhere someone else would offer something of it to her son.

"I'm giving a series of lectures at Chautauqua Institution this August," Brooker said. "I hate to suggest that you leave Mrs. Sweeney, but I wonder if you might not want to use my apartment for the month. You'd save money that way, and you could get some work done."

I just stood there.

"It must be awful trying to work in a motel."

"Well," I said, "I haven't been working."

"I'm going to be gone right through the last week of the month, because I have to spend some time in New York City too."

The president joined us then, wanting to introduce some people to Brooker, who nodded at them and was gracious and witty while I watched. There were two women in the group, one of them not much older than I, and as the president began to talk about the lack of rain and his garden, Brooker leaned toward me and, breathing the wine he had drunk, murmured something that I wasn't sure I could've heard correctly. I looked at him—he seemed to be awaiting a signal of agreement from me—and when I didn't respond he leaned close again, and, with a nod of his head in the direction of the younger of the two women, repeated himself. It was a phrase so nakedly obscene that I took a step back from him. He winked at me, then turned his charm in her direction, asking her if she liked the president's fine old house.

"Built in 1771," Dr. Keller said, looking at the ceiling as though the date might have been inscribed there.

"I love old houses," the young woman said. "That's what my field of study is. The American house."

Brooker offered her his hand and introduced himself, and then began an animated conversation with her about modern architecture. I stood there awhile, then moved off, through the hallway to the kitchen and out the door there. Some people were still on the lawn, but I went past them, to my car, feeling abruptly quite homesick and depressed. I drove around the college and through the town streets for a while, just trying to get the sense of where things were. The place my wife and I had rented was on the north end of town, in a group of old, run-down frame houses. Sitting in the idling car and gazing at it, I felt as though we had made a mistake. The place was really run-down. The porch steps sagged; it needed painting. I had agreed to fix the place up for a break in the amount of rent, and now the whole thing seemed like too much to have to do along with moving and starting a new job. I drove away feeling like someone leaving the scene of an accident.

When I got back to the motel, Mrs. Sweeney was waiting for me, and talking to her made me feel even worse. I kept hearing what Brooker had murmured in my ear. Mrs. Sweeney sensed that something was bothering me, and she was mercifully anxious not to intrude, or impose. She stayed only a few minutes, and then quietly excused herself and went on her way.

I had showered and was getting into bed before I remembered that Brooker had offered me his apartment. I was ready to doubt that he could've been sincere, and even so, when I called my wife, I found myself mentioning that I might be spending August as a house-sitter for none other than William Brooker.

"Who's William Brooker," she said.

I said, "You know who he is, Elaine."

"I'm not impressed," she said.

We didn't speak for a few seconds. Then I said, "So, do you miss me?"

"I miss you."

"What're you doing right now?" I asked.

"Talking to you."

With a feeling of suppressed irritation, I said, "What've you been doing all day?"

"Studying."

"The faculty orientation party was no fun," I said, and I went on to tell her about Brooker's murmured obscenity. Part of me simply wanted to express what I had felt about it all evening—that while I might have uttered exactly the same thing at one time or another, in Brooker's mouth and under those circumstances it was somehow more brutal than I could ever have meant it in my life. But there was also, I'm sure, the sense that my shock and disbelief would appeal to her.

"That doesn't seem like such an unusual thing for one man to say to another," she said. "Was she attractive?"

"You didn't hear the way he said it, Elaine."

"Did he slobber or something?"

Now I felt foolish. "Elaine, do you want to talk tonight?"

"Don't be mad," she said. "It really just doesn't sound like such an awful thing to me."

"Well," I said, "you weren't there."

"Are you going to stay in his apartment?" she asked.

"I don't know—I guess it'll save us money," I said, feeling wrong now, convinced that the whole question was pointless; that Brooker hadn't been serious, or that I had misinterpreted a gesture of hospitality anyone else would have known how to give the polite—and expected—refusal to.

"Why don't you hang up and go to sleep?" Elaine said. "You sound so tired."

"What if I get this apartment," I said. "Will you come out sooner?" And in the silence that followed, I added, "You could come out August first."

She said, "I'm in summer school, remember?"

"All right," I said, "the second week of August, then."

"We'll see."

"What's to keep you from coming then, Elaine?"

"We didn't plan it that way," she said.

Later, after we'd hung up and I'd been unable to fall asleep, I put my pants and shirt on and went out for a walk. Mrs. Sweeney was sitting on her little concrete slab of a porch, with a paperback book in her lap and a flyswatter in one hand, her stockings rolled down to her ankles, her hair in a white bandanna. She glanced over at me and smiled, and then went back to her reading. I went on up the sidewalk in my bare feet, and stood near the exit from the interstate, thinking about the fact that I was married, and that tonight my marriage felt like an old one, though we had been together only a little more than a year.

II

Elaine was trying to finish a master's degree in library science. The first time I saw her, she was wearing a swimsuit. I had just finished my first year of graduate school and was living in a small room above a garage, trying to write, and spending most of my afternoons at a lake a few miles west of the campus. There was a beach house and a restaurant on the lake, one of those places whose floors are covered with the sand that people track in from the beach, and whose atmosphere is suffused with the smell of suntan lotion. I was sitting alone at the counter, eating a hot dog, and two young women walked in, looking like health itself, tan and lithe and graceful in their bikinis.

They ordered ice cream cones and then walked to the back of the room to see what songs were on the jukebox. I sat gazing at them, as did the boy behind the counter—a high school kid with a lot of baby fat still on him, and with the funny round eyes of a natural clown. There wasn't anyone else in the place, and when the women strolled out finally, the boy put his hands down on the counter and let his head droop. "It's a tough job," he said, "but somebody's got to do it."

I laughed. We were for the moment in that exact state of agreement which may in fact be possible only between strangers. I got up and went out to the shaded part of the beach, where the two of them had settled at a picnic table. I had never done anything of the kind, but I was so struck by their beauty that I simply began speaking to them. I asked if they were students at the college and if they were going to summer school, and I asked how they liked the lake. They were polite, and they gave each other a few smiling, knowing glances, but we spent the rest of the afternoon together, and when I left them I asked to see them both again; it was all quite friendly, and we agreed to meet at a pizza parlor just off campus. That night, when I went there to meet them, only one of them showed up. This was Elaine. We had something to eat, and we went for a walk, and the odd thing to recall now is that I was a little disappointed that she, and not her friend, had come to meet me. I remember feeling a little guilty about this as the evening wore on and it became evident that Elaine and I were going to be seeing each other. As it turned out, her friend was leaving school, and I never saw her again; but even so, there were nights in that first year of our marriage when I would wake up next to Elaine and wonder about the friend. It was never anything but my mind wandering through possibility, of course, and yet when I think of Brooker, of the events that followed upon our first encounter at the faculty orientation party, my own woolgathering makes me feel rooted to the ground through the soles of my feet.

*

He phoned me early the next morning. I had been lying awake, thinking about calling Elaine, and when his call came through I thought it *was* Elaine. "I wondered what happened to you," he said.

I was vague. I think I was even a little standoffish. I said something about having things to do, errands to run.

"Listen," he said, "I wondered if you were still interested in house-sitting for me."

I hemmed and hawed a little, the thought having crossed my mind that I hadn't actually said I *was* interested; for some reason, now, accuracy seemed important: it was as if I might lose something to him if I allowed him to blur any of the lines between us.

He said, "I don't want to impose on you."

"No," I said, "really. I'm very glad you thought of me."

"You'd be doing me a favor," he said.

And so we agreed that I would come to the apartment for a drink that evening, at which time I could get a look at the place. His wife was arriving from New York in the afternoon, and if past experience meant anything at all she would not feel like entertaining a dinner guest; but a quiet, sociable drink was something else again.

"I could come another night," I said.

"No," he said after a pause, "tonight will be fine."

After we hung up, I went outside, and found Mrs. Sweeney hanging wash on a line in the yard.

"Have you looked at television this morning?" she said. "Did you see the news last night? You see that guy arrested for molesting that little girl?"

She didn't wait for me to answer.

"That's my ex-husband," she said. Her eyes were wide and frightened and tearful. "You believe that? My ex-husband." She turned to hang up a sheet, and I thought I heard her sniffle. "You think you know a person," she went on; she was looking at me now. "You live with a person and you think you know him—know the way he is. His—all the way to his soul. You think you understand a man's spirit when you look in his eyes and he's your live-in partner for three years. Three years," she said. "Do you believe it? And he was always the cleanest, nicest man you'd ever want to meet. Quiet and easy to get along with and sort of simple about things, and a good storyteller sometimes, when he felt like it. A little slow about work, sure—but."

"Maybe he's innocent," I said.

She stopped what she was doing and gave me a look almost of pity, except that there was impatience and frustration in it, too. "He confessed," she said. "He confessed to the whole thing. Can you imagine what this'll do to my boy, a thousand miles away from home, on some boat in the ocean, hearing that his stepfather did a terrible thing like that and then *confessed* to it?"

"Maybe the news won't get to him," I said.

"Oh, it'll get to him. I'll write and tell him about it. It'll get to him, all right." She put her apron full of clothespins in the basket at her feet and walked over to me. "I should be getting something for you to eat."

"No," I said, "I'm fine."

"I have a cook named Clara, but she's sick."

She had told me this on the day I registered—she'd repeated it three or four times since. I had begun to wonder what this Clara must be like to be missed so much.

"I'm fine," I told her.

She shook her head. "Do you believe it? A little girl." Then she turned and pointed at the motel office. "The paper's right inside the door there. It's on the front page if you want to read about it. My husband a rapist, for God's sake."

"It's a terrible thing," I said as she marched toward the office. I think she meant to get the newspaper and bring it out to me but then the phone rang in my room, and she said over her shoulder that I could come see it when I had the time. I went back into the room, certain that the call was from Elaine. I said "Howdy," into the telephone, and was greeted with a silence. "Hello?" I said.

"Uh, yes. This is William Brooker. Listen, I wanted to ask

you . . ." There was another silence, during which he sighed, like someone backing down from something. "Look, this is a little embarrassing. I mean I suppose it could wait until tonight. But I'd had a few drinks before I—before the party, you see."

"Yes?" I said, trying to sound only politely interested.

"Well—I said something last night—you know. We were all standing there and that extremely choice young lady was talking to Dr. Keller, and—you remember I said something a little off-color to you . . ."

"I didn't quite hear what it was," I lied.

"Oh. Well, I was wondering if you thought the young lady might've heard me. Or Dr. Keller."

"I wouldn't be able to say for sure."

"Yes, well. I shouldn't bother you with it. You say you didn't hear it at all?"

"That's right."

"I don't like to offend," he said.

And I was suddenly seized with a perverse desire to make him repeat the phrase that had so unnerved me the night before. "What was it, anyway?" I asked him.

"Oh, nothing. Just something a little—a silly little comment, you know. A joke. An impolite little aside. What I'd like to do to her—that sort of thing."

"Well," I said, wanting just as suddenly to let him off the hook, "I'm sure no one heard you."

"But—you said you *couldn't* be sure." Precision was Brooker's talent, someone had said.

"I'm reasonably sure, Professor Brooker. I mean if *I* couldn't hear you I don't think anyone else could."

"That's right," he said. "Good." I had the feeling that I had just been subjected to the tone he took in his classroom, leading a group of neophytes through the thicket of Twentieth-Century Politics.

"So," I said.

He said, "Well, I guess I'll see you tonight." Then, exactly as though it were an afterthought, he told me I ought to wear a suit and tie for the occasion.

"Excuse me?" I said.

"There'll be one or two other people here, if you don't mind."

"Not at all," I said. And I didn't really hear him as he talked about who his other guests would be, because I was thinking about the fact that I didn't have a suit *or* a tie, and so would have to go out and buy them. I had exactly twenty-two dollars in my pocket, and there was perhaps another forty in the checking account I'd opened only that week. The next installment of my advance wouldn't arrive for days.

Brooker had hung up before I could muster the courage to apprise him of this, and then I decided I wouldn't want him to know under any circumstances. I would simply go without if I had to go.

Of course I knew I would do no such thing. I would probably have been willing to steal what I needed; but as it turned out this wasn't necessary. Mrs. Sweeney's son was about my height and build, and he had left four suits behind—this was apparently his whole stock of them—along with about five hundred ties, all given to *him* by his former stepfather, the rapist and child molester, who according to Mrs. Sweeney had had a thing about ties, had collected them like somebody hoarding a thing that would soon be rare and hard to get. I chose a plain blue one, and a gray suit. I tried the suit on, standing in Mrs. Sweeney's spare room, and it fit well enough. Mrs. Sweeney made me wait while she ironed my shirt, and then that evening, after I'd got myself dressed and ready to go, she fussed with me, straightened the tie and brushed my arms and shoulders, her boy, going off to his first party in town. It seemed the appropriate thing to kiss her on the cheek before I left, and I'm afraid I embarrassed her.

"Good Lord," she said, but then she squeezed my elbow.

I almost asked what time she wanted me home.

III

Brooker's directions were characteristically precise. I had given myself a few minutes to allow for any trouble finding the place, and so I was early. I walked up the sidewalk in front of the building, already feeling stiff and uncomfortable in my suit and my rapist's tie, and Brooker came out on the landing and called to me. He was in shirt sleeves, the sleeves rolled up past his wrists.

"So glad you could make it," he said.

By the time I got up to him he had rolled the sleeves down and was buttoning them.

"I guess I'm a little early."

He ushered me inside and offered me a drink. Anything I wanted. I told him I'd wait awhile, and he excused himself and went upstairs. I sat in the living room, in the middle of his white sofa, my hands on my thighs, my back ramrod-stiff. It wasn't the sort of room you could relax in. There was a fireplace, and a baby grand piano, and on every available surface there were figurines and cut-glass shapes and statuary. The chairs and the love seat and the ottoman were not in the sort of proximity that would make conversation very easy, and the wallpaper was of a dark red hue that was really rather gloomy. I remembered that I had come to look at the place, then I had an image of me sitting there with the whole apartment to myself. Whatever else this room was, it was luxuriously appointed, and I knew I was going to enjoy the luxury of entering and leaving it as I pleased.

Now I sat back a little and breathed a satisfied sigh, while upstairs I heard Brooker and his wife moving around. Twice I heard her heels as she crossed from one room to another, and then she came down the stairs. She was a striking woman in her mid-forties, with wonderful square shoulders and deep, clear blue eyes, and she was wearing a white evening gown that made her skin look marvelously tan and smooth. She offered me her hand (I nearly brought it to my lips), and asked, in a voice that was warm and rich and full of humor, if I would come keep her company in the kitchen while she got things ready for the evening. Apart from being a little breathless at the sight of her, I was now beginning to wonder if I hadn't come more than a little early.

I said, "I must've got the time wrong, Mrs. Brooker."

"Call me Helen," she said, leading me into the kitchen. "And you shouldn't worry about being early—we're just running a little late."

The kitchen was a light-filled, high-ceilinged room that looked as though it might've been transported, brick by brick, board by board from one of the family farms in Brooker's native Minnesota. She indicated that I was to sit at the table in the center of the room, and then began opening cabinets and hutches, bringing out dishes, glasses, boxes of crackers, knives and forks.

"Can I help?" I said.

"Absolutely not. I could never stand servants in the house because I wanted to do it all myself, and as you can see I can't even let a guest be polite without launching into an explanation of this—quirk of mine." She paused. "Do you like the kitchen?"

"It's a very nice room," I said.

"Well, and you're going to be calling it home, aren't you."

"For a month. I guess so."

She went about her work, slicing cheese, arranging crackers on the plates, and making dip, and I sat watching her.

"William says your wife isn't with you."

"No."

"Too bad," she said. "Do you miss her?"

"Very much."

"William travels so much. It's just odd that we're both going this time."

"I'll take good care of things," I said.

She waved this away as if there could be no doubt about it,

and then without asking what I wanted she fixed me a glass of bourbon on ice. "If this isn't to your taste I'll drink it myself."

"It's fine," I said, and she gave me an odd look, as though my answer had surprised her. I sipped the whiskey, and she went back to setting things in order for the evening's guests, who were apparently arriving now—we could hear Brooker greeting someone out in the hall.

"William will think I stole you from him," she said. "Do you mind if I have a sip of your drink? I don't really want to have a whole one."

I handed her my glass. She took a long, slow sip, then breathed. I have loved the taste of whiskey since I was young and my father would take me out on the porch at home and let me sip it out of sight of my mother, and I have never seen anyone—nor, I believe, have I myself ever enjoyed a sip of whiskey as much as this stately and beautiful woman did that night in Brooker's kitchen.

"Very good," she said, and smiled, handing the glass back to me. There was something a little hurried about the way she did it, and then I realized that Brooker was coming down the hall. I put the drink down on the table in front of me and tried to look calm as he entered the room, leading Dr. Keller, who did not remember having met me, and who, again, asked if I was tenure-track. We had got past all that and in the next moment Brooker asked his wife if she wanted a glass of bourbon.

"Not on your life," she said.

"I always ask and she always refuses," Brooker said. "I don't know if I like disciplined people."

"Why don't *you* have some?" she said to him.

"No," he said, "I'm off it, too."

Dr. Keller also declined, and so now I was the only person in the group who was drinking. I found this a little irritating, and I made up my mind that I was going to sip the drink very slowly; I might even ask for another. I sat watching Mrs. Brooker put the finishing touches on a plateful of cheeses and cold cuts, while the two men stood talking about diets and diet drinks. Their conversation seemed so banal that I wondered if they weren't trading sides of a sort of running joke, but they were serious: Brooker's full attention was on the college president as he listed his various reasons for preferring iced tea without sugar over the sugarless colas. And then I noticed something else. Helen Brooker was staring at me. She had finished with everything and was simply standing there with her legs crossed at the ankles, gazing at me with all the frankness of a child. When I turned a little and met her gaze, she smiled and offered to refresh my glass.

It was an odd evening. The other guests arrived, two couples. They were people of Brooker's age and class, and Dr. Keller introduced the men as members of the Board of Visitors of the college.

"This is our writer," he said, presenting me to them. "Professor Brooker was so kind as to invite him here tonight."

The two men shook my hand, and their wives nodded at me from the snowy expanse of the couch. I sat in one of the wing chairs near the fireplace and was promptly forgotten. Brooker had begun to hold forth about the Kennedy years, and I noticed that his wife sat staring at her nails while he talked. She had heard it all before, of course, and she was doing a bad job of disguising her boredom. Finally she got up and carried a couple of empty plates into the kitchen, and when she came back out she had a glass of whiskey. She sat down next to the wives, and when she crossed her legs and let her high-heeled shoe slip to the toe of the dangling foot, my blood jumped. I went into the kitchen to pour my own whiskey, and I think I entertained for a moment the rather puerile fancy that she would make her way to me there, and that she might confess something to me, something I could console her for. But no one came, and in a little while I carried my fresh drink back to the chair by the fireplace.

The others were all drinking iced tea from a tray on the coffee table. I sipped my drink, and watched Helen Brooker sip hers. The talk was general now, and very stilted and hesitant; there seemed no common history for any of them to talk about—or there *was* a common history that all of them were avoiding as a subject for talk. In any case, I grew very tired and so deeply bored that I may even have nodded off once or twice. When Mrs. Brooker stood to go fix herself another drink, I got up too. I meant to leave, but before I could make my apologies she took me by the arm and walked with me into the kitchen.

"You haven't really seen the place," she said.

"It's fine," I said.

"We keep our bourbon in here to discourage our guests." She was pouring it into her glass. "Billy doesn't like trying to talk to drunks."

"Billy."

"Brooker." She tipped her head slightly to the side. "Doesn't it sound like a little innocent boy: Billy Brooker? That's what they called him, you know."

"Who?"

"The Kennedys."

"Did you know him then—when he was with the Kennedys?"

"I worked for him. I was his secretary."

"You must've been very young."

She took a sip of her drink. "Billy's thirteen years older than I am. He was forty-two and I was twenty-nine. I was just out of a very unhappy marriage, and of course he was—well, he was the famous Mr. Brooker, though I must say I was really in love with Jack Kennedy more than anything else. We were all in love with him—the whole staff. And of course I voted for him because I thought he was so handsome. A lot of women *and* men did that, you know."

"I wasn't old enough to vote, but I guess I would have," I said.

"You were fascinated with him." It was as though she were leading me toward something.

"I liked his speeches."

"He was an awful womanizer, you know."

"That's what they say."

"Are you a womanizer?" She smiled, swallowed some of her drink, turning to face her husband, who came into the room from the back door and stood for a moment, looking at her and then at me.

"Hogging the booze," he said.

"Here," said his wife, lazily handing him hers. "If I have any more I'll wind up with a headache."

"Cheers," Brooker said, and drank.

"Have our guests departed, Billy?"

"They've departed."

"I've got to go," I said.

"Why don't you have another drink?" Brooker said. "You haven't really seen the place yet."

So I stayed for another glass of bourbon, which was enough to make me a little bleary-eyed and giddy for the drive back to the motel. Brooker walked me through the upstairs rooms of the apartment, including his wife's reading room, as he called it (it looked like a bedroom), and his study. She excused herself and went off to another room to bed, leaving the smell of her perfume everywhere.

"Your wife is very beautiful," I said to him when she had gone.

"Yes," he said as if we had agreed on something quite unimportant.

The upstairs rooms were spacious and comfortable looking, and there was a television room I knew I would spend a lot of time in. I wasn't planning to try to do much writing. In fact, I have always been the sort of writer who works best out of a predictable routine, and with plenty of order and harmony around him. Brooker showed me his study last. It was a small book-lined room with a desk and two straight-backed chairs, and with exactly the harried, busy-paper look you'd expect it to have. "I've been working on something," he said to me, and took one of the pages from his desk. On the wall above the desk were photographs of Brooker among the powerful; and of his wife, wearing something flowing and diaphanous and white, in various balletic attitudes obviously meant to appear candid, and just as obviously posed for. Brooker apparently caught my interest in these photographs, for he put the page back down and touched the corner of the nearest photograph—of Helen standing in a bath of white light, her slender arms almost hidden in the liquid folds of the gown. He moved the frame just so, and then stared at the picture.

"Helen wanted to be an actress for a while," he said. "She wasn't bad."

"She's beautiful," I said, and realized that I was sounding more and more like a love-struck high school boy.

Rather drily Brooker said, "Yes, we agreed about that before." And then, giving me a fatherly smile: "I can bear any number of repetitions concerning the beauty of my wife, lad."

We went downstairs, and I declined what was—I was certain—a decidedly halfhearted offer of another drink; in any case, I thought it was time to leave. He stood in the light of the landing and asked if I was okay to drive, and I assured him I was, though I had my doubts. As much as I love the taste of bourbon, I have never been able to drink more than a glass or two without getting very unsteady on my feet. When I pulled out onto the highway there was an immediate blurring of the lines of the road ahead, and I held tight to the wheel, going very slow, feeling more sloshed every second.

Mrs. Sweeney was sitting under her yellow porch light, with her flyswatter and her book. She stood and walked over to me.

"My goodness," she said when I staggered.

I took her husband's tie off and held it out to her.

"I don't want it," she said.

I put it into the suit-coat pocket. "I'm sorry," I said. "I've had a little too much to drink."

"Your wife called," she said. "I waited up to tell you."

"You're very kind," I said.

"They showed pictures," Mrs. Sweeney said. "On the news. They showed him being taken into court. He was covering his face."

146

There wasn't anything I could think of to say to this.

"It was on the news. They think he killed a lot of little kids and buried them somewhere. I was married to him all that time."

I shook my head, and looked out at the road.

"Your wife called," she said. "I told her I'd wait up."

"Thank you, Mrs. Sweeney—and I wish there was something I could say about all this—"

"It's on the news," she said. "It's a big news story."

"I'll watch for it."

"They're going to come talk to me. The news people. They're going to ask me if I knew anything." She shook her head, turning. "You think you know a person."

In the room, I thought of calling Elaine, but what I did was lie across the bed, still wearing the borrowed suit, and, dreaming of a woman twenty years older than I was, I fell deeply, drunkenly asleep.

In the morning I woke to see a shadow move across my window, high up. I lay there with a dry mouth and a headache, watching it for a while, and finally I decided to investigate. As I came to my feet, I thought I heard Mrs. Sweeney's voice, and then other voices. Outside, across the way, on the grassy hill that led onto the interstate ramp and above which the sun had just risen, men were walking. Their shapes were all blazingly outlined, but I could see that they were combing the ground, searching. Mrs. Sweeney stood in the gravel lot, talking to one man while another filmed her, and there were police cars and news-media vans blocking the entrance to the motel. I went back into my room and turned on the television set, but it was too late for morning news; it was all movies and situation comedies and quiz shows. I started to go back out, and then decided not to. I didn't want to see whatever they would find out there, if they found anything at all.

IV

There was all that work to do on the house, and I was gone a lot during the next couple of days. I had an excuse to be gone, and I took it. One late night I arrived to find Mrs. Sweeney waiting up for me. She wanted to tell me about the interview with the news people, and her voice as she spoke was an exact blend of excitement and horror. The men searching the hillside had found nothing, she said. To think that murdered children might have been buried within yards of her own house; to think that she had been on the nightly news. "I told them," she said. "I made them understand that when Eddie lived with me he never did anything like hurting a little child."

"It's an awful thing," I said.

"I wrote a letter to my son. I don't know how to tell him."

"Would you like me to look at it?" I said.

She seemed puzzled by such a suggestion. "No," she said.

"Well, anything I can do to help."

She thanked me, but something about my offer to read the letter had made her nervous. I think she considered its contents too private even for the eyes of the faraway young man to whom it was addressed. The next day I stayed around the motel—I took a swim in the pool, and basked in the late-morning sun—and Mrs. Sweeney was uncharacteristically cool and distant. When she came to ask if I wanted lunch, I thought she was almost wary of me. I said I wasn't hungry, and thanked her, then went back to my room, certain that removing myself for the moment was the best thing for her peace of mind. In the room I napped and read magazines, and watched television. Mrs. Sweeney's husband was big news, all right. The authorities were turning up bodies all over the country. When I called Elaine, I told her about the man whose tie I now apparently owned, and though she feigned interest, I could tell that she was restive, wanted to hang up.

"So," I said, "tell me about your day."

"I studied."

"Anything else?"

"Nothing else."

"No movies? No television? No talk with friends?"

"I said nothing else."

"Is there anything you'd like to talk about?"

"You were telling me about the mad killer-rapist."

"Did I tell you about Brooker's wife?"

"Tell me about Brooker's wife."

"I'm in love with her."

"Wonderful."

"We're going to run away to Paris."

"Terrific."

"We're madly, desperately, spiritually and physically in love."

"I'm very happy for you."

"Elaine," I said.

"You have my blessing," she said.

"Are you coming out in August?" I asked. "We'll have their place all to ourselves."

"We can play Pretend."

"We can do anything you want," I said.

"All I know how to do is study."

"Are you coming out or not?" I said.

"Not."

"Come on, Elaine."

"Not, I'm afraid, is the truth."

"All right," I said, "why not?"

"Maybe I've decided I don't want to live in Virginia."

I didn't say anything then.

"What if I don't like Virginia?" she said.

"Elaine, you loved it. Remember? You picked out the house. You were all excited about fixing it up. I've been working on it all this time."

"I guess I'm getting cold feet. It's senior syndrome, or something."

"Are you serious?" I said.

"Half."

"You mean it."

"A little, yes."

"Are you telling me you might not come out here at all?"

"I don't know what I'm telling you. Don't badger me."

"I have a place for us both to stay until the house is ready. It's a very nice place, Elaine. It's luxurious, in fact."

"And it's famous."

"I don't understand your attitude about this. Yes, it is William Brooker's apartment, and William Brooker is widely known."

"He's famous."

"All right, goddammit, he's famous. Yes."

"Don't get mad," she said. "I'm too tired for anger over the telephone."

"Elaine," I said, "what's the matter?"

She paused, then sighed. "Nothing."

"No," I said, "what's the matter. Tell me."

"Nothing's the matter. I'm tired, and I don't feel like making any big decisions now, all right? I don't want to think about moving and all that. I'm trying to finish up a degree."

"All right, fine," I said.

She said, "Terrific."

We hung up simultaneously, I think. Then I called her back. We traded apologies and explanations. We were both under a lot of pressure; it was a new job, a new situation. She was so tired and beaten down by the work. She had been having anxiety attacks, and was beginning to wonder what it had all been for. I had upset her by talking about child murders and rape, and now the idea of living in a place where such things happened made her tremble. "I know, things like that happen anywhere, but I still feel jittery about living there and I was feeling jittery about it before you told me this horror story."

"It's just nerves," I said. "It's just getting settled, that's all. Once you get settled you'll see."

But in the silence that followed, I wondered if there weren't something more than nerves bothering her.

"Elaine?" I said.

"I don't know," she said. "I don't want to talk now. We'll talk later."

And again, we hung up almost simultaneously.

In the morning, I had breakfast in Mrs. Sweeney's small diner-kitchen. There were five or six other people staying at the motel now, and she was too busy to speak to me, except to say that her cook, Clara, would be coming back on in a few days, and it couldn't be a minute too soon. She made a gesture like a swoon of exhaustion. Outside, cars slowed going by, or pulled in and sat idling while the curious got out to stare and take pictures. Mrs. Sweeney's husband was a national story now—and each day brought new revelations about him: he had been killing people, mostly little girls, all his adult life. He had drifted across the country, killing as he went, years before settling in Virginia with Marilee Wilson. The psychiatrists who were conducting interviews with him found that he was completely without remorse, without any sense of the enormity of his crimes, and when he spoke about his victims he was chillingly direct and simple, a man describing uncomplicated work, something about which there were only the barest considerations of technique. Police officers from seven states would be converging on the small town jail where he was presently incarcerated; they would all be about the business of talking to the killer to clear away open files, unsolved cases. Some were guessing that it might take years for all the crimes to come to light, and estimated that the numbers were well into the hundreds.

Mrs. Sweeney was glad that business was better, but weary of all the questions, and she didn't like being stared at. The day her husband's picture appeared on the cover of a newsmagazine, she closed her shutters and put up the NO VACANCY sign.

"I don't care about the business any more," she told me. "I think I'll sell the place now, anyway."

This was about a week before I checked out. I hadn't told her yet that I would be leaving before the September date we had initially agreed on. She had come over from her place on the stoop, and headed me off from a night walk. We stood outside my room and watched the lights on the interstate beyond the crest of the hill across the way. "I used to get lonesome for him," she said, "nights like this."

I had the feeling that she was lonesome for him *now*, but I said nothing.

"Were you on your way somewhere?" she said.

"I was going to take a walk."

"It's a pretty night for a walk."

"Would you like to come with me?" I said, and knew immediately that I had embarrassed her again. "I mean I wouldn't mind company."

She mumbled something about having too much to do.

"Well," I said.

"You know what?" she said. "I don't believe him. I lived with him for three years. If he was like they say he was he would've killed *me*, wouldn't he?"

I said that seemed logical.

"But maybe with someone like that, there isn't really any logic to go by."

"That's probably true," I said.

"I'm going to sell this place and move out of the state." She walked off toward her yellow-lighted stoop.

I watched her go into the office, saw her shadow in the window, and there was something so bowed and unhappy and reproachful about the way she stood gazing out at me that I decided against the walk. I didn't want to find her waiting for me when I returned. I was sorry for everything, but I was in fact a little tired of her trouble; I had troubles of my own. I got into my car and drove over to the rental house, and worked for a few hours painting the rooms. While I worked, I thought about Elaine, and then I was thinking about Brooker's wife. It started as an idle daydream, but I found myself putting embellishments on it, and soon enough I was engaged in a full-fledged fantasy. I imagined that she drove by in the night and saw me in the curtainless windows of the rental house, that she came to the door and knocked, and I let her in. We strolled through the house, talking about what I planned to do with it once Elaine and I moved in, and then we said things that led to kissing. I was on a stepladder, with a roller in my hand, dripping paint, and I realized that I had been quite motionless, deep in this fantasy, for some time. I had seen myself removing Helen Brooker's white cocktail dress, sliding the straps down her shoulders, and I had kissed the soft untanned places on her belly. "Are you a womanizer?" she had asked me that night in her kitchen.

Before I was through, I imagined visiting her at the apartment—saw her arriving early from her travels while I was still alone and sleeping in her bed; I played out a small lubricious drama in which I told her that Elaine was staying behind, would not be joining me, and in which Helen Brooker became my mistress, visiting me every day in the rental house, full of appetite for me and the excitement of our illicitness. In other words, I conjured up a woman who bore no real relation to Helen Brooker—a dream woman who wished only to satisfy my whims.

When, a week later, I carried my suitcase up the sidewalk and the stairs to the landing of Brooker's apartment, I kept my eyes averted for fear of catching a glimpse of his wife, as if to see her would be to cause the whole business to come blurting out of me, the confession of a secret and obsessive lust; for I had kept my fantasies about her, had added to them, had suffered them in my sleep, along with crazy shifts of logic in which the mad mass killer Mr. Sweeney appeared, always in the guise of someone quite harmless at first, and then simply as himself, crouched in a kind of striped, shadowy corner, staring out. I had awakened from these dreams with a jolt, and with the sense that I had come into an area of my life that was utterly uncharted and dark. I found myself deciding against calling Elaine, or putting it off, and when she called me I was as uncommunicative and anxiety-ridden as she was. We had a few very unhappy, very gloomy discussions of plans for the end of summer, and we still hadn't established what she would do. For the time being, I was to move into the Brookers' apartment alone.

When I said goodbye to Mrs. Sweeney, she seemed oddly relieved to have me go. Her son was coming home on leave, she said, and it was too bad I wouldn't be able to meet him.

"Maybe I'll come visit," I said.

"That would be very nice," she said. But I think she was only being polite. I was the last of her customers, and she was closing up for good. She had even let Clara go. She told me this almost as an afterthought: it was too bad that someone like Clara had to go off and work for one of the big places, like Holiday Inn. She didn't think a big chain would appreciate someone of Clara's gifts. Everything was so cut-and-dried these days. She went on like this, tallying up my bill, and I knew she was glad I was leaving.

I didn't have to worry about seeing Brooker's wife, for she was already on her way north. Brooker told me this as he helped me inside with my things. He gave me his key, then called a taxi to come take him to the airport. When I offered to drive him there, he said, "Well, I should've thought of that. The taxi's on its way, though."

"Call and cancel it," I said. "I don't mind taking you."

He considered for a moment. "If you're sure about this, lad."

In the car, I caught the odor of alcohol on his breath. He sat staring out the passenger window, and I coasted along trying to think of something to say to him. I had hoped we might talk on the way, that I might get to know him better. Finally I said, "Will you be meeting your wife in New York?"

"I'm going to Toronto first. Overnight."

"Will she be at Chautauqua with you?"

"Part of the time, maybe. She has friends in the city—Chautauqua's a little too Victorian for her taste."

"Will you be lecturing about the Kennedy years?"

"Some."

"I wish I could've been around for some of that time."

"It wasn't all it was cracked up to be."

"You knew John Kennedy pretty well, didn't you?"

"He was my boss for a while. I knew him, all right."

"He looks so brilliant in all the films—you know, the speeches."

Brooker said nothing to this.

"Everybody who knew him wrote a book about him," I said. "Why didn't you?"

"I decided instead to give lectures. It means more money over a longer period of time. The colleges will pay handsomely for somebody like me to come tell them what they already suspect. After you get famous, lad, you'll be paid handsomely to come read from your work—it's a lot like that. All fiction. Don't tell anyone I said so, but the colleges are full of stupid, limited people, with a very few exceptions. And to be blunt about things, I might as well tell you that it's entirely possible I won't be teaching at our quaint little peaceful school after next year."

"Why not?" I said, breathing the alcohol again. And even so, I thought he would tell me about some grant or other, or plans to spend a year abroad. What he did say was so surprising that I took my eyes off the road a moment to look at him.

"It seems that I'm to be removed—for a few small indiscretions."

I was speechless.

"You must've noticed that I'm inclined to be a bit careless what I say."

If I could've said anything at all, I would have. I sat there staring out at the road and waiting for him to go on.

"The wife and I used to booze it up pretty good. She's got a lot better than I am, of course. But the two of us made a few powerful enemies. It doesn't matter now, you know, because I'm getting near retirement anyway. I guess you're wondering why I'm telling you all this."

"No," I said stupidly, as if I might've expected him to confide in me.

"The truth of the matter is that I did want to salvage something if I could. I mean I hoped that by showing some college spirit I might be able to persuade the Board to reconsider, but I don't think that's going to happen."

"They're *firing* you?" I said.

"Not exactly."

"You're tenured," I said, "aren't you?"

"I never accepted tenure, lad. I didn't want it. I've had a series of special contracts, each year."

I had pulled into the airport terminal. There was a small knot of people at the far gate, and I drove toward it. He already had the door open. "I hope you'll forgive me for deceiving you about—well, about work. I do like your stories, but I only read them to make this last try, so to speak. I mean I know you thought I was just one of those prescient types who read everything. I searched them out and read them because Helen thought it might impress the Board. I'm afraid it didn't even impress *you* quite as much as I could've hoped it would."

I had stopped the car.

"I guess not," he said, giving me a look.

I got out and helped him with his things, and when he was in line, waiting to board the plane, he shook my hand and told me to make myself at home in his place. I was to use everything just as if it were mine, and he would telephone now and again, if it was all right, just to be sure there wasn't any important mail, or phone calls that needed immediate attention. When I left him there, and started the drive back to town and my new surroundings, I felt as though I had been duped. And I don't mean I was bothered by the fact that he hadn't come upon my

work in the course of his normal habits of reading—that had
been too outlandish to believe in the first place, and I had
indeed been a little embarrassed all along at my own wish to
take him at his word; this is hard to explain, muddied as it is
by hindsight. In any case, my sense of having been duped had,
oddly, to do with Brooker's attitude in the few moments just
before I left him at the airport. It was as if I were somehow a
creation of his; as if everything I had thought and felt in the
few days since I first met him at the faculty orientation party
had been produced, orchestrated by him, with calculation and
in the certain knowledge that each gesture, each wave of his
baton would bring another shade of admiration out of me. I
must have looked like an adoring boy at that first meeting.

In any case, I returned to the empty apartment with a very
strong sense of dissatisfaction and displeasure concerning Mr.
William Brooker. I had decided that if he was a man who
deserved my respect, he was not the man of great qualities that
I had imagined him to be. And when, that evening, I took his
wife's picture down from the wall and carried it with me into
her reading room with its small, flower-fragrant bed, I thought
of him with something like the mixture of pity and disdain that
an adulterer feels for the man he has cuckolded.

V

Elaine decided not to come until the first of September—the
original moving date. I took this news quietly. I had stopped
all work on the rental house. I had stopped going out; I was
spending each day in the rooms of that apartment, watching
television, reading, sleeping, and gazing at what I could find of
photographs and belongings of Helen Brooker. I found a box
of pictures of her as a girl, and as a bright young student; I
found honors and trophies she had won in college, for her work
in the yearly stage play, or for her contributions to the literary
magazine; I found a stack of lurid-looking paperback books on

a shelf in her closet; and, best of all, I found a bundle of old letters and cards in the back of a bureau drawer—birthday greetings, Christmas cards, cards to accompany flowers, and a few thank-you notes, along with letters from her mother, from a sister in Connecticut, and, to my great fascination, from an ardent somebody who kept complaining that she never paid him enough attention. These love notes or complaints were all signed with the initial W.

Darling, one of them went, *I suppose you'll laugh when I say this, but someday you'll read what I've written to you, and remember me as your one truest friend; and you'll miss me. On that day you won't laugh. And wherever I am, I'll still love you. Always, W.*

Another said, *Helen, I have written a poem called "Sorry." It's about us. You said to keep in touch, and this is the only way I know how. The poem is simple: Could you spend Sunday / or just any one day / with me / she said / "Sorry." It goes on in this vein, so you see, Helen, I am not without humor concerning you and me. Love, W.*

It suddenly dawned on me as I read that W probably stood for William, and that these sophomoric and romantic missives were from the then senatorial staff worker William Brooker, already in his forties and sounding like a nineteen-year-old boy with a crush on his English teacher.

Helen, there's something in your eyes that makes me unable to speak, and the only thing I have is pen and paper. I'm not a poet, but if I were I'd find the words to make you see what happens to me every time you turn your head my way. I love you, Always, W.

This snooping of mine was exactly as undignified and sneaky as it sounds, and I suppose the only thing to be said about it now, once having admitted this, is that it was also a function of a kind of madness that had taken hold of me. At night I had begun to dream about Helen Brooker in a way that left me exhausted in the mornings, and there was always the haunting and shadowy figure of Sweeney, always the terrible fact of his passionless violence in the dreams. I had taken to following the development of the case on the local television stations, two of which were doing specials about him; and there were the continuing newspaper articles. And so in fact, Mr. Sweeney was part of the daytime, too. In the newspaper articles the reporters said Sweeney spoke in a soft, countrified voice about stabbing a girl through the heart, and my own heart shook in my chest, and yet I couldn't look away or stop reading or put my mind on my work. And when I wasn't following the news, I stalked the house for a woman's privacy.

When Elaine and I talked on the phone, our silences grew longer, and the suppressed irritations began to find terms of expression. We argued, or bickered, or teased each other into bickering, and finally she suggested that something was wrong with us which a separation might solve: she wanted to wait through the fall before coming east, if she came east at all. We could see how we felt in six months. I don't know if she thought much would change in that time, but I felt as though we were dissolving the marriage over the telephone, and I told her so. Her response was a very calm denial that this was so; she just wanted a little time. I even offered, near the end of the conversation, to come west; I said I was willing to give up the job. But of course this was a ridiculous idea, and in any case I didn't think I could bring myself to go through with it. If she wanted me to—which she did not.

So after a week in Brooker's apartment, I was fairly crazed: I was sure my wife was divorcing me; I was having a fantasy affair with a woman I had met only once in my life (there was something about being among her things; it was as if I were a ghost, haunting another ghost, and there was always the feeling that I *did* know her after all), and I was monitoring with avid and horrified fascination the story of Mr. Sweeney and his many victims. To put it simply, I was in no condition for what took place at the end of that first week. And to spare you any unnecessary suspense, I'll just say here that what happened was that I had a visitor, a woman I'd never seen before, someone close to my age or younger, who stood in the light of the

Brookers' landing and stared at me as if I had materialized out of the summer night.

I had been reading Brooker's vaguely plagiaristic love notes (*Helen, nothing is as intensely delicate as you are*), when the doorbell rang, so loudly and so suddenly—it seemed the tolling that calls the guilty to their punishment—that I let out a cry and nearly fell from the chair in which I sat, the letters and notes in a loose bundle on my lap. I almost dropped them all as I came to my feet, and for a confused minute I didn't know what to do with them; I thought this visitor would surely be Helen, or Brooker himself, and that I would be caught red-handed with the evidence of my spying. Finally I jammed everything under a cushion of the sofa and went to the door to peer out at whoever it was. In the dim light of the landing I made out enough of the face to know it wasn't either of the Brookers.

I opened the door.

She stared at me for some time before she spoke. "I am looking for Mrs. Brooker." As I have said, she was my age or younger, and she looked Spanish—her hair was very black, her eyes a facetless black. "I know they live here."

"Mrs. Brooker isn't here," I said.

She looked down a moment, apparently deciding something. Then she simply turned and started back down the steps.

"Excuse me," I said.

She stopped, looked back at me. "You are her son?"

I shook my head no.

"I need to talk to *her*, not him. You tell him that Maria Alvarez came to see Mrs. Brooker. You tell him that."

"Mr. Brooker is in New York State," I said.

"Remember the name," she said, going on, "Maria Alvarez."

I stood out on the landing and watched her cross the parking lot, moving very slowly, almost warily, as if she were afraid someone might spring out at her from behind one of the parked cars. But then it wasn't quite like that, either—for there was an element of discouragement about it, a kind of defeated dignity that made me wonder where she had come from and what she might be going back to. I almost called to her, though of course she probably would not have come back. She got into a small, beat-up Volkswagen bug and drove away, and I went back into Brooker's apartment and took up my invasion of Helen Brooker's personal life.

Later that evening, Brooker called, and I told him about his wife's visitor.

"Jesus Christ," Brooker said. "Jesus Christ."

I waited.

"She came to the door?"

"Yes," I said.

"And she asked for *Mrs.* Brooker?"

"Yes."

"Jesus Christ."

"She drove away in an old Volkswagen bug."

"Well, for Christ's sake."

I said nothing. For a moment there was just the faint interference on the line of another, distant conversation.

"Listen," he said. "If she comes back, tell her Mrs. Brooker and I are separated. Okay? We're not living together any more."

I stood there holding the receiver to my ear.

"Got that?" he said.

"You're separating?" I said.

He took a moment. "Just tell her that. Will you tell her that for me?"

I heard myself say I would.

"Did you tell her when we'd be home?"

"That didn't come up."

"Good."

"She probably won't be back," I said.

"Well, if she *comes* back, you'll remember to tell her Mrs. Brooker and I are separated. We've been separated for some time, you don't know how long."

"Mr. Brooker," I said, "are you asking me to lie for you?"

He took another moment to answer. "Just tell her we're separated. That'll be the truth."

"All right," I said.

"And then call me at this number if she does come back."

"I will," I said to him.

And then he had hung up. I sat for a long time by the phone, not really thinking about anything, and yet feeling low and lonely and sick at heart. Finally I called Elaine.

"Honey," I said, "I miss you."

She had fallen asleep studying, and was groggy and irritable. "Call me back," she mumbled, "okay?"

"Elaine, I'm going crazy here," I said.

"Call me back," she said sleepily, and then the line clicked.

The afternoon newspaper, in the third part of a four-part series about Mr. Sweeney, carried a summary of his early life. Apparently Mr. Sweeney had been raised by a self-styled freethinker, a man who believed in exposing children early to the realities of life, particularly the sexual realities: the senior Mr. Sweeney had made his young son take part in his own sexual escapades, had made him watch while he and the boy's mother and a friend of the boy's mother had relations. There were other unpleasant details: in Sweeney's own words, he could never be near a living, breathing human being without thinking of murder. Mostly, of course, he had chosen little girls because, he said, they were less trouble; everything was easier. In his early twenties he had been married to a young woman for about a month before he killed her, and in his late forties, after almost thirty years of drifting—during which he had spent stretches in prison for petty crimes and felonies, for vagrancy and public drunkenness, and during which he had also lived for a few intermittent years in Canada and Mexico— he had met and married one Marilee Wilson, a motel keeper, who for three years had somehow kept him happy, though he had continued to wander out in search of victims from time to time. In the words of Mr. Sweeney:

I should've probably killed her when we got separated, and I guess I would have if it wasn't for her changing the motel to my name and her boy being such a pal to me. We done a lot of going around, that kid and me, and I come close to telling him more than once that his stepdaddy weren't no ordinary stepdaddy. She's a lucky one, though. She don't know how lucky. I come close more'n a couple times.

Reading this, I thought of poor Mrs. Sweeney, who would certainly have read the same article, and must now be trembling to think what she had barely missed. And then I was thinking about them as a couple: there must have been moments of tenderness between them, moments when they were happy with each other. Mrs. Sweeney had talked about how she missed him.

I almost never can get really excited about sex with somebody unless they're dead.

I closed the newspaper and went upstairs to Mrs. Brooker's room. There were pictures of her on the bed, and I moved them to the nightstand and lay down. It was warm and bright in the room, the sun pouring through the chinks in the white curtain over the window, and through the curtain itself. I had most of the day ahead of me and I didn't have the energy to move. I thought of trying to write, but I felt empty, and anyway it would take energy to write. I could easily have imagined that I might never have another thing to say. At that moment, nothing seemed further from me than my own dearest and oldest interest. Indeed, the idea of writing stories seemed somehow so much beside the point that thinking about it even in this abstract way made me feel foolish.

I tried calling Elaine again, but there wasn't any answer.

Finally I went out, and drove myself over to the Sweeney Motel. I don't think I intended at first to go there. I remember I thought about riding around the campus, perhaps stopping in on one of my new colleagues. But the truth of the matter was that I hadn't liked any of them much. They had struck me as a closed group; their conversation in my presence had been full of in-jokes and references to things I couldn't know and therefore could not respond to. (During my years traveling and reading at the colleges I have come to see that this is a rudeness particular to academics, and that my first colleagues were no worse than most.)

So I wound up back at the Sweeney Motel, which was closed now, the windows all curtained and shut and the NO VACANCY sign replaced by a single large wooden plank with the word CLOSED painted on it in black. I pulled in and sat for a minute, looking the place over. Mrs. Sweeney came to her doorway as I got out of the car.

"What is it?" she said.

"Mrs. Sweeney," I said, "how are you?"

"I'm closed," she said. But then she recognized me.

"I just thought I'd—stop by."

She opened the door and stood back for me to enter. I was afraid I'd come at a bad time, and I apologized, or tried to, but she was already talking.

"My son got his leave canceled. And I know why—I wouldn't come here either if it was me."

The office was a mess. There were newspapers and magazines everywhere; on the television cabinet, glasses and dishes were stacked, and the tables were strewn with clothes. There wasn't anywhere to sit. Mrs. Sweeney cleared a place on the sofa, and then poured herself a tall glass of whiskey from one of several bottles of liquor on the coffee table.

"You want some?" she said.

I declined, and she sat down across from me, keeping her eyes on the TV screen, where a doctor and a nurse argued in an antiseptic-looking hallway. She drank her whiskey, licked her lips. It struck me that I had come there to stare at her, that no matter what I'd convinced myself with when I started out, my motives were no better than those of the merely curious. She was watching me, and I couldn't really return the look, couldn't meet her gaze. "So you're all closed up," I managed.

"Nothing else to do. My son's not coming home. I got people calling me all hours of the day and night. God almighty, you know *I* didn't kill anybody. It wasn't *me*, goddammit. I don't know anything. All I know is I was married to the guy three years and I never saw him hurt anyone or anything, and if he wasn't a real exciting man to have around the house he wasn't half bad, either. He left me alone mostly and he never expected much. It wasn't such a bad marriage and now I got to feel like I'm going to grow boils and horns if I miss him a little bit every now and then. People coming here wanting to know did he ever do anything that made me suspicious. I've had three husbands in my life and they all had things about them that you couldn't say was too normal. Who doesn't? Who's normal in private? He didn't seem a bit more strange than anybody else is when nobody's looking." She took a long pull of her drink. "Sure you don't want any?"

"No thank you," I said.

"I'm going to sell this place and move. Change my name back."

"I'm sorry your son isn't coming."

"He doesn't want to be *seen* in this town again."

I shook my head as if to say how unfortunate this was, but she thought I was disagreeing with her.

"I'm serious," she said. "He doesn't want to be seen. He won't ever come back here. He told me he wouldn't, and I can't say I blame him."

"No," I said, "I can understand that."

She stared at the television. There was a commercial on about sheer pantyhose, and then there was one about an airline. She took another drink of the whiskey and then leaned back in her chair. "I don't usually drink," she said. "I don't like the taste of it. I've just been taking it to calm down. You know, I just escaped death. More than once. He was going to kill me."

"I—I saw that," I said.

"Everybody saw it. You know he was with a lot of people here. He knew a lot of people and went to restaurants and fishing and all that, and even sat in church every week—we

165

were regulars, the two of us. And nobody else figured out what he was either, if you know what I mean. You'd think *somebody* would've noticed something."

"It's very strange," I said.

"And I'm not going to pretend I didn't like having him around because I did, and I don't care what they say."

I nodded agreement.

"You know," she said, 'You're the last tenant of the Sweeney Motel."

"Why don't you just call it the Wilson Motel again?"

She looked a little puzzled. "Oh, it was never the Wilson Motel. It was the All Nighter Motel."

This harmless piece of information had the effect of putting us both in a kind of musing calm. We might indeed have been mother and son, considering some fact or circumstance that had caught our attention. I reached over and poured a little of the whiskey into a cup on the coffee table.

"Let me get you a clean glass," she said.

I sat back and waited for her. On television a man in a bright T-shirt was biting into a hamburger, and the juices went flying. Mrs. Sweeney came back from her small kitchen and handed me a plastic tumbler, then poured far more whiskey than I wanted into it. We drank. I had an abrupt sense of how truly solitary my existence had become in the weeks since my arrival in Virginia.

"Well," Mrs. Sweeney said, "I sure didn't think you'd actually come back and visit me."

I smiled at her and held up my glass, as if to offer a toast.

"You know, I unplugged my phone. I don't even look at the mail, except to see if there's something from my boy."

Mrs. Sweeney had been leading her own solitary existence.

"I've got plenty of room," I said, "where I'm staying."

She swallowed her whiskey and looked at the television screen. "One time Sweeney killed a cat," she said.

I waited.

"We were on our way to Florida and the cat was in the road

and he just pulled right over it—swerved to get it." She took another swallow."Just—wham. Like that. No cat. A smear in the road behind us. And when I asked him why in the world he'd do a thing like that he said it was because he felt like it."

"So—" I said. "So that was—"

"That was scary," she said. "It scared the hell out of me."

"When was it?"

"Year after we were married."

I drank my own whiskey.

"You know why I divorced him?"

I shook my head.

"The laziness. I couldn't get him to do anything. All he wanted to do was watch television—Westerns. He loved Westerns. John Wayne and Randolph Scott. Horses and dust, and leather saddles and boots, and the cowboy hats. And—and clothes, you know, he loved clothes. He bought stuff he'd never wear even if he could've got around to it. Shoes and shirts and ties and belts, and pairs of socks. I couldn't get him to do anything around here that needed doing, so finally I just told him to pack his things and get out. Which he did." She was emphatic now. "Which he did. And he went as peaceful as a lamb. Now, you tell me."

I was beginning to feel the whiskey. I put my glass down and stood up. "Mrs. Sweeney, I have plenty of room where I'm staying—you're welcome to come stay there if you want to get away from here." I thought this was the least I could do.

"Isn't that nice of you," she said.

I said, "I mean it."

"Well," she said, rising. The whiskey had had its effect on her as well. She tottered, sat back down. "Stay and watch television for a while."

I didn't really have anywhere else to go, and yet I made my excuses and went out to my car, which was blazing hot in the afternoon sun, and drove back across the campus to William Brooker's apartment, where I intended to lie down and sleep off the effects of what I'd had to drink. As I climbed the stairs to the landing, already sweating profusely in the heat, I thought I caught a glimpse of someone peering at me from the other side of the building. When I looked, there wasn't anything, but I was pretty sure I hadn't imagined it. When I was at Brooker's door, I looked out at the parking lot, and saw the Volkswagen bug—the same one, with the same battered fender, the same rusty, gouged finish. Inside, in the cool of the air conditioning, I went straight to the bathroom and took a lukewarm shower, my mind made up to ignore all news and all thoughts of the Brookers or Elaine or poor Mrs. Sweeney, and when I was finished I got into Helen Brooker's bed and took a fitful, erotic-dreaming nap: someone, a woman, a spirit, was leading me into a velvet room.

I woke to the sound of the doorbell. It was dark. There was music coming from somewhere; the doorbell kept sounding, and I hurried down the stairs, trying to get my pants up without missing a step, or tripping over my own feet. "Just a minute," I said. I had no shirt; my eyes were sleep-filled and probably swollen. I opened the door, and of course even half asleep I knew it would be Maria Alvarez.

"Mrs. Brooker, please," she said, in that Spanish-soft voice.

"I should've told you—she's out of town," I answered, peering around the door at her. "They've been gone a few days now." And I was not too groggy to add, "They're separated."

She looked at me, then muttered something I couldn't catch.

"Excuse me?" I said.

"Separated?"

I nodded.

"*Sep*arated," she said, looking out at the dark. For perhaps a minute she simply stood there. "Separated." This time it was as if she were trying to hold back a laugh.

"That's right," I said.

"You know this," she said.

"Yes."

"Separated."

"Do you want to come in?" I asked, holding the door open a little more.

"In there?"

"Yes."

She seemed about to laugh again. "You're very kind, but no."

"I'm sorry," I said.

Her eyes took in the room behind me, and her expression seemed now only curious. "Mrs. Brooker—what is she like?"

"Why don't you come in?" I said.

"Mrs. Brooker is nice?"

"Yes."

"A nice woman. Poor Mrs. Brooker." And now she was laughing, though she tried to stifle it, holding her hand over her mouth. "Separated."

"Look," I said, "what is this about?"

She turned and went back down the stairs, still laughing, and when I followed her partway down she only went faster, until she was on the lawn, almost running.

"Miss?" I said. "Miss?" But she went on. The little, ragged-edged old car roared as she pulled out of the lot and on down the street.

That night, all night, I spent in Brooker's study, looking through his papers, his photographs, his files, for some sign of this young woman who had wanted to talk to his wife. I thought I knew why she wanted to talk to Helen Brooker, and I believed I understood exactly why Brooker had asked me to do what I had in fact done—to tell the lie that he had doubtless known would send the young woman away. Yet it was a fool thing to think I might find what I was looking for in the study of a man like Brooker, even knowing that he had a weakness for alcohol, and therefore might be expected to be careless; and if I did find the incriminating letter or note, I certainly had no plans for it—there wasn't anything at all that

I could possibly want with it. No, this rummaging through Brooker's papers was only another kind of undignified snooping, and the fact that I found nothing seemed finally to be a sort of judgment of me, as if my nosiness had earned me exactly what I deserved.

Even so, when I finally lay down in Helen Brooker's bed that early morning, I felt elated, and this is perhaps the most difficult thing to explain; I'm not even quite certain that I understand it now. I didn't know Brooker, really, at all: yet I had at his request relayed a bald lie to a young woman who had believed that lie, and then I had spent most of the night searching for evidence that, I suppose, would merely have proved what I felt I already knew—all of this just as undignified as my nocturnal voyeuristic journeys through Helen Brooker's private things . . . and even so, I felt this sense of elation. I remembered Helen Brooker saying to me about Jack Kennedy, "He was an awful womanizer, you know." And perhaps I was merely feeling the excitement of interest, to have been privy to something Brooker would want hidden.

VI

Dearest Helen,

J. says he likes your eyes best. He especially likes tall, leggy types, very smart, very sexy. All of which you are. I think he has designs on you and so you must be very careful this April. I've been working on a speech for the visit to B. Harbor. Lots of ward types there. I wish you'd call me once in a while; I mean one could get the feeling you're not letting the absence grow your heart fonder, or words to that effect.

Love, W.

Brooker called late the next morning. I had been up for an hour or so, hiding the signs of my recent strangeness—putting Helen Brooker's photographs where they belonged, her letters and cards back in their bundled order (though I had taken the time to copy down a few things to take with me, things I knew would be of interest to me later, most notably the one set out above, with its reference to a J. that simply must be Jack), and rearranging the casual disorder of Brooker's study. I had mostly finished all this—there were just a few envelopes to be put away—and was taking a short break to watch the morning report. (For the first time in many mornings, no mention was made of Sweeney.)

"Well," Brooker said, through the hiss of long distance. "Did she come back?"

"She came back," I said.

"Jesus Christ."

"I told her you were separated."

"Did she buy it?"

I thought of the first time I had seen him, of the confidence with which he had leaned toward me to murmur his obscenity. And then in an odd shift of mind I had an image of that boy behind the counter at the beach house and restaurant, the day I met Elaine.

"Well?" Brooker said.

"She believed what I told her," I said.

"She bought it."

"Yes."

"When did she come back?"

"Last night. I think she's watching this place."

"Jesus Christ."

"Mr. Brooker, what is she to you?"

"Listen, why didn't you call me last night?"

"It was too late. It was late. What is she to you, Mr. Brooker?"

"She's nothing. Don't pay any attention," he said.

"Well, then what does she want?"

After a moment, he said, "She was a student of mine. She had a problem."

I waited.

"She got the wrong idea of things—the way things were. And now she wants to make trouble for me."

"Did you by any chance have an affair with her?"

"She's just a kid," he said.

I could feel the adrenaline running at the back of my neck. "Yes," I said, "but did you?"

After another pause he said, "Look, I appreciate your help. You *do* have the use of my apartment. I don't think that entitles you to make assumptions about my affairs."

"I think I have to know what the situation *is* if I'm going to be of any more help," I said.

There was still another pause. "I told you," he said. "She got the wrong idea of things. There's something unstable about her that I should've seen—she's of *age*, if that's what you're getting at."

"Does your wife know about her?"

"Jesus Christ," he said, "what is this?"

"She says she wants to talk to your wife—she was asking questions about your wife."

"Look, I can't talk about this any more. You told her we were separated and you said she bought it—did she buy it or not?"

"I guess she bought it," I said.

"Well, then—fine. If she comes back again will you call me?"

"Do you want to talk to her?"

"Jesus Christ, no. Call me *after* she shows up again, if she does. And if she bought what you told her she probably won't."

"All right," I said.

He muttered, "Jesus Christ," then thanked me for my help, and we said goodbye. The line on his end closed; I listened until the dial tone started.

Outside, the parking lot was ablaze, the sun reflecting too brightly off the cars for me to see much. I went out and walked around the building, hoping that I might find her waiting on one of the landings, or behind one of the parched-looking sycamores in the grassy square across from the main entrance. There wasn't a soul, it seemed, anywhere. All the windows of the building were closed against the heat, and the little park for children was empty; a hot breeze disturbed some sheets on a line that had been strung across one of the landings. Cars going by on the road looked as if they were trailing fire.

In the morning, there was another article about Sweeney. He had talked to police from surrounding states, and apparently all of his stories were checking out; authorities were finding remains where he said he'd left them. In describing these burial sites, the article said, he often fell into a kind of reverie, and his crimes became nouns. *That one, yeah, that would be a knife. And, let's see, oh, this one's a strangle.*

I read all this with the same sick fascination, and then called Elaine. She was in bed; she had been down with a cold. "I miss you," she said.

I had the TV on, the midday news, and was lying back in Brooker's easy chair. "Elaine," I said, "I'm going out of my mind."

"Maybe our separation isn't going to work out," she said.

"Are you finished with everything?" I asked. And then I didn't hear what she said, because the local news was showing film of Maria Alvarez standing out on the roof of the college library building. I sat there with Elaine's familiar sleepy voice in my ear and understood what I was seeing. It was Maria Alvarez. Before I could get out of the chair, the picture shifted, everything changed: a crowd of police and firemen were gathered around a broken shape under a blanket in the street.

I pulled the telephone from its table, reaching to turn the TV up, and when I did get the sound up there was only the announcer, a man looking far too calm for what his camera crew had just shown, talking about the morning's tragedy with a series of eyewitnesses, who all reported the same thing. The poor girl jumped. They had seen it all; they were afraid, and their voices shook, and the announcer remained calm, holding the microphone to their mouths.

I don't remember what I said to Elaine. It's entirely possible that I blurted out everything I knew of Brooker and his trouble, speaking, no doubt, with that peculiar clarity that horror sometimes provides an otherwise cloudy mind. But it wasn't long before I was dialing the number Brooker had given me, and having trouble accomplishing it because my hands were shaking so. I don't think I quite expected to get through to him at this hour, and I left a little pause of surprise when he answered.

"Yes?" he said.

"What did you do to her, Brooker?"

"Who is this?"

"Did you tell her you were in love with her?"

He said nothing for a moment. Then, "I can't talk now."

"For God's sake," I said, "I *lied* to her for you. My God, I don't believe this—I told her your lie, and sent her on her way. I helped you do it."

"Now, hold on," he said. "She had a lot of trouble—there were things that had nothing to do with me or any lie. For God's sake, what's happened?"

"Jesus Christ," I said.

"Let's calm down," William Brooker said. "Just tell me what she did."

That night I slept on the sofa in the guest room. In his horror, Brooker had been fatherly and philosophical: there was nothing to be done, nothing *he* could do, at any rate; he was very sorry for the troubled Miss Alvarez, he had tried his best to help her, but in the end he was powerless. He hadn't known her very well, in fact, and perhaps no one ever really gets to know a suicide. Miss Alvarez had wandered into a seminar he had taught as a visiting lecturer the previous fall in Atlanta, and he had seen right away that she was barely holding on. He described his concern for her, his work with her while she was his student; it was all very much a professional relationship, candid and above board, he said; and of course it was quite clear that he was lying. I told him I couldn't talk any more, and hung the phone up. I didn't care what he thought about this, and I don't mean that I was as full of moral outrage as I must have sounded. For the facts of the matter are that something had occurred to me concerning my own part in it all, and I simply wanted no more to do with anyone or anything for a time. What occurred to me was the unpleasant truth that I had held something back in the first minute Maria Alvarez had stood staring at me in the dim light of the landing. She had asked to see Mrs. Brooker and I had said only that Mrs. Brooker wasn't there; I had kept back what I knew about where Helen Brooker was and how long she would be gone, and I had done so, without having to think about it, because of course I understood in an instant what Maria Alvarez had come for, and what she would want with William Brooker's wife. I had, then, already begun the lie that Brooker would later ask me to complete—and this not out of friendship for the man, or loyalty to his interests, but out of something else.

In the days that followed, Brooker called two or three times, wanting to get what details he could. I told him I would not be staying in his apartment any more, and so there were practical things to consider as well. He didn't say much about his own parts in the affair, and yet I was able to piece together a version of it from what he *did* say: Maria Alvarez comes to him looking for what she imagines he can give her; she's pathologically unhappy, but he doesn't see this. He sees her shapely figure and Spanish-dark features, her deep black eyes. He charms her, seduces her, then finds that she is quite mad, quite unable to understand the casual way he means this sort of thing, and he decides it is necessary to evade her. The rest is, of course, an unfortunate chain of events over which he has no control. If only the world weren't the way it is. I had no trouble at all imagining the whole scenario.

What I never imagined had to do with Helen Brooker. She

showed up on a Friday afternoon from New York, having set out at the request of her husband, to make certain that things were in order for my departure. (We had no signed agreement, and Brooker was a thorough man.) She came breezing into the living room, where I lay on the white sofa in a bath of letters and photographs—the whole history of William and Helen Brooker. She went into the kitchen and poured us both a bourbon, then came and stood over me, holding my drink out, her eyes not quite settling on what I had in my hands and on my lap. I took the drink, and she sipped hers, still standing over me. "I suppose writers have to be spies," she said. "It must be a perfectly seedy little part of the job."

I put my drink on the end table and began to gather up the photographs.

"Did you find anything of interest?" she said.

I said, "No."

"How unfortunate."

"One of the perfectly seedy little risks of the job," I said.

She took another drink. "Do you suppose I ought to look for a way to get you?"

"I guess you'll do what you want to do."

"You're not even sorry, are you?"

"Yes," I said, "in fact I am. I'm quite sorry."

"To think I believed you were charming. It turns out you're just a writer."

I had got everything in a stack, and had put it carefully, as if it were fragile, aside. "I wish I could tell you how sorry I *really* am," I said. When I remember this now, it seems clear that I didn't have much respect for her any more, and it all had to do with what I thought she did not know about her husband.

"Are you referring," she said, "to Miss Alvarez?"

I looked at her. There was nothing at all in her eyes.

"Of course you are."

"You know," I said.

"William has always been like a child in a candy store when

it comes to women." She finished her drink, and then, precisely as though I were no longer there, put away the papers and letters and photographs. I went upstairs and packed my things, and she followed me, stood in the doorway of the room, her room, watching me. She had fixed herself another drink.

"This is where you slept?"

"Yes."

"That's fascinating."

"I had to sleep somewhere," I said.

"You don't think much of us, do you? Or of me."

I didn't say anything to this.

"I suppose I should go jump off a building, the way that poor girl did."

"Mrs. Brooker," I said, "you wondered if I was sorry about—about prying the way I did. What about you? What about your husband? There's a young woman dead, Mrs. Brooker. What about that?"

"Your indignation is touching," she said.

We didn't say much else to each other before I left. She stood by with the air of someone who has dealt the telling blow, sipping her drink now and again, tapping the toe of one shoe on the hardwood floor. As I went down the stairs she said, "They all deserve whatever they get." It was as if she were hurling it at me as I scurried away; as if she wanted to chase me with it. There was no anger or pain in her voice—only scorn. And my answer was exactly the kind of stupid, reflexive thing one regrets later, thinking of the smart things one could have said if only one had been able to summon the presence of mind, or the courage, or the calm. I said, "I'm sorry I ever saw you." And of course the fact is that if I'd had had an hour to think of something I would no doubt have found nothing better: I was to begin a teaching job in less than two weeks, and I couldn't imagine anything I might have to say to anyone.

I drove around the city for a while that evening. I don't know what I thought I might see in those quiet streets, the fine old houses and shaded lawns. I suppose I needed simply to get a feeling for the town as something continuous, something—well, ongoing and unabstract, too: children playing in the splashed blue shade of a sycamore; a dog barking from behind a white picket fence.

When it grew too dark to see, I stopped at a package store and bought myself a bottle of whiskey. I intended to get drunk, of course, but I didn't. I went to the rental house and worked all night painting the bedroom and the guest room. Oh, I had some of the whiskey, all right. I had enough to make me sleep in spite of a feeling so desperate and hopeless that, in the morning when I woke and remembered it, I thought of drinking more of the whiskey to keep it at bay. But it was immediately upon me again, and I made myself go about the business of cleaning up the rooms, even as my conviction grew that I would not be living in that house. I had no sense of it—even with all my work on it—as a place where I might be with Elaine, one of a pair of tenants, at home.

A little later, when I headed over to the Western Union office to wire Elaine for the money to fly back to the Midwest, I had my mind half made up to tell her I was coming back for good, that I would not be taking the job after all. In fact, it was Elaine who, that week, insisted that we go through everything as planned, that we travel east to take up residence in the rental house.

VII

That fall, I saw Brooker now and again, from a distance, as I'm sure most people on the campus ever saw him. He left the college, that spring, and the faculty bulletin said he was starting his retirement, along with his lovely wife, Helen, in Key West. The Sweeney Motel was torn down before the year was out, and I never saw Mrs. Sweeney again. The last thing I heard about her infamous husband was that he was an object of study: the doctors were hoping to find some clue to him.

Elaine and I remained in the rental house for almost two years, and then bought a place, a little bigger, and a lot older, on the other side of the campus. I would never have believed that I might stay at a small college like that, but we did stay more than seven years. All four of our children, two boys and two girls, were born there. Sometimes at night I wake up from a dream that I'm holed up in a place like Brooker's apartment, and then our room feels like a little cave in the dark. If I can't go back to sleep I get myself up and go look at the children. I tuck their blankets over their shoulders, remove their books or toys from their beds; I perform the tasks of a father in the night. Elaine sleeps so soundly that my kiss never wakes her. Our life together is full and perhaps often enough a little too busy; there are times when I think we just miss each other. But that is probably true of any couple.

Whenever I think of that end of summer so long ago, when I took flight from an oppression that might have unhinged me, I remember the slow, lonely hours in the air—the sense that the world below me was little more than a savage place where the weak were fed upon by the strong—and the nervous feeling when I arrived, the fear that my marriage really was over for all my indulgence in those fantasies of betrayal, and our mutual neglect. And the way it felt to see Elaine standing in the white light of the airport terminal, waiting for me.

How good it was to see her.

As I walked up the ramp toward her, lugging my packed suitcase and my unhappy experience like the same great weight, I understood at least that I loved her, and I remember my sense of wonder about this. I remember also that I thought of Sweeney, and of Brooker; that Sweeney and Brooker occurred to me then as though they were, together, the opposing principle—a naked manifestation of the forces that would always be lurking in the darker corners of the spirit. I put this from my mind, and stepped forward to greet her. "Darling," I said. I couldn't believe how familiar and wonderful she looked.

She smiled as if to say we would be all right now.

There was a thing in us both that moved us in each other's direction, that made us recognizable to each other. Whatever our complications, this obdurate fact remained.

"You look beat," she said, and she reached across the little space that divided us.

Wedlock

Honeymoon night, Howard locked the motel room door, flopped down on the bed, and, clasping his hands behind his head, regarded her for a moment. He was drunk. They were both drunk. They had come from the Starlight Room, where they had danced and had too much champagne. They had charmed the desk clerk, earlier, with their teasing and their radiant, happy faces. The desk clerk was a woman in her mid-fifties, who claimed a happy, romantic marriage herself.

"Thirty-five years and two months," she'd said, beaming.

"Not even thirty-five hours," Howard had said. His face when he was excited looked just like a little boy's. "But it's not Lisa's first one."

"No," Lisa said, embarrassed. "I was married before."

"Well, it's this one that counts," the desk clerk had said.

Lisa, twenty-five years old, three years older than her new husband, had felt vaguely sorry to have the woman know this rather personal detail about her past. She was nervous about it; it felt like something that wasn't cleared up, quite, though she hadn't seen Dorsey in at least two years—hadn't seen him in person, that is. He had called that once, and she'd told Howard about it. She'd complained to Howard about it, and even so had felt weirdly as if she were telling lies to him. Many times over the weeks of her going with Howard she'd wished the first marriage had never happened, for all her talk with her friends at work about what an experience it was, being married to a rock-'n'-roll singer and traveling around the country in that miserable van, with no air-conditioning and no windows.

Somehow she'd kept her sense of humor about the whole bad three years.

And tonight she'd made Howard laugh, talking about being on the road, traipsing from one motel to another and riding all those miles in a van with people she wouldn't cross the sidewalk to see; it was astonishing how quickly dislikes and tensions came out in those circumstances. You just went from place to place and smiled and performed and shook hands and hung around and you hated everybody you were with most of the time, and they hated you right back. It was worse, and somehow more intimate, than hatred between family members because for one thing you didn't hold back the stuff that scraped the raw places; you didn't feel compelled to keep from hitting someone in the sweet spot, as she liked to call it. You just went ahead and hit somebody's weakest point, and you kept hitting it until you drew blood. She'd kept on about it because he was staring at her with his boy's eyes, all dreamy and half-drunk, and finally they were both laughing, both potted, feeling goofy and special and romantic, like the couple in the happy end of a movie, walking arm in arm down the long corridor of the motel to their room. They had come stumbling in, still holding onto each other, and finally Howard had lurched toward the bed and dropped there.

Where he now crossed his ankles and smiled at her, murmuring, "So."

She said, "So."

"Nobody knows where we are."

"Right," she said.

"We're—" He made a broad gesture. "Hidden away."

"Hidden away."

"Just the two of us."

"Just us, right."

"Strip," he said.

She looked at him, looked into his innocent, chilly blue eyes.

"Want to play a game?"

"A game," she said.

"Let's play charades."

"Okay."

"You start," he said.

"No, you start."

"I'm really sick of starting all the time," he said. "I start the car and I start—" He seemed confused. "The car."

They laughed.

He got up and went to the bathroom door. "I know—wait a minute. I'll come out and you tell me who I am."

She waited. He staggered through the door. He was a very funny, very good-natured young man. It was what she loved about him.

"Here I come," he sang.

She sang back, "I'm ready when you are."

When he danced out of the bathroom, he lost his balance and stumbled onto the bed. As he bounced there, she laughed, holding her sides and leaning against the door.

"One more time," he said, then paused and put one finger over his lips. "Shhhhh. It's necessary to be very quiet."

She said, "Right. Shhhh."

"I don't guess you could tell who it was from the first time."

She shook her head. She was laughing too hard to speak.

"Sure?"

"Stumbly?" she said.

"Stumbly."

"Isn't that one of the Seven Dwarfs?"

"Stumbly," he said, looking around. He seemed out of breath, but of course it was the champagne. "Hey, how do I know? I never even met Sleeping Beauty."

"Snow White," she said.

He said, "Right," and threw himself onto the bed, bouncing again, lying flat on his back with his legs and arms outspread. She let herself slide down against the door, and her dizziness felt good, as though she were floating in deep space, held up by clouds.

He'd come off the bed. "Okay, let's try again."

"Snow White," she said.

183

He laughed. "Now watch. You'll know who it is."

Again he went into the bathroom.

"I'm ready," she said.

He peeked out at her, held one finger to his lips again. "Shhhh."

"Shhhh," she said.

Once more he was gone. She made herself comfortable against the door, letting her legs out and folding her arms. It seemed to her now that in all the three years with Dorsey she had never had such a lighthearted time. Everything with Dorsey had been freighted with his drive to make it big, his determination to live out some daydream he'd had when he was thirteen. Married to him, traveling with him, watching him pretend to be single and listening to him complain at night about bad bookings, stupid sidemen, the road, and the teen hops where kids asked over and over for the cheap radio stuff—living with all this, she had never felt the kind of uncomplicated pleasure-in-the-moment that she had experienced from the beginning with Howard, who was quite unlike Dorsey in all the important ways. Oddly enough, for all Dorsey's rock-band outrageousness and all his talk of personal freedom, she felt much less constrained around Howard, who was a plumber's apprentice and had no musical or artistic talent whatsoever. From the beginning, she'd felt comfortable with him, as though he were a younger brother she'd grown up with. The fact that he *was* younger wasn't as important, finally, as the fact that he made her feel like laughing all the time, and was wonderfully devoid of the kinds of anxiety that always plagued Dorsey. Worries about health, about the world situation, the environment, the future. The trouble, finally, was that Dorsey had never learned how to have fun, how to let go and just see what happened.

Dorsey would never have allowed this, for instance, getting tight and being a sort of spectacle to the other guests at the hotel. She remembered that Howard had stopped someone in the hall—a squat-looking balding man in a blue bathing suit with a towel wrapped around his neck and shower clogs under one arm—and, with a voice soaked in portent, announced that all the moons were unfavorable. Somehow he'd managed it with such good-natured goofiness that the man had simply smiled and walked on.

"Hey," she said now. "What're you doing in there?"

"I'm transforming," he said. "You won't believe it."

"I'm getting sleepy."

"Guess who this is," he said.

"I'm waiting."

When he came out this time, he had removed his shirt, and his shoes and socks. He came slowly, bending down to peer in all directions, looking very suspicious and wary. "Well?" he said, barely able to keep his feet.

"I don't know. Not Stumbly?"

"No," he said. "Look close." And he paraded past her again.

"God, I can't get it."

"Groucho. Ever see him walk? Groucho Marx. Look."

"Oh."

"Okay," he said, smiling, straightening with exaggerated dignity. "I'd like to see you try it."

"I want to see you do Stumbly again."

"Hey," he said. "You think your mother likes me as much as she liked old Dorsey?"

"Better," she said.

"Can't understand how a lady could like somebody like that."

"She liked his hands." Lisa said. "Isn't that silly? I think that's silly. She liked his beautiful hands."

"Do I have beautiful hands?" he wanted to know.

"Beautiful," she said.

"Okay. Try this one." He lurched into the bathroom again.

"Howard?" she said. "My mother likes you a lot."

"She thinks you're robbing the cradle."

185

"Oh, don't be ridiculous."

"True."

"That's just dumb. If anything, she's jealous."

"Of my hands."

"I think she likes your tush, in fact."

"Well, that's nice to know, anyway."

She said, "Hey, what's taking so long?"

He said, "Just wait."

"I'm getting dizzy and sleepy."

"Wait."

When he appeared again, he had crossed his eyes and was clutching an imaginary something to his chest. She laughed. "Harpo."

"No."

"Stumbly."

"There's no such thing as Stumbly."

"Okay," she said, laughing, delighting in him. "Who then?"

"How could you say Harpo?"

"I'm sorry."

"Harpo," he said. "Jeez."

"All right, who is it, then?"

"It's my uncle Mark."

"I never met your uncle Mark."

"Never met Stumbly, either."

She laughed again. "You win."

"No," he said. "Who's this?" And he went back into the bathroom.

She waited, a little impatiently now. She was beginning to feel uncomfortable, and she didn't want to get too sleepy. In fact, there was a heavy, buzzing sensation in her ears when she closed her eyes.

"Boo," he said. He had mussed his hair and made it stand on end, and he was wearing his shirt like a cape around his neck. He went through the pantomime motions of lighting a cigarette, and then she saw that he meant her to understand it was dope, not tobacco. He fake-puffed, rolled his eyes, breathed with a thick, throaty rasping, and held his index finger and thumb in the pose of passing a joint. "Well?" he said.

"I'm thinking."

"This is no ordinary cigarette."

"I can't think of his name. The Supreme Court guy."

"Wrong," he said, smoothing his hair down. He went back into the bathroom, but then leaned out, holding on to the frame, and smiled at her. "You know what you get when you cross a doctor with a ground hog?"

"A court date," she said, laughing.

"Somebody told you," he said.

"Is that *it*?"

"Six more weeks of golf," he said.

"I don't get it. Tell me another one."

"You know what you get if you mix rock 'n' roll and Dorsey?" His eyebrows went up. He seemed to be taking great delight in the question. "You get stumbly."

"Howard," she said.

He disappeared into the bathroom again.

"Hey," she called, getting to her feet. This time he leaned out the door, bending low, so that he was looking at her from a horizontal angle. He tipped an imaginary hat and said, "You slept with Dorsey before you got married, huh. That's the stumbly truth, sort of."

"Stop talking about Dorsey," she said. "Stop that."

He grinned at her. "Wouldn't be surprised if you went out and met him while we were engaged. I mean, you know. Talking to him on the phone and stuff. You and old Dorsey maybe decided to play a little for old times' sake. A little stumbly on the side?"

"What?" she said to him. "What?"

He lifted his chin slightly, as if to challenge her.

"Look," she said, "this isn't funny. I know you don't mean it but it's not in the least bit amusing."

He had disappeared past the frame.

"Howard," she said.

Now he let himself fall out of the frame, catching himself at the last possible second with one hand. Again, he tipped an imaginary hat. "Dorsey has beautiful hands, and you made some rock 'n' roll behind my back."

"Howard, stop this."

He was laughing; he had pulled himself up and was out of sight again. She moved toward the bed, so that she could see into where he was. But now he came out, walking unsteadily, carrying his folded shirt and pants.

"Howard," she said.

He turned to her, his face an impassive, confident mask. "Wait," he said.

"Howard, say you're sorry."

"You're sorry." he said.

"I mean it," she told him.

He went to the bed and dropped down on it again, clasped his hands behind his head, and seemed to wait for her to speak. But he spoke first. "Strip."

"What?"

"Go ahead. Strip for me."

She said nothing.

"Come on. Dance—turn me on a little."

"Look," she said.

"Hey—look," he said. "I mean it. I really want you to." His face was bright and innocent looking and friendly, as if he were a child asking for candy. She had a moment of doubting that she could have heard everything quite exactly.

"Honey," she said. "You're teasing me."

He crossed his legs. "I'm not teasing—come on, this is our honeymoon, right? I've been waiting for this."

"You—" she began.

"Look, what's the situation here," he said.

"You're not like this, Howard, now stop it."

"Well," he said. "Maybe I am teasing."

"Don't tease like that any more," she told him. "I don't like it."

188

"Aren't you drunk?" he said. He was lying there staring at her. "Didn't you strip for Dorsey?"

She turned, started fumbling with the door.

"Hey," he said.

She couldn't get the door to work; at some point she'd put the chain on. He got off the bed and came up behind her. She was crying. He wrapped his arms around her, was holding her, kissing the back of her neck. "Let go of me," she said.

"Don't be mad."

"Let go of me, Howard."

He stepped back. She pulled the hair away from her face, feeling sour now—sodden and dizzy and alone. She was leaning against the door, crying, and he simply stood there with that open-faced boy's expression, staring at her. "Hey," he said. "I was just teasing you."

"Teasing," she said. "Teasing. Right. Jesus Christ."

"I was teasing. Didn't you know I was teasing?"

She looked at him.

"Hey," he said. "Come on." He took hold of her elbow, was leading her back into the room, and she had an eerie, frightful moment of sensing that he considered himself to be in a kind of mastery over her. She resisted, pulled away from him. "Don't touch me."

"Hey," he said not unkindly. "I said I was sorry."

"You said those horrible things—"

He sat down on the bed and locked his hands between his knees. "Let's start over, okay? This is supposed to be a honeymoon night."

She stood there.

"We were having so much fun. Weren't we? Weren't we having fun?"

It was impossible to return his gaze. Impossible to look into those blue boy's eyes.

"I got drunk, okay? I went too far."

"I don't feel good," she said. "I have to go to the bathroom."

"Want me to go for you?"

"No." She was crying, holding it in, moving toward the

bathroom door. The light in that little tiled space looked like refuge. He stood and moved in front of her, reaching to hold the door open. "Oh, hey," he said. "I've got one."

She halted, sniffled, felt the closeness of the room.

"Do you have to go really bad?"

"I just want to be alone for a while," she said.

"You don't have to go?"

"Howard, for God's sake."

"Well, no—but look. I've got one more. You've got to see it. It's funny. Stay here."

"I don't want to play any more," she told him.

"Yeah, but wait'll you see this one."

"Oh, stop it," she said, crying. "Please."

"You'll see," he told her, turning his bright, happy expression away, moving into the bathroom ahead of her and hunching down, working himself up somehow.

"Oh, please," she said, crying, watching him with his back turned there in the bright light of the bathroom.

"Wait, now," he said. "Let me think a minute. I'll have one in a minute." He wavered slightly and brought his hands up to his face. "It'll be funny," he said. "Don't look. I'm thinking."

"Just let's go to sleep," she told him.

"Let me concentrate," he said. "Jesus. I promise you'll like it and laugh."

She waited, feeling a deeper and deeper sense of revulsion. It was the champagne, of course; she'd had so much of it and they were both drunk, and people said and did things when they'd had too much. She was trying to keep this clear in her mind, feeling the sickness start in her and watching him in his bent, agitated posture. He turned slightly and regarded her. "Don't stare," he said. "I can't concentrate if you stare."

"What are you doing?" she asked him. But she had barely spoken; the words had issued forth from her like a breath.

"I had it a minute ago," he said, hunching his shoulders, shifting slightly, running his hands through his hair. Watching this, she had an unpleasant little thought, which arrived almost idly in the boozy haze and irritation of the moment, but which quickly blossomed into a fright more profound than she could have dreamed—and which some part of her struggled with a deep shudder to blot out—that he looked like one of those scarily adept comedians on television, the ones who faced away from the camera and gyrated a moment, then whirled around and were changed, had become the semblance of someone else, spoke in an accent or with a different voice, or had donned a mask or assumed a contorted facial expression, looking like anyone at all but themselves.

Design

The Reverend Tarmigian was not well. You could see it in his face—a certain hollowness, a certain blueness in the skin. His eyes lacked luster and brightness. He had a persistent dry, deep cough; he'd lost a lot of weight. And yet on this fine, breezy October day he was out on the big lawn in front of his church, raking leaves. Father Russell watched him from the window of his study, and knew that if he didn't walk over there and say something to him about it, this morning—like so many recent mornings—would be spent fretting and worrying about Tarmigian, seventy-two years old and out raking leaves in the windy sun. He had been planning to speak to the old man for weeks, but what could you say to a man like that? An institution in Point Royal, old Tarmigian had been pastor of the neighboring church—Faith Baptist, only a hundred or so yards away on the other side of Tallawaw Creek—for more than three decades. He referred to himself in conversation as the Reverend Fixture. He was a stooped, frail man with wrinkled blue eyes and fleecy blond hair that showed freckled scalp in the light; there were dimples in his cheeks. One of his favorite jokes—one of the many jokes he was fond of repeating—was that he had the eyes of a clown built above the natural curve of a baby's bottom. He'd touch the dimples and smile, saying a thing like that. And the truth was he tended to joke too much—even about the fact that he was apparently taxing himself beyond the dictates of good health for a man his age.

It seemed clear to Father Russell—who was all too often worried about his own health, though he was thirty years younger than Tarmigian—that something was driving the older man to these stunts of killing work: raking leaves all morning in the fall breezes; climbing on a ladder to clear drainspouts; or, as he had done one day last week, lugging a bag of mulch across the road and up the hill to the little cemetery where his wife lay buried, as if there weren't plenty of people within arm's reach on any Sunday who would have done it gladly for him (and would have just as gladly stood by while he said his few quiet prayers over the grave). His wife had been dead twenty years, he had the reverential respect of the whole countryside, but something was driving the man and, withal, there was often a species of amused cheerfulness about him almost like elation, as though he were keeping some wonderful secret.

It was perplexing; it violated all the rules of respect for one's own best interest. And today, watching him rake leaves, Father Russell determined that he would speak to him about it. He would simply confront him—broach the subject of health and express an opinion. Father Russell understood enough about himself to know that this concern would seem uncharacteristically personal on his part—it might even be misconstrued in some way—but as he put a jacket on and started out of his own church, it was with a small thrill of resolution. It was time to interfere, regardless of the age difference and regardless of the fact that it had been Father Russell's wish to find ways of avoiding the company of the older man.

Tarmigian's church was at the top of a long incline, across a stone bridge over Tallawaw Creek. It was a rigorous walk, even on a cool day, as this one was. The air was blue and fragrant in the mottled shade, and there were little patches of steam on the creek when the breezes were still. The Reverend Tarmigian stopped working, leaned on the handle of the rake and watched Father Russell cross the bridge.

"Well, just in time for coffee."

"I'll have tea," Father Russell said, a little out of breath from the walk.

"You're winded," said Tarmigian.

"And you're white as a sheet."

It was true. Poor Tarmigian's cheeks were pale as death. There were two blotches on them, like bruises—caused, Father Russell was sure, by the blood vessels that were straining to break in the old man's head. He indicated the trees all around, burnished looking and still loaded with leaves, and even now dropping some of them, like part of an argument for the hopelessness of this task the old man had set for himself.

"Why don't you at least wait until they're finished?" Father Russell demanded.

"I admit, it's like emptying the ocean with a spoon." Tarmigian put his rake down and motioned for the other man to follow him. They went through the back door into the older man's tidy little kitchen, where Father Russell watched him fuss and worry, preparing the tea. When it was ready, the two men went into the study to sit among the books and talk. It was the old man's custom to take an hour every day in this book-lined room, though with this bad cold he'd contracted, he hadn't been up to much of anything recently. It was hard to maintain his old fond habits, he said. He felt too tired, or too sick. It was just an end-of-summer cold, of course, and Tarmigian dismissed it with a wave of his hand. Yet Father Russell had observed the weight loss, the coughing; and the old man was willing to admit that lately his appetite had suffered.

"I can't keep anything down," he said. "Sort of keeps me discouraged from trying, you know? So I shed the pounds. I'm sure when I get over this flu—"

"Medical science is advancing," said the priest, trying for sarcasm. "They have doctors now with their own offices and instruments. It's all advanced to a sophisticated stage. You can even get medicine for the flu."

"I'm fine. There's no need for anyone to worry."

Father Russell had seen denial before: indeed, he saw some version of it almost every day, and he had a rich understanding of the psychology of it. Yet Tarmigian's statement caused a surprising little clot of anger to form in the back of his mind and left him feeling vaguely disoriented, as if the older man's blithe neglect of himself were a kind of personal affront.

Yet he found, too, that he couldn't come right out and say what he had come to believe: that the old man was jeopardizing his own health. The words wouldn't form on his lips. So he drank his tea and searched for an opening—a way of getting something across about learning to relax a bit, learning to take it easy. There wasn't a lot to talk about beyond Tarmigian's anecdotes and chatter. The two men were not particularly close: Father Russell had come to his own parish from Boston only a year ago, believing this small Virginia township to be the accidental equivalent of a demotion (the assignment, coming really like the drawing of a ticket out of a hat, was less than satisfactory). He had felt almost immediately that the overfriendly, elderly clergyman next door was a bit too southern for his taste—though Tarmigian was obviously a man of broad experience, having served in missions overseas as a young man, and it was true that he possessed a kind of simple, happy grace. So while the priest had spent a lot of time in the first days trying to avoid him for fear of hurting his feelings, he had learned finally that Tarmigian was unavoidable, and had come to accept him as one of the mild irritations of the place in which he now found himself. He had even considered that the man had a kind of charm, was amusing and generous. He would admit that there had been times when he found himself surprised by a faint stir of gladness when the old man could be seen on the little crossing bridge, heading down to pay another of his casual visits as if there were nothing better to do than to sit in Father Russell's parlor and make jokes about himself.

The trouble now, of course, was that everything about the old man, including his jokes, seemed tinged with the something terrible that the priest feared was happening to him. And here Father Russell was, watching him cough, watching him hold up one hand as if to ward off anything in the way of advice or concern about it. The cough took him deep, so that he had to gasp to get his breath back; but then he cleared his throat, sipped more of the tea and, looking almost frightfully white around the eyes, smiled and said, "I have a good one for you, Reverend Russell. I had a couple in my congregation—I won't name them, of course—who came to me yesterday afternoon, claiming they were going to seek a divorce. You know how long they've been married? They've been married fifty-two years. Fifty-two years and they say they can't stand each other. I mean can't stand to be in the same room with each other."

Father Russell was interested in spite of himself—and in spite of the fact that the old man had again called him "Reverend." This would be another of Tarmigian's stories, or another of his jokes. The priest felt the need to head him off. "That cough," he said.

Tarmigian looked at him as if he'd merely said a number or recited a day's date.

"I think you should see a doctor about it."

"It's just a cold, Reverend."

"I don't mean to meddle," said the priest.

"Yes, well. I was asking what you thought about a married couple can't stand to be in the same room together after fifty-two years."

Father Russell said, "I guess I'd have to say I have trouble believing that."

"Well, believe it. And you know what I said to them? I said we'd talk about it for a while. Counseling, you know."

Father Russell said nothing.

"Of course," said Tarmigian, "as you know, we permit divorce. Something about an English king wanting one badly enough to start his own Church. Oh, that was long ago, of course. But we do allow it when it seems called for."

"Yes," Father Russell said, feeling beaten.

"You know, I don't think it's a question of either one of

196

them being interested in anybody else. There doesn't seem to be any romance or anything—nobody's swept anybody off anybody's feet."

The priest waited for him to go on.

"I can't help feeling it's a bit silly." Tarmigian smiled, sipped the tea, then put the cup down and leaned back, clasping his hands behind his head. "Fifty-two years of marriage, and they want to untie the knot. What do you say, shall I send them over to you?"

The priest couldn't keep the sullen tone out of his voice. "I wouldn't know what to say to them."

"Well—you'd tell them to love one another. You'd tell them that love is the very breath of living or some such thing. Just as I did."

Father Russell muttered, "That's what I'd have to tell them, of course."

Tarmigian smiled again. "We concur."

"What was their answer?"

"They were going to think about it. Give themselves some time to think, really. That's no joke, either." Tarmigian laughed, coughing. Then it was just coughing.

"That's a terrible cough," said the priest, feeling futile and afraid and deeply irritable. His own words sounded to him like something learned by rote.

"You know what I think I'll tell them if they come back?"

He waited.

"I think I'll tell them to stick it out anyway, with each other." Tarmigian looked at him and smiled. "Have you ever heard anything more absurd?"

Father Russell made a gesture, a wave of the hand, that he hoped the other took for agreement.

Tarmigian went on: "It's probably exactly right—probably exactly what they should do, and yet such odd advice to think of giving two people who've been together fifty-two years. I mean, when do you think the phrase 'sticking it out' would stop being applicable?"

197

Father Russell shrugged and Tarmigian smiled, seemed to be awaiting some reaction.

"Very amusing," said Father Russell.

But the older man was coughing again.

From the beginning there had been things Tarmigian said and did which unnerved the priest. Father Russell was a man who could be undone by certain kinds of boisterousness, and there were matters of casual discourse he simply would never understand. Yet often enough over the several months of their association, he had entertained the suspicion that Tarmigian was harboring a bitterness, and that his occasional mockery of himself was some sort of reaction to it, if it wasn't in fact a way of releasing it.

Now Father Russell sipped his tea and looked away out the window. Leaves were flying in the wind. The road was in blue shade, and the shade moved. There were houses beyond the hill, but from here everything looked like a wilderness.

"Well," Tarmigian said, gaining control of himself. "Do you know what my poor old couple say is their major complaint? Their major complaint is they don't like the same TV programs. Now, can you imagine a thing like that?"

"Look," the priest blurted out. "I see you from my study window—you're—you don't get enough rest. I think you should see a doctor about that cough."

Tarmigian waved this away. "I'm fit as a fiddle, as they say. Really."

"If it's just a cold, you know," said Father Russell, giving up. "Of course—" He could think of nothing else to say.

"You worry too much," Tarmigian said. "You know, you've got bags under your eyes."

True.

In the long nights Father Russell lay with a rosary tangled in his fingers and tried to pray, tried to stop his mind from playing tricks on him: the matter of greatest faith was and had been for a very long time now that every twist or turn of his body held a symptom, every change signified the onset of disease. It was all waiting to happen to him, and the anticipation of it sapped him, made him weak and sick at heart. He had begun to see that his own old propensity for morbid anxiety about his health was worsening, and the daylight hours required all his courage. Frequently he thought of Tarmigian as though the old man were in some strange way a reflection of his secretly held, worst fear. He recalled the lovely sunny mornings of his first summer as a curate, when he was twenty-seven and fresh and the future was made of slow time. This was not a healthy kind of thinking. It was middle age, he knew. It was a kind of spiritual dryness he had been taught to recognize and contend with. Yet each morning his dazed wakening—from whatever fitful sleep the night had yielded him—was greeted with the pall of knowing that the aging pastor of the next-door church would be out in the open, performing some strenuous task as if he were in the bloom of health. When the younger man looked out the window, the mere sight of the other building was enough to make him sick with anxiety.

On Friday Father Russell went to St. Celia Hospital to attend to the needs of one of his older parishioners, who had broken her hip in a fall, and while he was there a nurse walked in and asked that he administer the sacrament of extreme unction to a man in the emergency room. He followed her down the hall and the stairs to the first floor, and while they walked she told him the man had suffered a heart attack, that he was already beyond help. She said this almost matter of factly, and Father Russell looked at the delicate curve of her ears, thinking about design. This was, of course, an odd thing to be contemplating at such a somber time, yet he cultivated the thought, strove to concentrate on it, gazing at the intricacy of the nurse's red-veined ear lobe. Early in his priesthood, he had taught himself to make his mind settle on other things during moments

requiring him to look upon sickness and death—he had worked
to foster a healthy appreciation of, and attention to, insignifi-
cant things which were out of the province of questions of
eternity and salvation, and the common doom. It was what he
had always managed as a protection against too clear a memory
of certain daily horrors—images that could blow through him
in the night like the very winds of fright and despair—and if
over the years it had mostly worked, it had recently been in
the process of failing him. Entering the crowded emergency
room, he was concentrating on the whorls of a young woman's
ear as an instrument for hearing, when he saw Tarmigian
sitting in one of the chairs near the television, his hand
wrapped in a bandage, his pallid face sunk over the pages of a
magazine.

Tarmigian looked up, then smiled, held up the bandaged
hand. There wasn't time for the two men to speak. Father
Russell nodded at him and went on, following the nurse,
feeling strangely precarious and weak. He looked back over his
shoulder at Tarmigian, who had simply gone back to reading
the magazine, and then he was attending to what the nurse
had brought him to see: she pulled a curtain aside to reveal a
gurney with two people on it—a man and a woman of roughly
the same late middle age—the woman cradling the man's head
in her arms and whispering something to him.

"Mrs. Simpson," the nurse said, "here's the priest."

Father Russell stood there while the woman regarded him.
She was perhaps fifty-five, with iron-gray hair and small, round,
wet eyes. "Mrs. Simpson," he said to her.

"He's my husband," she murmured, rising, letting the man's
head down carefully. His eyes were open wide, as was his
mouth. "My Jack. Oh, Jack. Jack."

Father Russell stepped forward and touched her shoulder,
and she cried, staring down at her husband's face.

"He's gone," she said. "We were talking, you know. We
were thinking about going down to see the kids. And he just
put his head down. We were talking about how the kids never
come to visit and we were going to surprise them."

"Mrs. Simpson," the nurse said, "would you like a sedative? Something to settle your nerves—"

This had the effect of convincing the poor woman about what had just taken place: the reality of it sank into her features as the color drained from them. "No," she said in a barely audible whisper, "I'm fine."

Father Russell began quickly to say the words of the sacrament, and she stood by him, gazing down at the dead man.

"I—I don't know where he is," she said. "He just put his head down." Her hands trembled over the cloth of her husband's shirt, which was open wide at the chest, and it was a moment before Father Russell understood that she was trying to button the shirt. But her hands were shaking too much. She patted the shirt down, then bowed her head and sobbed. Somewhere in the jangled apparatus of the room something was beeping, and he heard air rushing through pipes; everything was obscured in the intricacies of procedure. And then he was simply staring at the dead man's blank countenance, all sound and confusion and movement falling away from him. It was as though he had never looked at anything like this before; he remained quite still, in a profound quiet, for some minutes before Mrs. Simpson got his attention again. She had taken him by the wrist.

"Father," she was saying. "Father, he was a good man. God has taken him home, hasn't He?"

Father Russell turned to face the woman, to take her hands into his own and to whisper the words of hope.

"I think seeing you there—at the hospital," he said to Tarmigian. "It upset me in an odd way."

"I cut my hand opening the paint jar," Tarmigian said. He was standing on a stepladder in the upstairs hallway of his rectory, painting the crown molding. Father Russell had walked out of his church in the chill of first frost and made his way across the little stone bridge and up the incline to the old man's door, had knocked and been told to enter, and, entering, finding no one, had reached back and knocked again.

"Up here," came Tarmigian's voice.

And the priest had climbed the stairs in a kind of torpor, his heart beating in his neck and face. He had blurted out that he wasn't feeling right, hadn't slept at all well, and finally he'd begun to hint at what he could divine as to why. He was now sitting on the top step, hat in hand, still carrying with him the sense of the long night he had spent, lying awake in the dark, seeing not the dead face of poor Mrs. Simpson's husband but Tarmigian holding up the bandaged hand and smiling. The image had wakened him each time he had drifted toward sleep.

"Something's happening to me," he said now, unable to believe himself.

The other man reached high with the paint brush, concentrating. The ladder was rickety.

"Do you want me to hold the ladder?"

"Pardon me?"

"Nothing."

"Did you want to know if I wanted you to hold the ladder?"

"Well, do you?"

"You're worried I'll fall."

"I'd like to help."

"And did you say something is happening to you?"

Father Russell was silent.

"Forget the ladder, son."

"I don't understand myself lately," said the priest.

"Are you making me your confessor or something there, Reverend?"

"I—I can't—"

"Because I don't think I'm equipped."

"I've looked at the dead before," said Father Russell. "I've held the dying in my arms. I've never been very much afraid of it. I mean I've never been morbid."

"Morbidity is an indulgence."

"Yes, I know."

"Simply refuse to indulge yourself."

"I'm forty-three—"

"A difficult age, of course. You don't know whether you fit with the grown-ups or the children." Tarmigian paused to cough. He held the top step of the ladder with both hands, and his shoulders shook. Everything tottered. Then he stopped, breathed, wiped his mouth with the back of one hand.

Father Russell said, "I meant to say, I don't think I'm worried about myself."

"Well, that's good."

"I'm going to call and make you an appointment with a doctor."

"I'm fine. I've got a cold. I've coughed like this all my life."

"Nevertheless."

Tarmigian smiled at him. "You're a good man—but you're learning a tendency."

No peace.

Father Russell had entered the priesthood without the sort of fervent sense of vocation he believed others had. In fact, he'd entertained serious doubts about it right up to the last year of seminary—doubts that, in spite of his confessor's reassurances to the contrary, he felt were more than the normal upsets of seminary life. In the first place, he had come to it against the wishes of his father, who had cherished dreams of a career in law for him; and while his mother applauded the decision, her own dream of grandchildren was visibly languishing in her eyes as the time for his final vows approached. Both parents had died within a month of each other during his last year of studies, and so there had been times when he'd had to contend with the added problem of an apprehension that he might unconsciously be learning to use his vocation as a form of refuge. But finally, nearing the end of his training, seeing the completion of the journey, something in him rejoiced, and he came to believe that this was what having a true vocation was:

no extremes of emotion, no real perception of a break with the world, though the terms of his faith and the ancient ceremony that his training had prepared him to celebrate spoke of just that. He was even-tempered and confident, and when he was ordained, he set about the business of being a parish priest. There were matters to involve himself in, and he found that he could be energetic and enthusiastic about most of them. The life was satisfying in ways he hadn't expected, and if in his less confident moments some part of him entertained the suspicion that he was not progressing spiritually, he was also not the sort of man to go very deeply into such questions: there were things to do. He was not a contemplative. Or he hadn't been.

Something was shifting in his soul.

Nights were terrible. He couldn't even pray now. He stood at his rectory window and looked at the light in the old man's window, and his imagination presented him with the belief that he could hear the faint rattle of the deep cough, though he knew it was impossible across that distance. When he said the morning mass, he leaned down over the host and had to work to remember the words. The stolid, calm faces of his parishioners were almost ugly in their absurd confidence in him, their smiles of happy expectation and welcome. He took their hospitality and their care of him as his due, and felt waves of despair at the ease of it, the habitual taste and lure of it, while all the time his body was aching in ways that filled him with dread and reminded him of Tarmigian's ravaged features.

Sunday morning early, it began to rain. Someone called, then hung up before he could answer. He had been asleep, the loud ring at that hour had frightened him, changed his heartbeat. He took his own pulse, then stood at his window and gazed at the darkened shape of Tarmigian's church. That morning after the second mass, exhausted, miserable, filled with apprehension, he crossed the bridge in the rain, made his way up the hill, and knocked on the old man's door. There wasn't any answer. He peered through the window on the porch and saw that there were dishes on the table in the kitchen, which was visible through the arched hallway off the living room. Tarmigian's Bible lay open on the arm of the easy chair. Father Russell knocked loudly and then walked around the building, into the church itself. It was quiet. The wind stirred outside and sounded like traffic whooshing by. Father Russell could feel his own heartbeat in the pit of his stomach. He sat down in the first pew of Tarmigian's church and tried to calm himself. Perhaps ten minutes went by, and then he heard voices. The old man was coming up the walk outside, talking to someone. Father Russell stood, thought absurdly of trying to hide, but then the door was opened and Tarmigian walked in, accompanied by an old woman in a white woolen shawl. Tarmigian had a big umbrella, which he shook down and folded, breathing heavily from the walk and looking, as always, even in the pall of his decline, amused by something. He hadn't seen Father Russell yet, though the old woman had. She nodded and smiled broadly, her hands folded neatly over a small black purse.

"Well," Tarmigian said. "To what do we owe this honor, Reverend?"

It struck Father Russell that they might be laughing at him. He dismissed this thought and, clearing his throat, said, "I—I wanted to see you." His own voice sounded stiffly formal and somehow foolish to him. He cleared his throat again.

"This is Father Russell," Tarmigian said loudly to the old woman. Then he touched her shoulder and looked at the priest. "Mrs. Aldenberry."

"God bless you," Mrs. Aldenberry said.

"Mrs. Aldenberry wants a divorce," Tarmigian murmured.

"Eh?" she said. Then, turning to Father Russell, "I'm hard of hearing."

"She wants her own television set," Tarmigian whispered.

"Pardon me?"

"And her own room."

"I'm hard of hearing," she said cheerfully to the priest. "I'm deaf as a post."

"Irritates her husband," Tarmigian said.

"I'm sorry," said the woman, "I can't hear a thing."

Tarmigian guided her to the last row of seats, and she sat down there, folded her hands in her lap. She seemed quite content, quite trustful, and the old minister, beginning to stutter into a deep cough, winked at Father Russell—as if to say this was all very entertaining. "Now," he said, taking the priest by the elbow, "let's get to the flattering part of all this— you walking over here getting yourself all wet because you're worried about me."

"I just wanted to stop by," Father Russell said. He was almost pleading. The old man's face, in the dim light, looked appallingly bony and pale.

"Look at you," said Tarmigian. "You're shaking."

Father Russell could not speak.

"Are you all right?"

The priest was assailed by the feeling that the older man found him somehow ridiculous—and he remembered the initial sense he'd had, when Tarmigian and Mrs. Aldenberry had entered, that he was being laughed at. "I just wanted to see how you were doing," he said.

"I'm a little under the weather," Tarmigian said, smiling.

And it dawned on Father Russell, with the force of a physical blow, that the old man knew quite well he was dying.

Tarmigian indicated Mrs. Aldenberry with a nod of his head. "Now I have to attend to the depths of this lady's sorrow. You know, she says she should've listened to her mother and not married Mr. Aldenberry fifty-two years ago. She's revising her own history; she can't remember being happy in all that time, not now, not after what's happened. Now you think about that a bit. Imagine her standing in a room slapping her forehead and saying 'What a mistake!' Fifty-two years. Oops. A mistake. She's glad she woke up in time. Think of it! And I'll tell you, Reverend, I think she feels lucky."

Mrs. Aldenberry made a prim, throat-clearing sound, then stirred in her seat, looking at them.

"Well," Tarmigian said, straightening, wiping the smile from his face. He offered his hand to the priest. "Shake hands. No. Let's embrace. Let's give this poor woman an ecumenical thrill."

Father Russell shook hands, then walked into the old man's extended arms. It felt like a kind of collapse. He was breathing the odor of bay rum and talcum and something else, too, something indefinable and dark, and to his astonishment he found himself fighting back tears. The two men stood there while Mrs. Aldenberry watched, and Father Russell was unable to control the sputtering and trembling that took hold of him. When Tarmigian broke the embrace, the priest turned away, trying to compose himself. Tarmigian was coughing again.

"Excuse me," said Mrs. Aldenberry. She seemed quite tentative and upset.

Tarmigian held up one hand, still coughing, and his eyes had grown wide with the effort to breathe.

"Hot honey with a touch of lemon and whiskey," she said, to no one in particular. "Works like a charm."

Father Russell thought about how someone her age would indeed learn to feel that humble folk remedies were effective in stopping illness. It was logical and reasonable, and he was surprised by the force of his own resentment of her for it. He stood there wiping his eyes and felt his heart constrict with bitterness.

"Well," Tarmigian said, getting his breath back.

"Hot toddy," said Mrs. Aldenberry. "Never knew it to fail." She was looking from one to the other of the two men, her expression taking on something of the look of tolerance. "Fix you up like new," she said, turning her attention to the priest, who could not stop blubbering. "What's—what's going on here?"

Father Russell had a moment of sensing that everything Tarmigian had done or said over the past year was somehow freighted with this one moment, and it took him a few seconds to recognize the implausibility of such a thing: no one could have planned it, or anticipated it, this one seemingly aimless gesture of humor—out of a habit of humorous gestures, and from a brave old man sick to death—that could feel so much like health, like the breath of new life.

He couldn't stop crying. He brought out a handkerchief and covered his face with it, then wiped his forehead. It had grown quiet. The other two were gazing at him. He straightened, caught his breath. "Excuse me."

"No excuse needed," Tarmigian said, looking down. His smile seemed vaguely uncertain now, and sad. Even a little afraid.

"What is going on here?" the old woman wanted to know.

"Why, nothing at all out of the ordinary," Tarmigian said, shifting the small weight of his skeletal body, clearing his throat, managing to speak very loudly, very gently, so as to reassure her, but making certain, too, that she could hear him.

The fireman's wife

Jane's husband, Martin, works for the fire department. He's on four days, off three; on three, off four. It's the kind of shift work that allows plenty of time for sustained recreation, and during the off times Martin likes to do a lot of socializing with his two shift mates, Wally Harmon and Teddy Lynch. The three of them are like brothers: they bicker and squabble and compete in a friendly way about everything, including their common hobby, which is the making and flying of model airplanes. Martin is fanatical about it—spends way too much money on the two planes he owns, which are on the worktable in the garage, and which seem to require as much maintenance as the real article. Among the arguments between Jane and her husband—about money, lack of time alone together, and housework—there have been some about the model planes, but Jane can't say or do much without sounding like a poor sport: Wally's wife, Milly, loves watching the boys, as she calls them, fly their planes, and Teddy Lynch's ex-wife, before they were divorced, had loved the model planes too. In a way, Jane is the outsider here: Milly Harmon has known Martin most of his life, and Teddy Lynch was once point guard to Martin's power forward on their high school basketball team. Jane is relatively new, having come to Illinois from Virginia only two years ago, when Martin brought her back with him from his reserve training there.

This evening, a hot September twilight, they're sitting on lawn chairs in the dim light of the coals in Martin's portable grill, talking about games. Martin and Teddy want to play Risk, though they're already arguing about the rules. Teddy says that a European version of the game contains a wrinkle that makes it more interesting, and Martin is arguing that the game itself was derived from some French game.

"Well, go get it," Teddy says, "and I'll show you. I'll bet it's in the instructions."

"Don't get that out now," Jane says to Martin.

"It's too long," Wally Harmon says.

"What if we play cards," Martin says.

"Martin doesn't want to lose his bet," Teddy says.

"We don't have any bets, Teddy."

"Okay, so let's bet."

"Let's play cards," Martin says. "Wally's right. Risk takes too long."

"I feel like conquering the world," Teddy says.

"Oh, Teddy," Milly Harmon says. "Please shut up."

She's expecting. She sits with her legs out, holding her belly as thought it were unattached, separate from her. The child will be her first, and she's excited and happy; she glows, as if she knows everyone's admiring her.

Jane thinks Milly is spreading it on a little thick at times: lately all she wants to talk about is her body and what it's doing.

"I had a dream last night," Milly says now. "I dreamed that I was pregnant. Big as a house. And I woke up and I was. What I want to know is, was that a nightmare?"

"How did you feel in the dream?" Teddy asks her.

"I said. Big as a house."

"Right, but was it bad or good?"

"How would you feel if you were big as a house?"

"Well, that would depend on what the situation was."

"The situation is, you're big as a house."

"Yeah, but what if somebody was chasing me? I'd want to be big, right?"

"Oh, Teddy, please shut up."

"I had a dream," Wally says. "A bad dream. I dreamed I died. I mean, you know, I was dead—and what was weird was that I was also the one who had to call Milly to tell her about it."

"Oh, God," Milly says. "Don't talk about this."

"It was weird. I got killed out at sea or something. Drowned, I guess. I remember I was standing on the deck of this ship talking to somebody about how it went down. And then I was calling Milly to tell her. And the thing is, I talked like a stranger would—you know, 'I'm sorry to inform you that your husband went down at sea.' It was weird."

"How did you feel when you woke up?" Martin says.

"I was scared. I didn't know who I was for a couple of seconds."

"Look," Milly says, "I don't want to talk about dreams."

"Let's talk about good dreams," Jane says. "I had a good dream. I was fishing with my father out at a creek—some creek that felt like a real place. Like if I ever really did go fishing with my father, this is where we would have fished when I was small."

"What?" Martin says after a pause, and everyone laughs.

"Well," Jane says, feeling the blood rise in her face and neck, "I never—my father died when I was just a baby."

"I dreamed I got shot once," Teddy says. "Guy shot me with a forty-five automatic as I was running downstairs. I fell and hit bottom, too. I could feel the cold concrete on the side of my face before I woke up."

Milly Harmon sits forward a little and says to Wally, "Honey, why did you have to tell about having a dream like that? Now I'm going to dream about it, I just know it."

"I think we all ought to call it a night," Jane says. "You guys have to get up at six o'clock in the morning."

"What're you talking about?" Martin says. "We're going to play cards, aren't we?"

"I thought we were going to play Risk," Teddy says.

"All right," Martin says, getting out of his chair. "Risk it is."

Milly groans, and Jane gets up and follows Martin into the house. "Honey," she says. "Not Risk. Come on. We'd need four hours at least."

He says over his shoulder, "So then we need four hours."

"Martin, I'm tired."

He's leaning up into the hall closet, where the games are stacked. He brings the Risk game down and turns, holding it in both hands like a tray. "Look, where do you get off, telling everybody to go home the way you did?"

She stands there staring at him.

"These people are our friends, Jane."

"I just said I thought we ought to call it a night."

"Well *don't* say—all right? It's embarrassing."

He goes around her and back out to the patio. The screen door slaps twice in the jamb. She waits a moment and then moves through the house to the bedroom. She brushes her hair, thinks about getting out of her clothes. Martin's uniforms are lying across the foot of the bed. She picks them up, walks into the living room with them, and drapes them over the back of the easy chair.

"Jane," Martin calls from the patio. "Are you playing or not?"

"Come on, Jane," Milly says. "Don't leave me alone out here."

"What color armies do you want?" Martin asks.

She goes to the patio door and looks out at them. Martin has lighted the tiki lamps; everyone's sitting at the picnic table in the moving firelight. "Come on," Martin says, barely concealing his irritation. She can hear it, and she wants to react to it—wants to let him know that she is hurt. But they're all waiting for her, so she steps out and takes her place at the table. She chooses green for her armies, and she plays the game to lose, attacking in all directions until her forces are so badly depleted that when Wally begins to make his own move she's the first to lose all her armies. This takes more than an hour. When she's out of the game, she sits for a while, cheering Teddy on against Martin, who is clearly going to win; finally she excuses herself and goes back into the house. The glow from the tiki lamps makes weird patterns on the kitchen wall. She pours herself a glass of water and drinks it down; then she pours more and swallows some aspirin. Teddy sees this as he comes in for more beer, and he grasps her by the elbow and asks if she wants something a little better than aspirin for a headache.

"Like what?" she says, smiling at him. She's decided a smile is what one offers under such circumstances; one laughs things off, pretends not to notice the glazed look in the other person's eyes.

Teddy is staring at her, not quite smiling. Finally he puts his hands on her shoulders and says, "What's the matter, lady?"

"Nothing," she says. "I have a headache. I took some aspirin."

"I've got some stuff," he says. "It makes America beautiful. Want some?"

She says, "Teddy."

"No problem," he says. He holds both hands up and backs away from her. Then he turns and is gone. She hears him begin to tease Martin about the French rules of the game. Martin is winning. He wants Wally Harmon to keep playing, and Wally wants to quit. Milly and Teddy are talking about flying the model airplanes. They know about an air show in Danville on Saturday. They all keep playing and talking, and for a long time Jane watches them from the screen door. She smokes half a pack of cigarettes, and she paces a little. She drinks three glasses of orange juice, and finally she walks into the bedroom and lies down with her face in her hands. Her forehead feels hot. She's thinking about the next four days, when Martin will be gone and she can have the house to herself. She hasn't been married even two years, and she feels crowded; she's depressed and tired every day. She never has enough time to herself. And yet when she's alone, she feels weak and afraid. Now she hears someone in the hallway and she sits up, smoothes her hair back from her face. Milly Harmon comes in with her hands cradling her belly.

"Ah," Milly says. "A bed." She sits down next to Jane and then leans back on her hands. "I'm beat," she says.

"I have a headache," Jane says.

Milly nods. Her expression seems to indicate how unimportant she finds this, as if Jane had told her she'd already got over a cold or something. "They're in the garage now," she says.

"Who?"

"Teddy, Wally, Martin. Martin conquered the world."

"What're they doing?" Jane asks. "It's almost midnight."

"Everybody's going to be miserable in the morning," Milly says.

Jane is quiet.

"Oh," Milly says, looking down at herself. "He kicked. Want to feel it?"

She takes Jane's hand and puts it on her belly. Jane feels movement under her fingers, something very slight, like one heartbeat.

"Wow," she says. She pulls her hand away.

"Listen," Milly says. "I know we can all be overbearing sometimes. Martin doesn't realize some of his responsibilities yet. Wally was the same way."

"I just have this headache," Jane says. She doesn't want to talk about it, doesn't want to get into it. Even when she talks to her mother on the phone and her mother asks how things are, she says it's all fine. She has nothing she wants to confide.

"You feel trapped, don't you," Milly says.

Jane looks at her.

"Don't you?"

"No."

"Okay—you just have a headache."

"I do," Jane says.

Milly sits forward a little, folds her hands over the roundness of her belly. "This baby's jumping all over the place."

Jane is silent.

"Do you believe my husband and that awful dream? I wish he hadn't told us about it—now I know I'm going to dream something like it. You know pregnant women and dreams. It makes me shake just thinking of it."

"Try not to think of it," Jane says.

Milly waits a moment and then clears her throat and says, "You know, for a while there after Wally and I were married, I thought maybe I'd made a mistake. I remember realizing that I didn't like the way he laughed. I mean, let's face it, Wally laughs like a hyena. And somehow that took on all kinds of importance—you know, I had to absolutely like everything about him or I couldn't like anything. Have you ever noticed the way he laughs?"

Jane has never really thought about it. But she says nothing now. She simply nods.

"But you know," Milly goes on, "all I had to do was wait. Just—you know, wait for love to come around and surprise me again."

"Milly, I have a headache. I mean, what do you think is wrong, anyway?"

"Okay," Milly says, rising.

Then Jane wonders whether the other woman has been put up to this conversation. "Hey," she says, "did Martin say something to you?"

"What would Martin say?"

"I don't know. I mean, I really don't know, Milly. Jesus Christ, can't a person have a simple headache?"

"Okay," Milly says. "Okay."

"I like the way everyone talks around me here, you know it?"

"Nobody's talking around you—"

"I think it's wonderful how close you all are."

"All right," Milly says, standing there with her hands folded under the bulge of her belly. "You just look so unhappy these days."

"Look," Jane says, "I have a headache, all right? I'm going to go to bed. I mean, the only way I can get rid of it is to lie down in the dark and be very quiet—okay?"

"Sure, honey," Milly says.

"So—goodnight, then."

"Right," Milly says. "Goodnight." She steps toward Jane and kisses her on the cheek. "I'll tell Martin to call it a night. I know Wally'll be miserable tomorrow."

"It's because they can take turns sleeping on shift," Jane says.

"I'll tell them," Milly says, going down the hall.

Jane steps out of her jeans, pulls her blouse over her head, and crawls under the sheets. She turns the light off and closes her eyes. She can't believe how bad it is. She hears them all saying goodnight, and she hears Martin shutting the doors and turning off the lights. In the dark she waits for him to get to her. She's very still, lying on her back with her hands at her sides. He goes into the bathroom at the end of the hall. She hears him cough, clear his throat. He's cleaning his teeth. Then he comes to the entrance of the bedroom and stands in the light of the hall.

"I know you're awake," he says.

She doesn't answer.

"Jane," he says.

She says, "What?"

"Are you mad at me?"

"No."

"Then what's wrong?"

"I have a headache."

"You always have a headache."

"I'm not going to argue now, Martin. So you can say what you want."

He moves toward her, is standing by the bed. He's looming above her in the dark. "Teddy had some dope."

She says, "I know. He offered me some."

"I'm flying," Martin says.

She says nothing.

"Let's make love."

"Martin," she says. Her heart is beating fast. He moves a little, staggers taking off his shirt. He's so big and quick and powerful; nothing fazes him. When he's like this, the feeling she has is that he might do anything. "Martin," she says.

"All right," he says. "I won't. Okay? You don't have to worry your little self about it."

"Look," she says.

But he's already headed into the hall.

"Martin," she says.

He's in the living room. He turns the television on loud. A rerun of *Kojak*. She hears Theo calling someone sweetheart. "Sweetheart," Martin says. When she goes to him, she finds that he's opened a beer and is sitting on the couch with his legs out. The beer is balanced on his stomach.

"Martin," she says. "You have to start your shift in less than five hours."

He holds the beer up. "Baby," he says.

In the morning he's sheepish, obviously in pain. He sits at the kitchen table with his hands up to his head while she makes coffee and hard-boiled eggs. She has to go to work, too, at a car dealership in town. All day she sits behind a window with a circular hole in the glass, where people line up to pay for whatever the dealer sells or provides, including mechanical work, parts, license plates, used cars, rental cars, and, of course, new cars. Her day is long and exhausting, and she's already feeling as though she worked all night. The booth she has to sit in is right off the service bay area, and the smell of exhaust and grease is everywhere. Everything seems coated with a film of grime. She's standing at her sink, looking at the sun coming up past the trees beyond her street, and without thinking about it she puts the water on and washes her hands. The idea of the car dealership is like something clinging to her skin.

"Jesus," Martin says. He can't eat much.

She's drying her hands on a paper towel.

"Listen," he says, "I'm sorry, okay?"

"Sorry?" she says.

"Don't press it, all right? You know what I mean."

"Okay," she says, and when he gets up and comes over to

put his arms around her, she feels his difference from her. She kisses him. They stand there.

"Four days," he says.

When Teddy and Wally pull up in Wally's new pickup, she stands in the kitchen door and waves at them. Martin walks down the driveway, carrying his tote bag of uniforms and books to read. He turns around and blows her a kiss. This morning is like so many other mornings. They drive off. She goes back into the bedroom and makes the bed, and puts his dirty uniforms in the wash. She showers and chooses something to wear. It's quiet. She puts the radio on and then decides she'd rather have the silence. After she's dressed, she stands at the back door and looks out at the street. Children are walking to school in little groups of friends. She thinks about the four days ahead. What she needs is to get into the routine and stop thinking so much. She knows that problems in a marriage are worked out over time.

Before she leaves for work she goes out into the garage to look for signs of Teddy's dope. She doesn't want someone stumbling on incriminating evidence. On the worktable along the back wall are Martin's model planes. She walks over and stands staring at them. She stands very still, as if waiting for something to move.

At work her friend Eveline smokes one cigarette after another, apologizing for each one. During Martin's shifts Jane spends a lot of time with Eveline, who is twenty-nine and single and wants very much to be married. The problem is she can't find anyone. Last year, when Jane was first working at the dealership, she got Eveline a date with Teddy Lynch. Teddy took Eveline to Lum's for hot dogs and beer, and they had fun at first. But then Eveline got drunk and passed out—put her head down on her arms and went to sleep like a child asked to take a nap in school. Teddy put her in a cab for home and then called Martin to laugh about the whole thing. Eveline was so humiliated by the experience that she goes out of her way to avoid Teddy—doesn't want anything to do with him or with any of Martin's friends, or with Martin, for that matter. She will come over to the house only when she knows Martin is away at work. And when Martin calls the dealership and she answers the phone, she's very stiff and formal, and she hands the phone quickly to Jane.

Today things aren't very busy, and they work a crossword together, making sure to keep it out of sight of the salesmen, who occasionally wander in to waste time with them. Eveline plays her radio and hums along with some of the songs. It's a long, slow day, and when Martin calls Jane feels herself growing anxious—something is moving in the pit of her stomach.

"Are you still mad at me?" he says.

"No," she tells him.

"Say you love me."

"I love you."

"Everybody's asleep here," he says. "I wish you were with me."

She says, "Right."

"I do," he says.

"Okay."

"You don't believe me?"

"I said *okay*."

"Is it busy today?" he asks.

"Not too."

"You're bored, then."

"A little," she says.

"How's the headache?"

"Just the edge of one."

"I'm sorry," he says.

"It's not your fault."

"Sometimes I feel like it is."

"How's *your* head?" she says.

"Terrible."

"Poor boy."

"I wish something would happen around here," he says. "A lot of guys snoring."

"Martin," she says, "I've got to go."

"Okay."

"You want me to stop by tonight?" she asks.

"If you want to."

"Maybe I will."

"You don't have to."

She thinks about him where he is: she imagines him, comfortable, sitting on a couch in front of a television. Sometimes, when nothing's going on, he watches all the soaps. He was hooked on *General Hospital* for a while. That he's her husband seems strange, and she thinks of the nights she's lain in his arms, whispering his name over and over, putting her hands in his hair and rocking with him in the dark. She tells him she loves him, and hangs the phone up. Eveline makes a gesture of frustration and envy.

"Nuts," Eveline says. "Nuts to you and your lovey-dovey stuff."

Jane is sitting in a bath of cold inner light, trying to think of her husband as someone she recognizes.

"Let's do something tonight," Eveline says. "Maybe I'll get lucky."

"I'm not going with you if you're going to be giving strange men the eye," Jane says. She hasn't quite heard herself. She's surprised when Eveline reacts.

"How dare you say a nasty thing like that? I don't know if I want to go out with someone who doesn't think any more of me than *that*."

"I'm sorry," Jane says, patting the other woman's wrist. "I didn't mean anything by it, really. I was just teasing."

"Well, don't tease that way. It hurts my feelings."

"I'm sorry," Jane says again. "Please—really." She feels near crying.

"Well, okay," Eveline says. "Don't get upset. I'm half teasing myself."

Jane sniffles, wipes her eyes with the back of one hand.

"What's wrong, anyway?" Eveline says.

"Nothing," Jane says. "I hurt your feelings."

That evening they ride in Eveline's car over to Shakey's for a pizza, and then stroll down to the end of the block, to the new mini-mall on Lincoln Avenue. The night is breezy and warm. A storm is building over the town square. They window-shop for a while, and finally they stop at a new corner café, to sit in a booth by the windows, drinking beer. Across the street one of the movies has ended, and people are filing out, or waiting around. A few of them head this way.

"They don't look like they enjoyed the movie very much," Eveline says.

"Maybe they did, and they're just depressed to be back in the real world."

"Look, what is it?" Eveline asks suddenly.

Jane returns her gaze.

"What's wrong?"

"Nothing."

"Something's wrong," Eveline says.

Two boys from the high school come past, and one of them winks at Jane. She remembers how it was in high school—the games of flirtation and pursuit, of ignoring some people and noticing others. That seemed like such an unbearable time, and it's already years ago. She watches Eveline light yet another cigarette and feels very much older than her own memory of herself. She sees the person she is now, with Martin, somewhere years away, happy, with children, and with different worries. It's a vivid daydream. She sits there fabricating it, feeling it for what it is and feeling, too, that nothing will change: the Martin she sees in the daydream is nothing like the man she lives with. She thinks of Milly Harmon, pregnant and talking about waiting to be surprised by love.

"I think I'd like to have a baby," she says. She hadn't known she would say it.

Eveline says, "Yuck," blowing smoke.

"Yuck," Jane says. "That's great. Great response, Evie."

They're quiet awhile. Beyond the square the clouds break up into tatters, and lightning strikes out. They hear thunder, and the smell of rain is in the air. The trees in the little park across from the theater move in the wind, and leaves blow out of them.

"Wouldn't you like to have a family?" Jane says.

"Sure."

"Well, the last time I checked, that meant having babies."

"Yuck," Eveline says again.

"Oh, all right—you just mean because of the pain and all."

"I mean yuck."

"Well, what does 'yuck' mean, okay?"

"What *is* the matter with you?" Eveline says. "What difference does it make?"

"I'm trying to have a normal conversation," Jane says, "and I'm getting these weird one-word answers, that's all. I mean what's 'yuck,' anyway? What's it mean?"

"Let's say it means I don't want to talk about having babies."

"I wasn't talking about you."

Each is now a little annoyed with the other. Jane has noticed that whenever she talks about anything that might border on plans for the future, the other woman becomes irritatingly sardonic and close mouthed. Eveline sits there smoking her cigarette and watching the storm come. From beyond the square they hear sirens, which seem to multiply. The whole city seems to be mobilizing. Jane thinks of Martin out there where all those alarms are converging. How odd to know where your husband is by a sound everyone hears. She remembers lying awake nights last year, hearing sirens and worrying about what might happen. And now, through a slanting sheet of rain, as though something in these thoughts has produced her, Milly Harmon comes, holding an open magazine above her head. She sees Jane and Eveline in the

222

window and waves at them. "Oh, God," Eveline says. "Isn't that Milly Harmon?"

Milly comes into the café and stands for a moment, shaking water from herself. Her hair is wet, as are her shoulders. She pushes her hair away from her forehead, and wipes the rain away with the back of one hand. Then she walks over and says, "Hi, honey," to Jane, bending down to kiss her on the side of the face. Jane manages to seem glad to see her. "You remember my friend Eveline from work," she says.

"I think I do, sure," Milly says.

"Maybe not," Eveline says.

"No, I think I do."

"I have one of those faces that remind you of somebody you never met," Eveline says.

Jane covers this with a laugh as Milly settles on her side of the booth.

Milly is breathless, all bustle and worry, arranging herself, getting comfortable. "Do you hear that?" she says about the sirens. "I swear, it must be a big one. I wish I didn't hear the sirens. It makes me so jumpy and scared. Wally would never forgive me if I did, but I wish I could get up the nerve to go see what it is."

"So," Eveline says, blowing smoke, "how's the baby coming along?"

Milly looks down at herself. "Sleeping now, I think."

"Wally—is it Wally?"

"Wally, yes."

"Wally doesn't let you chase ambulances?"

"I don't chase ambulances."

"Well, I mean—you aren't allowed to go see what's what when you hear sirens?"

"I don't want to see."

"I guess not."

"He's seen some terrible things. They all have. It must be terrible sometimes."

"Right," Eveline says. "It must be terrible."

Milly waves her hand in front of her face. "I wish you wouldn't smoke."

"I was smoking before you came," Eveline says. "I didn't know you were coming."

Milly looks confused for a second. Then she sits back a little and folds her hands on the table. She's chosen to ignore Eveline. She looks at Jane and says, "I had that dream last night."

Jane says, "What dream?"

"That Wally was gone."

Jane says nothing.

"But it wasn't the same, really. He'd left me, you know—the baby was born and he'd just gone off. I was so mad at him. And I had this crying little baby in my lap."

Eveline swallows the last of her beer and then gets up and goes out to stand near the line of wet pavement at the edge of the awninged sidewalk.

"What's the matter with her?" Milly asks.

"She's just unhappy."

"Did I say something wrong?"

"No—really. It's nothing." Jane says.

She pays for the beer. Milly talks to her for a while, but Jane has a hard time concentrating on much of anything now, with sirens going and Eveline standing out there at the edge of the sidewalk. Milly goes on, talking nervously about Wally's leaving her in her dream and how funny it is that she woke up mad at him, that she had to wait a few minutes and get her head clear before she could kiss him good morning.

"I've got to go," Jane says. "I came in Eveline's car."

"Oh, I'm sorry—sure. I just stepped in out of the rain myself."

They join Eveline outside, and Milly says she's got to go get her nephews before they knock down the ice-cream parlor. Jane and Eveline watch her walk away in the rain, and Eveline says, "Jesus."

"She's just scared," Jane says. "God, leave her alone."

"I don't mean anything by it," Eveline says. "A little malice, maybe."

Jane says nothing. They stand there watching the rain and lightning, and soon they're talking about people at work, the salesmen and the boys in the parts shop. They're relaxed now; the sirens have stopped and the tension between them has lifted. They laugh about one salesman who's apparently interested in Eveline. He's a married man—an overweight, balding, middle-aged Texan who wears snakeskin boots and a string tie, and who has an enormous fake-diamond ring on the little finger of his left hand. Eveline calls him Disco Bill. And yet Jane thinks her friend may be secretly attracted to him. She teases her about this, or begins to, and then a clap of thunder so frightens them both that they laugh about it, off and on, through the rest of the evening. They wind up visiting Eveline's parents, who live only a block from the café. Eveline's parents have been married almost thirty years, and, sitting in their living room, Jane looks at their things—the love seat and the antique chairs, the handsome grandfather clock in the hall, the paintings. The place has a lovely *tended* look about it. Everything seems to stand for the kind of life she wants for herself: an attentive, loving husband; children; and a quiet house with a clock that chimes. She knows this is all very dreamy and childish, and yet she looks at Eveline's parents, those people with their almost thirty years' love, and her heart aches. She drinks four glasses of white wine and realizes near the end of the visit that she's talking too much, laughing too loudly.

It's very late when she gets home. She lets herself in the side door of the house and walks through the rooms, turning on all the lights, as is her custom—she wants to be sure no one is hiding in any of the nooks and crannies. Tonight she looks at everything and feels demeaned by it. Martin's clean uniforms are lying across the back of the lounge chair in the living room.

The TV and the TV trays are in one corner, next to the coffee table, which is a gift from Martin's parents, something they bought back in the fifties, before Martin was born. Martin's parents live on a farm ten miles outside town, and for the past year Jane has had to spend Sundays out there, sitting in that living room with its sparse, starved look, listening to Martin's father talk about the weather, or what he had to eat for lunch, or the wrestling matches he watches on TV. He's a kindly man but he has nothing whatever of interest to say, and he seems to know it—his own voice always seems to surprise him at first, as if some profound inner silence had been broken; he pauses, seems to gather himself, and then continues with the con- sidered, slow cadences of oration. He's tall and lean and powerful looking; he wears coveralls, and he reminds Jane of those pictures of hungry, bewildered men in the Dust Bowl thirties—with their sad, straight, combed hair and their des- peration. Yet he's a man who seems quite certain about things, quite calm and satisfied. His wife fusses around him, making sure of his comfort, and he speaks to her in exactly the same soft, sure tones he uses with Jane.

Now, sitting in her own living room, thinking about this man, her father-in-law, Jane realizes that she can't stand another Sunday afternoon listening to him talk. It comes to her like a chilly premonition, and quite suddenly, with a kind of tidal shifting inside her, she feels the full weight of her unhappiness. For the first time it seems unbearable, like something that might drive her out of her mind. She breathes, swallows, closes her eyes and opens them. She looks at her own reflection in one of the darkened windows of the kitchen, and then she finds herself in the bedroom, pulling her things out of the closet and throwing them on the bed. Something about this is a little frantic, as though each motion fed some impulse to go further, go through with it—use this night, make her way somewhere else. For a long time she works, getting the clothes out where she can see them. She's lost herself in the practical matter of getting packed. She can't decide what to take, and then she can't find a suitcase or an overnight bag. Finally she settles on one of Martin's travel bags, from when he was in the Reserves. She's hurrying, stuffing everything into the bag, and when the bag is almost full she stops, feeling spent and out of breath. She sits down at her dressing table for a moment, and now she wonders if perhaps this is all the result of what she's had to drink. The alcohol is wearing off. She has the beginning of a headache. But she knows that whatever she decides to do should be done in the light of day, not now, at night. At last she gets up from the chair and lies down on the bed to think. She's dizzy. Her mind swims. She can't think, so she remains where she is, lying in the tangle of clothes she hasn't packed yet. Perhaps half an hour goes by. She wonders how long this will go on. And then she's asleep. She's nowhere, not even dreaming.

She wakes to the sound of voices. She sits up and tries to get her eyes to focus, tries to open them wide enough to see in the light. The imprint of the wrinkled clothes is in the skin of her face; she can feel it with her fingers. And then she's watching as two men bring Martin in through the front door and help him lie down on the couch. It's all framed in the perspective of the hallway and the open bedroom door, and she's not certain that it's actually happening.

"Martin?" she murmurs, getting up, moving toward them. She stands in the doorway of the living room, rubbing her eyes and trying to clear her head. The two men are standing over her husband, who says something in a pleading voice to one of them. He's lying on his side on the couch, both hands bandaged, a bruise on the side of his face as if something had spilled there.

"Martin," Jane says.

And the two men move, as if startled by her voice. She realizes she's never seen them before. One of them, the younger one, is already explaining. They're from another company.

227

"We were headed back this way," he says, "and we thought it'd be better if you didn't hear anything over the phone." While he talks, the older one is leaning over Martin, going on about insurance. He's a big square-shouldered man with an extremely rubbery look to his face. Jane notices this, notices the masklike quality of it, and she begins to tremble. Everything is oddly exaggerated—something is being said, they're telling her that Martin burned his hands, and another voice is murmuring something. Both men go on talking, apologizing, getting ready to leave her there. She's not fully awake. The lights in the room hurt her eyes; she feels a little sick to her stomach. The two men go out on the porch and then look back through the screen. "You take it easy, now," the younger one says to Jane. She closes the door, understands that what she's been hearing under the flow of the past few moments is Martin's voice muttering her name, saying something. She walks over to him.

"Jesus," he says. "It's awful. I burned my hands and I didn't even know it. I didn't even feel it."

She says, "Tell me what happened."

"God," he says. "Wally Harmon's dead. God. I saw it happen."

"Milly—" she begins. She can't speak.

He's crying. She moves to the entrance of the kitchen and turns to look at him. "I saw Milly tonight." The room seems terribly small to her.

"The Van Pickel Lumberyard went up. The warehouse. Jesus."

She goes into the kitchen and runs water. Outside the window above the sink she sees the dim street, the shadows of houses without light. She drinks part of a glass of water and then pours the rest down the sink. Her throat is still very dry. When she goes back into the living room, she finds him lying on his side, facing the wall.

"Martin?" she says.

"What?"

But she can't find anything to tell him. She says, "God—

poor Milly." Then she makes her way into the bedroom and begins putting away the clothes. She doesn't hear him get up, and she's startled to find him standing in the doorway, staring at her.

"What're you doing?" he asks.

She faces him, at a loss—and it's her hesitation that gives him his answer.

"Jane?" he says, looking at the travel bag.

"Look," she tells him, "I had a little too much to drink tonight."

He just stares at her.

"Oh, this," she manages. "I—I was just going through what I have to wear."

But it's too late. "Jesus," he says, turning from her a little.

"Martin," she says.

"What."

"Does—did somebody tell Milly?"

He nods. "Teddy. Teddy stayed with her. She was crazy. Crazy."

He looks at his hands. It's as if he just remembered them. They're wrapped tight; they look like two white clubs. "Jesus, Jane, are you—" He stops, shakes his head. "Jesus."

"Don't," she says.

"Without even talking to me about it—"

"Martin, this is not the time to talk about anything."

He's quiet a moment, standing there in the doorway. "I keep seeing it," he says. "I keep seeing Wally's face. The—the way his foot jerked. His foot jerked like with electricity and he was—oh, Christ, he was already dead."

"Oh, don't," she says. "Please. Don't talk. Stop picturing it."

"They gave me something to make me sleep," he says. "And I won't sleep." He wanders back into the living room. A few minutes later she goes to him there and finds that whatever the doctors gave him has worked. He's lying on his back, and he looks smaller somehow, his bandaged hands on his chest, his face pinched with grief, with whatever he's dreaming. He twitches and mutters something and moans. She turns the light off and tiptoes back to the bedroom. She's the one who won't sleep. She gets into the bed and huddles there, leaving the light on. Outside the wind gets up—another storm rolls in off the plains. She listens as the rain begins, and hears the far-off drumming of thunder. The whole night seems deranged. She thinks of Wally Harmon, dead out in the blowing, rainy dark. And then she remembers Milly and her bad dreams, how she looked coming from the downpour, the wet street, with the magazine held over her head—her body so rounded, so weighted down with her baby, her love, the love she had waited for, that she said had surprised her. These events are too much to think about, too awful to imagine. The world seems cruelly immense now, and remorselessly itself. When Martin groans in the other room, she wishes he'd stop, and then she imagines that it's another time, that she's just awakened from a dream and is trying to sleep while they all sit in her living room and talk the hours of the night away.

In the morning she's awake first. She gets up and wraps herself in a robe and then shuffles into the kitchen and puts coffee on. For a minute it's like any other morning. She sits at the table to wait for the coffee water to boil. He comes in like someone entering a stranger's kitchen—his movements are tentative, almost shy. She's surprised to see that he's still in his uniform. He says, "I need you to help me go to the bathroom. I can't get my pants undone." He starts trying to work his belt loose.

"Wait," she says. "Here, hold on."

"I have to get out of these clothes, Jane. I think they smell like smoke."

"Let me do it," she says.

"Milly's in the hospital—they had to put her under sedation."

"Move your hands out of the way," Jane says to him.

She has to help with everything, and when the time comes

for him to eat, she has to feed him. She spoons scrambled eggs
into his mouth and holds the coffee cup to his lips, and when
that's over with, she wipes his mouth and chin with a damp
napkin. Then she starts bathwater running and helps him out
of his underclothes. They work silently, and with a kind of
embarrassment, until he's sitting down and the water is right.
When she begins to run a soapy rag over his back, he utters a
small sound of satisfaction and comfort. But then he's crying
again. He wants to talk about Wally Harmon's death. He says
he has to. He tells her that a piece of hot metal the size of an
arrow dropped from the roof of the Van Pickel warehouse and
hit poor Wally Harmon in the top of the back.

"It didn't kill him right away," he says, sniffling. "Oh, Jesus.
He looked right at me and asked if I thought he'd be all right.
We were talking about it, honey. He reached up—he—over
his shoulder. He took ahold of it for a second. Then he—then
he looked at me and said he could feel it down in his stomach."

"Don't think about it," Jane says.

"Oh, God." He's sobbing. "God."

"Martin, honey—"

"I've done the best I could," he says. "Haven't I?"

"Shhh," she says, bringing the warm rag over his shoulders
and wringing it, so that the water runs down his back.

They're quiet again. Together they get him out of the tub,
and then she dries him off, helps him into a pair of jeans.

"Thanks," he says, not looking at her. Then he says, "Jane."

She's holding his shirt out for him, waiting for him to turn
and put his arms into the sleeves. She looks at him.

"Honey," he says.

"I'm calling in," she tells him. "I'll call Eveline. We'll go be
with Milly."

"Last night," he says.

She looks straight at him.

He hesitates, glances down. "I—I'll try and do better." He
seems about to cry again. For some reason this makes her feel
abruptly very irritable and nervous. She turns from him, walks

231

into the living room and begins putting the sofa back in order. When he comes to the doorway and says her name, she doesn't answer, and he walks through to the kitchen door.

"What're you doing?" she says to him.

"Can you give me some water?"

She moves into the kitchen and he follows her. She runs water, to get it cold, and he stands at her side. When the glass is filled, she holds it to his mouth. He swallows, and she takes the glass away. "If you want to talk about anything—" he says.

"Why don't you try to sleep awhile?" she says.

He says, "I know I've been talking about Wally—"

"Just please—go lie down or something."

"When I woke up this morning, I remembered everything, and I thought you might be gone."

"Well, I'm not gone."

"I knew we were having some trouble, Jane—"

"Just let's not talk about it now," she says. "All right? I have to go call Eveline." She walks into the bedroom, and when he comes in behind her she tells him very gently to please go get off his feet. He backs off, makes his way into the living room. "Can you turn on the television?" he calls to her.

She does so. "What channel do you want?"

"Can you just go through them a little?"

She's patient. She waits for him to get a good look at each channel. There isn't any news coverage; it's all commercials and cartoons and children's shows. Finally he settles on a rerun of *The Andy Griffith Show*, and she leaves him there. She fills the dishwasher and wipes off the kitchen table. Then she calls Eveline to tell her what's happened.

"You poor thing," Eveline says. "You must be so relieved. And I said all that bad stuff about Wally's wife."

Jane says, "You didn't mean it," and suddenly she's crying. She's got the handset held tight against her face, crying.

"You poor thing," Eveline says. "You want me to come over there?"

"No, it's all right—I'm all right."

"Poor Martin. Is he hurt bad?"

"It's his hands."

"Is it very painful?"

"Yes," Jane says.

Later, while he sleeps on the sofa, she wanders outside and walks down to the end of the driveway. The day is sunny and cool, with little cottony clouds—the kind of clear day that comes after a storm. She looks up and down the street. Nothing is moving. A few houses away someone has put up a flag, and it flutters in a stray breeze. This is the way it was, she remembers, when she first lived here—when she first stood on this sidewalk and marveled at how flat the land was, how far it stretched in all directions. Now she turns and makes her way back to the house, and then she finds herself in the garage. It's almost as if she's saying goodbye to everything, and as this thought occurs to her, she feels a little stir of sadness. Here on the worktable, side by side under the light from the one window, are Martin's model airplanes. He won't be able to work on them again for weeks. The light reveals the miniature details, the crevices and curves on which he lavished such care, gluing and sanding and painting. The little engines are lying on a paper towel at one end of the table; they smell just like real engines, and they're shiny with lubrication. She picks one of them up and turns it in the light, trying to understand what he might see in it that could require such time and attention. She wants to understand him. She remembers that when they dated, he liked to tell her about flying these planes, and his eyes would widen with excitement. She remembers that she liked him best when he was glad that way. She puts the little engine down, thinking how people change. She knows she's going to leave him, but just for this moment, standing among these things, she feels almost peaceful about it. There's no need to hurry. As she steps out on the lawn, she realizes she can take the time to think clearly about when and where; she can even change her mind. But she doesn't think she will.

He's up. He's in the hallway—he had apparently wakened and found her gone. "Jesus," he says. "I woke up and you weren't here."

"I didn't go anywhere," she says, and she smiles at him.

"I'm sorry," he says, starting to cry. "God, Janey, I'm so sorry. I'm all messed up here. I've got to go to the bathroom again."

She helps him. The two of them stand over the bowl. He's stopped crying now, though he says his hands hurt something awful. When he's finished he thanks her, and then tries a joke. "You don't have to let go so soon."

She ignores this, and when she has him tucked safely away, he says quietly, "I guess I better just go to bed and sleep some more if I can."

She's trying to hold onto the feeling of peace and certainty she had in the garage. It's not even noon, and she's exhausted. She's very tired of thinking about everything. He's talking about his parents; later she'll have to call them. But then he says he wants his mother to hear his voice first, to know he's all right. He goes on—something about Milly and her unborn baby, and Teddy Lynch—but Jane can't quite hear him: he's a little unsteady on his feet, and they have trouble negotiating the hallway together.

In their bedroom she helps him out of his jeans and shirt, and she actually tucks him into the bed. Again he thanks her. She kisses his forehead, feels a sudden, sick-swooning sense of having wronged him somehow. It makes her stand straighter, makes her stiffen slightly.

"Jane?" he says.

She breathes. "Try to rest some more. You just need to rest now." He closes his eyes and she waits a little. He's not asleep. She sits at the foot of the bed and watches him. Perhaps ten minutes go by. Then he opens his eyes.

"Janey?"

"Shhh," she says.

He closes them again. It's as if he were her child. She thinks of him as he was when she first saw him, tall and sure of himself in his uniform, and the image makes her throat constrict.

At last he's asleep. When she's certain of this, she lifts herself from the bed and carefully, quietly withdraws. As she closes the door, something in the flow of her own mind appalls her, and she stops, stands in the dim hallway, frozen in a kind of wonder: she had been thinking in an abstract way, almost idly, as though it had nothing at all to do with her, about how people will go to such lengths leaving a room—wishing not to disturb, not to awaken, a loved one.

Consolation

Late one summer afternoon, Milly Harmon and her older sister Meg, spend a blessed, uncomplicated hour at a motel pool in Philadelphia, sitting in the shade of one of the big umbrella tables. They drink tropical punch from cans, and Milly nurses the baby, staring out at the impossibly silver agitation of water around the body of a young, dark swimmer, a boy with Spanish black hair and eyes. He's the only one in the pool. Across the way, an enormous woman in a red terry-cloth bikini lies on her stomach in the sun, her head resting on her folded arms. Milly's sister puts her own head down for a moment, then looks at Milly. "I feel fat," she says, low. "I look like that woman over there, I just know it."

"Be quiet, Milly says. "Your voice carries."

"Nobody can hear us," Meg says. She's always worried about weight, though she's nothing like the woman across the way. Her thighs are heavy, her hips wide, but she's bigboned, as their mother always says; she's not built to be skinny. Milly's the one who's skinny. When they were growing up, Meg often called her "stick." Sometimes it was an endearment and sometimes it was a jibe, depending on the circumstances. These days, Meg calls her "honey" and speaks to her with something like the careful tones of sympathy. Milly's husband was killed last September, when Milly was almost six months pregnant, and the two women have traveled here to see Milly's in-laws, to show them their grandchild, whom they have never seen.

The visit hasn't gone well. Things have been strained and awkward. Milly is exhausted and discouraged, so her sister has worked everything out, making arrangements for the evening, preserving these few hours in the day for the two of them and

236

the baby. In a way, the baby's the problem: Milly would never have suspected that her husband's parents would react so peevishly, with such annoyance, to their only grandson—the only grandchild they will ever have.

Last night, when the baby started crying at dinner, both the Harmons seemed to sulk, and finally Wally's father excused himself and went to bed—went into his bedroom and turned a radio on. His dinner was still steaming on his plate; they hadn't even quite finished passing the food around. The music sounded through the walls of the small house, while Milly, Wally's mother, and Meg sat through the meal trying to be cordial to each other, the baby fussing between them.

Finally Wally's mother said, "Perhaps if you nurse him."

"I just did," Milly told her.

"Well, he wants *something*."

"Babies cry," Meg put in, and the older woman looked at her as though she had said something off-color.

"Hush," Milly said to the baby. "Be quiet." Then there seemed nothing left to say.

Mrs. Harmon's hands trembled over the lace edges of the tablecloth. "Can I get you anything?" she said.

At the end of the evening she took Milly by the elbow and murmured, "I'm afraid you'll have to forgive us, we're just not used to the commotion."

"Commotion," Meg said as they drove back to the motel. "Jesus. Commotion."

Milly looked down into the sleeping face of her son. "My little commotion," she said, feeling tired and sad.

Now Meg turns her head on her arms and gazes at the boy in the pool. "Maybe I'll go for a swim," she says.

"He's too young for you," Milly says.

Meg affects a forlorn sigh, then sits straight again. "You want me to take Zeke for a while?" The baby's name is Wally, after his dead father, but Meg calls him Zeke. She claims she's always called every baby Zeke, boy or girl, but she's especially fond of the name for *this* baby. Even Milly uses the name occasionally, as an endearment.

"He's not through nursing," Milly says.

It's been a hot day. Even now, at almost six o'clock, the sky is pale blue and crossed with thin, fleecy clouds that look like filaments of steam. Meg wants a tan, or says she does, but she's worn a kimono all afternoon, and hasn't moved out of the shade. She's with Milly these days because her marriage is breaking up. It's an amicable divorce; there are no children. Meg says the whole thing simply collapsed of its own weight. Neither party is interested in anyone else, and there haven't been any ugly scenes or secrets. They just don't want to be married to each other any more, see no future in it. She talks about how civilized the whole procedure has been, how even the lawyers are remarking on it, but Milly thinks she hears some sorrow in her voice. She thinks of two friends of hers who have split up twice since the warehouse fire that killed Wally, and whose explanations, each time, have seemed to preclude any possibility of reconciliation. Yet they're now living together, and sometimes, when Milly sees them, they seem happy.

"Did I tell you that Jane and Martin are back together?" she asks Meg.

"Again?"

She nods.

"Tied to each other on a rock in space," Meg says.

"What?"

"Come on, let me hold Zeke," Meg reaches for the baby. "He's through, isn't he?"

"He's asleep."

Meg pretends to pout, extending her arm across the table and putting her head down again. She makes a yawning sound. "Where are all the boys? Let's have some fun here anyway— right? Let's get in a festive mood or something."

Milly removes the baby's tight little sucking mouth from her breast and covers herself. The baby sleeps on, still sucking. "Look at this," she says to her sister.

Meg leans toward her to see. "What in the world do you think is wrong with them?"

She's talking about Wally's parents, of course. Milly shrugs. She doesn't feel comfortable discussing them. She wants the baby to have both sets of grandparents, and a part of her feels that this ambition is in some way laudatory—that the strange, stiff people she has brought her child all this way to see ought to appreciate what she's trying to do. She wonders if they harbor some resentment about how before she would marry their son she'd extracted a promise from him about not leaving Illinois, where her parents and her sister live. It's entirely possible that Wally's parents unconsciously blame her for Wally's death, for the fact that his body lies far away in her family's plot in a cemetery in Lincoln, Illinois.

"Hey," Meg says.

"What."

"I asked a question. You drove all the way out here to see them and let them see their grandson, and they act like it's some kind of bother."

"They're just tired," Milly says. "Like we are."

"Seven hundred miles of driving to sit by a motel pool."

"They're not used to having a baby around," Milly says. "It's awkward for them, too." She wishes her sister would stop. "Can't we just not worry it all to death?"

"Hey," Meg says. "It's your show."

Milly says, "We'll see them tonight and then we'll leave in the morning and that'll be that, okay?"

"I wonder what they're doing right now. You think they're watching the four o'clock movie or something? With their only grandson two miles away in a motel?"

In a parking lot in front of a group of low buildings on the other side of the highway, someone sets off a pack of firecrackers—they make a sound like small machine-gun fire.

"All these years of independence," Meg says. "So people like us can have these wonderful private lives."

Milly smiles. It's always been Meg who defined things, who spoke out and offered opinions. Milly thinks of her sister as someone who knows the world, someone with experience she herself lacks, though Meg is only a little more than a year older. So much of her own life seems somehow duplicitous to her, as if the wish to please others and to be well thought of had somehow dulled the edges of her identity and left her with nothing but a set of received impressions. She knows she loves the baby in her lap, and she knows she loved her husband— though during the four years of her marriage she was confused much of the time, and afraid of her own restlessness. It was only in the weeks just before Wally was taken from her that she felt most comfortably in love with him, glad of his presence in the house and worried about the dangerous fire-fighting work that was, in fact, the agency of his death. She doesn't want to think about this now, and she marvels at how a moment of admiration for the expressiveness of her sister could lead to remembering that her husband died just as she was beginning to understand her need for him. She draws a little shuddering breath, and Meg frowns.

"You looked like something hurt you," Meg says. "You were thinking about Wally."

Milly nods.

"Zeke looks like him, don't you think?"

"I wasted so much time wondering if I loved him," Milly says.

"I think he was happy," her sister tells her.

In the pool the boy splashes and dives, disappears; Milly watches the shimmery surface. He comes up on the other side, spits a stream of water, and climbs out. He's wearing tight, dark blue bathing trunks.

"Come on," Meg says, reaching for the baby. "Let me have him."

"I don't want to wake him," Milly says.

Meg walks over to the edge of the pool, takes off her sandals, and dips the toe of one foot in, as though trying to gauge how cold the water is. She comes back, sits down, drops the sandals between her feet, and steps into them one by one. "You know what I think it is with the Harmons?" she says. "I think it's the war. I think the war got them. That whole generation."

Milly ignores this, and adjusts, slightly, the weight of the baby in her lap. "Zeke," she says. "Pretty Zeke."

The big woman across the way has labored up off her towel and is making slow progress out of the pool area.

"Wonder if she's married," Meg says. "I think I'll have a pool party when the divorce is final."

The baby stirs in Milly's lap. She moves slightly, rocking her legs.

"We ought to live together permanently," Meg says.

"You want to keep living with us?"

"Sure, why not? Zeke and I get along. A divorced woman and a widow. And one cool baby boy."

They're quiet a while. Somewhere off beyond the trees at the end of the motel parking lot, more firecrackers go off. Meg stands, stretches. "I knew a guy once who swore he got drunk and slept on top of the Tomb of the Unknown Soldier. On Independence Day. Think of it."

"You didn't believe him," Milly says.

"I believed he had the idea. Whole culture's falling apart. Whole goddam thing."

"Do you really want to stay with us?" Milly asks her.

"I don't know. That's an idea, too." She ambles over to the pool again, then walks around it, out of the gate, to the small stairway leading up to their room. At the door of the room she turns, shrugs, seems to wait. Milly lifts the baby to her shoulder, then rises. Meg is standing at the railing on the second level, her kimono partway open at the legs. Milly, approaching her, thinks she looks wonderful, and tells her so.

"I was just standing here wondering how long it'll take to drive you crazy if we keep living together," Meg says, opening the door to the room. Inside, in the air conditioning, she flops down on the nearest bed. Milly puts the baby in the Port-a-Crib and turns to see that the telephone message light is on. "Hey, look," she says.

Meg says, "Ten to one it's the Harmons canceling out."

"No bet," Milly says, tucking the baby in. "Oh, I just want to go home, anyway."

Her sister dials the front desk, then sits cross-legged with pillows at her back, listening. "I don't believe this," she says.

It turns out that there are two calls: one from the Harmons, who say they want to come earlier than planned, and one from Meg's estranged husband, Larry, who has apparently traveled here from Champaign, Illinois. When Meg calls the number he left, he answers, and she waves Milly out of the room. Milly takes the baby, who isn't quite awake, and walks back down to the pool. It's empty; the water is perfectly smooth. She sits down, watches the light shift on the surface, clouds moving across it in reflection.

It occurs to her that she might have to spend the rest of the trip on her own, and this thought causes a flutter at the pit of her stomach. She thinks of Larry, pulling this stunt, and she wonders why she didn't imagine that he might show up, her sister's casual talk of the divorce notwithstanding. He's always been prone to the grand gesture: once, after a particularly bad quarrel, he rented a van with loudspeakers and drove up and down the streets of Champaign, proclaiming his love. Milly remembers this, sitting by the empty pool, and feels oddly threatened.

It isn't long before Meg comes out and calls her back. Meg is already trying to make herself presentable. What Larry wants, she tells Milly, what he pleaded for, is only that Meg agree to see him. He came to Philadelphia and began calling all the Harmons in the phone book, and when he got Wally's parents, they gave him the number of the motel. "The whole thing's insane," she says, hurriedly brushing her hair. "I don't get it. We're almost final."

"Meg, I need you now," Milly says.

"Don't be ridiculous," says her sister.

"What're we going to do about the Harmons?"

"Larry says they asked him to say hello to you. Can you feature that? I mean, what in the world is that? It's like they don't expect to see you again."

"Yes," Milly says. "But they're coming."

"He called before, you know."

"Mr. Harmon?"

"No—Larry. He called just before we left. I didn't get it. I mean, he kept hinting around and I just didn't get it. I guess I told him we were coming to Philly."

The baby begins to whine and complain.

"Hey, Zeke," Meg says. She looks in the mirror. "Good Lord, I look like war," and then she's crying. She moves to the bed, sits down, still stroking her hair with the brush.

"Don't cry," Milly says. "You don't want to look all red eyed, do you?"

"What the hell," Meg says. "I'm telling you, I don't care about it. I mean—I don't care. He's such a baby about everything."

Milly is completely off balance. She has been the one in need on this trip, and now everything's turned around. "Here," she says, offering her sister a Kleenex. "You can't let him see you looking miserable."

"You believe this?" Meg says. "You think I should go with him?"

"He wants to take you somewhere?"

"I don't know."

"What about the Harmons?"

Meg looks at her. "What about them?"

"They're on their way here, too."

"I can't handle the Harmons any more," Meg tells her.

"Who asked you to handle them?"

"You know what I mean."

"Well—are you just going to go off with Larry?"

"I don't know what he wants."

"Well, for God's sake, Meg. He wouldn't come all this way just to tell you hello."

"That's what he said. He said 'Hello'."

"*Meg.*"

"I'm telling you, honey, I just don't have a clue."

In a little while Larry arrives, looking sheepish and expectant. Milly lets him in, and accepts his clumsy embrace, explaining that Meg is in the bathroom changing out of her bathing suit.

"Hey," he says, "I brought mine with me."

"She'll be through in a minute."

"Is she mad at me?" he asks.

"She's just changing," Milly tells him.

He looks around the room, walks over to the Port-a-Crib, and stands there making little cooing sounds at the baby. "He's smiling at me. Look at that."

"He smiles a lot." She moves to the other side of the crib and watches him make funny faces at the baby.

Larry is a fair, willowy man, and though he's older than Milly, she has always felt a tenderness toward him for his obvious unease with her, for the way Meg orders him around, and for his boyish romantic fragility—which, she realizes now, reminds her a little of Wally. It's in the moment that she wishes he hadn't come here that she thinks of this, and abruptly she has an urge to reach across the crib and touch his wrist, as if to make up for some wrong she's done. He leans down and puts one finger into the baby's hand. "Look at that," he says. "Quite a grip. Boy's going to be a linebacker."

"He's small for his age," Milly tells him.

"It's not the size. It's the strength."

She says nothing. She wishes Meg would come out of the bathroom. Larry pats the baby's forehead, then moves to the windows and, holding the drapes back, looks out.

"Pretty," he says. "Looks like it'll be a nice clear night for fireworks."

For the past year or so, Larry has worked in a shoe store in Urbana, and he's gone through several other jobs, though he often talks about signing up for English courses at the junior college and getting started on a career. He wants to save money for school, but in five years he hasn't managed to save enough for one course. He explains himself in terms of his appetite for life: he's unable to put off the present, and frugality sometimes suffers. Meg has often talked about him with a kind of wonder at his capacity for pleasure. It's not a thing she would necessarily want to change. He can make her laugh, and he writes poems to her, to women in general, though according to Meg they're not very good poems.

The truth is, he's an amiable, dreamy young man without an ounce of objectivity about himself, and what he wears on this occasion seems to illustrate this. His bohemian dress is embarrassingly like a costume—the bright red scarf and black beret and jeans; the sleeveless turtleneck shirt, its dark colors bleeding into each other across the front.

"So," he says, turning from the windows. "Are the grand-parents around?"

She draws in a breath, deciding to tell him about the Harmons, but Meg comes out of the bathroom at last. She's wearing the kimono open, showing the white shorts and blouse she's changed into.

Larry stands straight, clears his throat. "God, Meg. You look great," he says.

Meg flops down on the bed nearest the door and lights a cigarette. "Larry, what're you trying to pull here?"

"Nothing," he says. He hasn't moved. He's standing by the windows. "I just wanted to see you again. I thought Philadelphia on the Fourth might be good."

"Okay," Meg says, drawing on the cigarette.

"You know me," he says. "I have a hard time saying this sort of stuff up close."

"What sort of stuff, Larry."

"I'll take Zeke for a walk," Milly says.

"I can't believe this," Meg says, blowing smoke.

Milly gathers up the baby, but Larry stops her. "You don't have to go."

"Stay," Meg tells her.

"I thought I'd go out and meet the Harmons."

"Come on, tell me what you're doing here," Meg says to Larry.

"You don't know?"

"What if I need you to tell me anyway," she says.

He hesitates, then reaches into his jeans and brings out a piece of folded paper. "Here."

Meg takes it, but doesn't open it.

"Aren't you going to read it?"

"I can't read it with you watching me like that. Jesus, Larry—what in the world's going through your mind?"

"I started thinking about it being final," he says, looking down. Milly moves to the other side of the room, to her own bed, still holding the baby.

"I won't read it with you standing here," Meg says.

Larry reaches for the door. "I'll be outside," he says.

Milly, turning to sit with her back to them, hears the door close quietly. She looks at Meg, who's sitting against the headboard of the other bed, the folded paper in her lap.

"Aren't you going to read it?"

"I'm embarrassed for him."

Milly recalls her own secret embarrassment at the unattractive, hyena-like note poor Wally struck every time he laughed. "It was probably done with love," she says.

Meg offers her the piece of paper across the space between the two beds. "You read it to me."

"I can't do that, Meg. It's private. I shouldn't even be here."

Meg opens the folded paper, and reads silently. "Jesus," she says. "Listen to this."

"Meg," Milly says.

"You're my sister. Listen. 'When I began to think our time was really finally up/My chagrined regretful eyes lumbered tightly shut.' Lumbered, for God's sake."

Milly says nothing.

"My eyes lumbered shut."

And quite suddenly the two of them are laughing. They laugh quietly, or they try to. Milly sets Zeke down on his back, and pulls the pillows of the bed to her face in an attempt to muffle herself, and when she looks up she sees Meg on all fours with her blanket pulled over her head and, beyond her Larry's faint shadow through the window drapes. He's pacing. He stops and leans on the railing, looking out at the pool.

"Shhh," Meg says, finally. "There's more." She sits straight, composes herself, pushes the hair back from her face, and holds up the now crumpled piece of paper. "Oh," she says. "Ready?"

"Meg, he's right there."

Meg looks. "He can't hear anything."

"Whisper," Milly says.

Meg reads. "'I cried and sighed under the lids of these lonely eyes/Because I knew I'd miss your lavish thighs.'"

For a few moments they can say nothing. Milly, coughing and sputtering into the cotton smell of the sheets, has a moment of perceiving, by contrast, the unhappiness she's lived with these last few months, how bad it has been—this terrible time—and it occurs to her that she's managed it long enough not to notice it, quite. Everything is suffused in an ache she's grown accustomed to, and now it's as if she's flying in the face of it all. She laughs more deeply than she ever has, laughs even as she thinks of the Harmons, and of her grief. She's woozy from lack of air and breath. At last she sits up, wipes her eyes with part of the pillowcase, still laughing. The baby's fussing, so she works to stop, to gain some control of herself. She realizes that Meg is in the bathroom, running water. Then Meg comes out and offers her a wet washcloth.

"I didn't see you go in there."

"Quiet," Meg says. "Don't get me started again."

Milly holds the baby on one arm. "I have to feed Zeke some more."

"So once more I don't get to hold him."

They look at each other.

"Poor Larry," Meg says. "Married to a philistine. But—just maybe—he did the right thing, coming here."

"You don't suppose he heard us."

"I don't suppose it matters if he did. He'd never believe we could laugh at one of his *poems*."

"Oh, Meg—that's so mean."

"It's the truth. There are some things honey, that love just won't change."

Now it's as if they are both suddenly aware of another context for these words—both thinking about Wally. They gaze at each other. But then the moment passes. They turn to the window and Meg says, "Is Larry out there? What'll I tell him anyway?" She crosses the room and looks through the little peephole in the door. "God," she says, "the Harmons are here."

Mrs. Harmon is standing in front of the door with Larry, who has apparently begun explaining himself. Larry turns and takes Meg by the arm as she and Milly come out. "All the way from Champaign to head it off," he says to Mrs. Harmon. "I hope I just avoided making the biggest mistake of my life."

"God," Meg says to him. "If only you had money." she laughs at her own joke. Mrs. Harmon steps around her to take the baby's hand. She looks up at Milly. "I'm afraid we went overboard," she says. "We went shopping for the baby."

Milly nods at her. There's confusion now: Larry and Meg are talking, seem about to argue. Larry wants to know what Meg thinks of the poem, but Milly doesn't hear what she says to him. Mrs. Harmon is apologizing for coming earlier than planned.

"It's only an hour or so," Milly says, and then wonders if that didn't sound somehow ungracious. She can't think of anything else to say. And then she turns to see Mr. Harmon laboring up the stairs. He's carrying a giant teddy bear with a red ribbon wrapped around its thick middle. He has it over his shoulder, like a man lugging a body. The teddy bear is bigger than he is, and the muscles of his neck are straining as he sets it down. "This is for Wally," he says with a smile that seems sad. His eyes are moist. He puts one arm around his wife's puffy midriff and says, "I mean—if it's okay."

"I don't want to be divorced," Larry is saying to Meg.

Milly looks at the Harmons, at the hopeful, nervous expressions on their faces, and then she tries to give them the satisfaction of her best appreciation: she marvels at the size and the softness of the big teddy, and she holds the baby up to it, saying, "See? See?"

"It's quite impractical, of course," says Mr. Harmon.

"We couldn't pass it up," his wife says. "We have some other things in the car."

"I don't know where we'll put it," says Milly.

"We can keep it here," Mrs. Harmon hurries to say. She's holding on to her husband, and her pinched, unhappy features make her look almost frightened. Mr. Harmon raises the hand that had been around her waist and lightly, reassuringly, clasps her shoulder. He stands there, tall and straight in that intentionally ramrod-stiff way of his—the stance, he would say, of an old military man, which happens to be exactly what he is. His wife stands closer to him, murmurs something about the fireworks going off in the distance. It seems to Milly that they're both quite changed; it's as if they've come with bad news and are worried about hurting her with more of it. Then she realizes what it is they are trying to give her, in what is apparently the only way they know how, and she remembers that they have been attempting to get used to the loss of their only child. She feels her throat tighten, and when Larry reaches for her sister, putting his long, boy's arms around Meg, it's as if this embrace is somehow the expression of what they all feel. The Harmons are gazing at the baby now. Still arm in arm.

"Yes," Milly tells them, her voice trembling. "Yes, of course. You—we could keep it here."

Meg and Larry are leaning against the railing, in their embrace. It strikes Milly that she's the only one of these people without a lover, without someone to stand with. She lifts the baby to her shoulder and looks away from them all, but only for a moment. Far off, the sky is turning dusky; it's getting near the time for rockets and exploding blooms of color.

"Dinner for everyone," Mr. Harmon says, his voice full of brave cheerfulness. He leans close to Milly, and speaks to the child. "And you, young fellow, you'll have to wait awhile."

"We'll eat at the motel restaurant and then watch the fireworks," says Mrs. Harmon. "We could sit right here on the balcony and see it all."

Meg touches the arm of the teddy bear. "Thing's as big as a *real* bear," she says.

"I feel like fireworks," Larry says.

"They put on quite a show," says Mr. Harmon. "There used to be a big field out this way—before they widened the street. Big field of grass, and people would gather—"

"We brought Wally here when he was a little boy," Mrs. Harmon says. "So many—such good times."

"They still put on a good show," Mr. Harmon says, squeezing his wife's shoulder.

Milly faces him, faces them, fighting back any sadness. In the next moment, without quite thinking about it, she steps forward slightly and offers her child to Mrs. Harmon. Mrs. Harmon tries to speak, but can't. Her husband clears his throat, lifts the big teddy bear as if to show it to everyone again. But he, too, is unable to speak. He sets it down, and seems momentarily confused. Milly lightly grasps his arm above the elbow, and steps forward to watch her mother-in-law cradle the baby. Mrs. Harmon makes a slight swinging motion, looking at her husband, and then at Milly. "Such a pretty baby," she says.

Mr. Harmon says, "A handsome baby."

Meg and Larry move closer. They all stand there on the motel balcony with the enormous teddy bear propped against

the railing. They are quiet, almost shy, not quite looking at
each other, and for the moment it's as if, like the crowds
beginning to gather on the roofs of the low buildings across the
street, they have come here only to wait for what will soon be
happening in every quarter of the city of brotherly love.

The eyes of love

This particular Sunday in the third year of their marriage, the Truebloods are leaving a gathering of the two families—a cookout at Kenneth's parents' that has lasted well into the night and ended with his father telling funny stories about being in the Army in Italy just after the war. The evening has turned out to be exactly the kind of raucous, beery gathering Shannon said it would be, trying to beg off going. She's pregnant, faintly nauseous all the time, and she's never liked all the talk. She's heard the old man's stories too many times.

"They're good stories," Kenneth said that morning as she poured coffee for them both.

"I've heard every one of them at least twice," said Shannon. "God knows how many times your mother has heard them."

He said, "You might've noticed everybody laughing when he tells them, Shannon. Your father laughs until I start thinking about his heart."

"He just wants to be a part of the group."

"He chokes on it," Kenneth said, feeling defensive and oddly embarrassed, as if some unflattering element of his personality had been cruelly exposed. "Jesus, Shannon. Sometimes I wonder what goes through your mind."

"I just don't feel like listening to it all," she told him. "Does it have to be a statement of some kind if I don't go? Can't you just say I'm tired?"

"Your father and sisters are supposed to be there."

"Well, I'm pregnant—can't I be tired?"

"What do you think?" Kenneth asked her, and she shook her head, looking discouraged and caught. "It's just a cook-

252

out," he went on. "Cheer up—maybe no one will want to talk."

"That isn't what I mean, and you know it," she said.

Now she rolls the window down on her side and waves at everybody. "See you," she calls as Kenneth starts the car. For a moment they are sitting in the roar and rattle of the engine, which backfires and sends up a smell of burning oil and exhaust. Everyone's joking and calling to them, and Kenneth's three brothers begin teasing about the battered Ford Kenneth lacks the money to have fixed. As always he feels a suspicion that their jokes are too much at his expense, home from college four years and still out of a job in his chosen field, there being no college teaching jobs to be had anywhere in the region. He makes an effort to ignore his own misgiving, and anyway most of what they say is obliterated by the noise. He races the engine, and everyone laughs. It's all part of the uproar of the end of the evening, and there's good feeling all around. The lawn is illuminated with floodlights from the top of the house, and Kenneth's father stands at the edge of the sidewalk with one arm over *her* father's broad shoulders. Both men are a little tight.

"Godspeed," Kenneth's father says, with a heroic wave.

"Goodbye," says Shannon's father.

The two men turn and start unsteadily back to the house, and the others, Kenneth's mother and brothers and Shannon's two younger sisters, are applauding and laughing at the dizzy progress they make along the walk. Kenneth backs out of the driveway, waves at them all again, honks the horn, and pulls away.

Almost immediately his wife gives forth a conspicuous expression of relief, sighing deeply and sinking down in the seat. This makes him clench his jaw, but he keeps silent. The street winds among trees in the bright fan of his headlights; it's going to be a quiet ride home. He's in no mood to talk now.

She murmurs something beside him in the dark, but he chooses to ignore it. He tries to concentrate on driving, staring out at the road as if alone. After a little while she puts the radio on, looks for a suitable station, and the noise begins to irritate him, but he says nothing. Finally she gives up, turns the radio off. The windshield is dotting with rain. They come to the end of the tree-lined residential street, and he pulls out toward the city. Here the road already shimmers with water, the reflected lights of shops and buildings going on into the closing perspective of brightnesses ahead.

"Are you okay to drive?" she asks.

"What?" he says, putting the wipers on.

"I just wondered. You had a few beers."

"I had three beers."

"You had a few."

"Three," he says. "And I didn't finish the last one. What're you doing, counting them now?"

"Somebody better count them."

"I had three goddam beers," he says.

In fact, he hadn't finished the third beer because he'd begun to experience heartburn shortly after his father started telling the stories. He's sober all right, full of club soda and coffee, and he feels strangely lucid, as if the chilly night with its rain-smelling breezes has brought him wider awake, somehow. He puts both hands on the wheel and hunches forward slightly, meaning to ignore her shape, so quiet beside him. He keeps right at the speed limit, heading into the increasing rain, thinking almost abstractly about her.

"What're you brooding about?" she says.

The question surprises him. "I don't know," he says. "I'm driving."

"You're mad at me."

"No."

"Sure?" she asks.

"I'm sure."

.

What he is sure of is that the day has been mostly ruined for him: the entire afternoon and evening spent in a state of vague tension, worrying about his wife's mood, wondering about what she might say or do or refuse to do in light of that mood. And the vexing thing is that toward the end, as he watched her watch his father tell the stories, the sense of something guilty began to stir in his soul, as if this were all something he had betrayed her into having to endure and there was something lurid or corrupt about it—an immoral waste of energy somehow, like a sort of spiritual gluttony. He's trying hard not to brood about it, but he keeps seeing her in the various little scenes played out during the course of the day—her watchfulness during his own clowning with his brothers and her quiet through the day-long chatter of simple observation and remarking that had gone on with her father and sisters, with Kenneth's parents. In each scene she seemed barely able to contain her weariness and boredom.

At one point while his father was basking in the laughter following a story about wine and a small boy in Rome who knew where the Germans had stored untold gallons of it, Kenneth stared at Shannon until she saw him, and when for his benefit she seemed discreetly to raise one eyebrow (it was just between them), her face, as she looked back at his father, took on a glow of tolerance along with the weariness it had worn—and something like affectionate exasperation, too.

Clearly she meant it as a gift to him, for when she looked at him again she smiled.

He might've smiled back. He had been laughing at something his father said. Again, though, he thought he saw the faintest elevation of one of her eyebrows.

This expression, and the slight nod of her head, reminded him with a discomforting nostalgic stab (had they come so far from there?) of the look she had given him from the other side of noisy, smoky rooms in rented campus houses, when they were in graduate school and had first become lovers and moved with a crowd of radical believers and artists, people who were somehow most happy when they were wakeful and ruffled in the drugged hours before dawn—after the endless far-flung hazy discussions, the passionate sophomoric talk of philosophy and truth and everything that was wrong with the world and the beautiful changes everyone expected.

Someone would be talking, and Shannon would somehow confide in him with a glance from the other side of the room. There had been a thrill in receiving this look from her, since it put the two of them in cahoots; it made them secret allies in a kind of dismissal, a superiority reserved for the gorgeous and the wise. And this time he thought for a moment that she was intending the look, intending for him to think about those other days, before the job market had forced them to this city and part-time work for his father; before the worry over rent and the pregnancy had made everything of their early love seem quite dreamy and childish. He almost walked over to take her hand. But then a moment later she yawned deeply, making no effort to conceal her sleepiness, and he caught himself wishing that for the whole of the evening he could have managed not to look her way at all. With this thought in his mind, he did walk over to her. "I guess you want to go."

"For two hours," she said.

"You should've told me."

"I think I did."

"No," he said.

"I'm too tired to think," she told him.

Now, driving through the rainy night, he glances over at her and sees that she's simply staring out the passenger window, her hands open in her lap. He wants to be fair. He reminds himself that she's never been the sort of person who feels comfortable—or with whom one feels comfortable—at a party: something takes hold of her; she becomes objective and heavily intellectual, sees everyone as species, somehow, everything as behavior. A room full of people laughing and having a good innocent time is nevertheless a manifestation of some kind of

pecking order to her: such a gathering means nothing more
than a series of meaningful body languages and gestures,
nothing more than the forms of competition, and, as she has
told him on more than one occasion, she refuses to allow
herself to be drawn in; she will not play social games. He
remembers now that in their college days he considered this
attitude of hers to be an element of her sharp intelligence, her
wit. He had once considered that the two of them were above
the winds of fashion, intellectual and otherwise; he had once
been proud of this quirk of hers.

It's all more complicated than that now, of course. Now he
knows she's unable to help the fear of being with people in
congregation, that it's all a function of her having been refused
affection when she was a child, of having been encouraged to
compete with her many brothers and sisters for the attentions
of her mother, who over the years has been in and out of
mental institutions, and two of whose children, Shannon's
older sisters, grew sexually confused in their teens and later
underwent sex-change operations. They are now two older
brothers. Shannon and Kenneth have made jokes about this,
but the truth is, she comes from a tremendously unhappy
family. The fact that she's managed to put a marriage together
is no small accomplishment. She's fought to overcome the
confusion and troubles of her life at home, and she's mostly
succeeded. When her father finally divorced her mother,
Shannon was the one he came to for support; it was Shannon
who helped get him situated with the two younger sisters; and
it was Shannon who forgave him all the excesses he had been
driven to by the mad excesses of her mother. Shannon doesn't
like to talk about what she remembers of growing up, but
Kenneth often thinks of her as a little girl in a house where
nothing is what it ought to be. He would say she has a right to
her temperament, her occasional paranoia in groups of
people—and yet for some time now, in spite of all efforts not
to, he's felt only exasperation and annoyance with her about
it.

As he has felt annoyance about several other matters: her late unwillingness to entertain; her lack of energy; and her reluctance to have sex. She has only begun to show slightly, yet she claims she feels heavy and unsexy. He understand this, of course, but it worries him that when they're sitting together quietly in front of the television set and she reaches over and takes his hand—a simple gesture of affection from a woman expecting a child—he finds himself feeling itchy and irritable, aware of the caress as a kind of abbreviation, an abridgement: she doesn't mean it as a prelude to anything. He wants to be loving and gentle through it all, and yet he can't get rid of the feeling that this state of affairs is what she secretly prefers.

When she moves on the front seat next to him, her proximity actually startles him.

"What?" she says.

"I didn't say anything."

"You jumped a little."

"No," he says.

"All right." She settles down in the seat again.

A moment later he looks over at her. He wants to have the sense of recognition and comfort he has so often had when gazing upon her. But her face looks faintly deranged in the bad light, and he sees that she's frowning, pulling something down into herself. Before he can suppress it, anger rises like a kind of heat in the bones of his face. "Okay, what is it?" he says.

"I wish I was in bed."

"You *didn't* say anything to me about going," he says.

"Would you have listened?"

"I would've listened, sure," he says. "What kind of thing to say is that?"

She's silent, staring out her window.

"Look," he says, "just exactly what is it that's bothering you?"

She doesn't answer right away. "I'm tired," she tells him without quite turning to look at him.

"No, really," he says. "I want to hear it. Come on, let it out."

Now she does turn. "I told you this morning. I just don't like hearing the same stories all the time."

"They aren't all the same," he says, feeling unreasonably angry.

"Oh, of course they are. God—you were asking for them. Your mother deserves a medal."

"I like them. Mom likes them. Everybody likes them. Your father and your sisters like them."

"Over and over," she mutters, looking away again. "I just want to go to sleep."

"You know what your problem is?" he says. "You're a *critic*. That's what your problem is. Everything is something for you to evaluate and *decide* on. Even me. Especially me."

"You," she says.

"Yes," he says. "Me. Because this isn't about my father at all. It's about us."

She sits staring at him. She's waiting for him to continue. On an impulse, wanting to surprise and upset her, he pulls the car into a 7-Eleven parking lot and stops.

"What're you doing?" she says.

He doesn't answer. He turns the engine off and gets out, walks through what he is surprised to find is a blowing storm across to the entrance of the store and in. It's noisy here—five teenagers are standing around a video game while another is rattling buttons and cursing. Behind the counter an old man sits reading a magazine and sipping from a steaming cup. He smiles as Kenneth approaches, and for some reason Kenneth thinks of Shannon's father, with his heavy red hands and unshaven face, his high-combed double crown of hair and missing front teeth. Shannon's father looks like the Ukrainian peasant farmer he's descended from on the un-Irish side of that family. He's a stout, dull man who simply watches and listens. He has none of the sharp expressiveness of his daughter, yet it seems to Kenneth that he is more friendly—even, somehow, more tolerant. Thinking of his wife's boredom as a kind of aggression, he buys a pack of cigarettes, though he and Shannon quit smoking more than a year ago. He returns to the car, gets in without looking at her, dries his hands on his shirt, and tears at the cigarette pack.

"Oh," she says. "Okay—great."

He pulls out a cigarette and lights it with the dashboard lighter. She's sitting with her arms folded, still hunched down in the seat. He blows smoke. He wants to tell her, wants to set her straight somehow; but he can't organize the words in his mind yet. He's too angry. He wants to smoke the cigarette and then measure everything out for her, the truth as it seems to be arriving in his heart this night: that she's manipulative and mean when she wants to be, that she's devious and self-absorbed and cruel of spirit when she doesn't get her way—looking at his father like that, as if there were something sad about being able to hold a room in thrall at the age of seventy-five. Her own father howling with laughter the whole time. . .

"When you're through with your little game, I'd like to go home," she says.

"Want a cigarette?" he asks.

"This is so childish, Kenneth."

"Oh?" he says. "How childish is it to sit and *sulk* through an entire party because people don't conform to your wishes and—well, Jesus, I'm sorry, I don't think I quite know what the hell you wanted from everybody today. Maybe you could fill me in on it a little."

"I want some understanding from you," she says, beginning to cry.

"Oh, no," says Kenneth. "You might as well cut that out. I'm not buying that. Not the way you sat yawning at my father tonight as if he was senile or something and you couldn't even be bothered to humor him."

"*Humor* him. Is that what everyone's doing?"

"You know better than that, Shannon. Either that or you're blind."

"All right," she says. "That was unkind. Now I don't feel like talking any more, so let's just drop it."

He's quiet a moment, but the anger is still working in him. "You know the trouble with you?" he says. "You don't see anything with love. You only see it with your *brain.*"

"Whatever you say," she tells him.

"Everything's locked up in your *head,*" he says, taking a long drag of the cigarette and then putting it out in the ashtray. He's surprised by how good he feels—how much in charge, armed with being right about her: he feels he's made a discovery, and he wants to hold it up into the light and let her look at it.

"God, Kenneth. I felt sick all day. I'm pregnant."

He starts the car. "You know those people that live behind us?" he says. The moment has become almost philosophical to him.

She stares at him with her wet eyes, and just now he feels quite powerful and happy.

"Do you?" he demands.

"Of course I do."

"Well, I was watching them the other day. The way he is with the yard—right? We've been making such fun of him all summer. We've been so *smart* about his obsession with weeds and trimming and the almighty grass."

"I guess it's really important that we talk about these people now," she says. "Jesus."

"I'm telling you something you need to hear," Kenneth says. "Goddammit."

"I don't want to hear it now," she says. "I've been listening to talk all day. I'm tired of talk."

And Kenneth is shouting at her. "I'll just say this and then I'll shut up for the rest of the goddam year if that's what you want!"

She says nothing.

"I'm telling you about these people. The man was walking around with a little plastic baggie on one hand, picking up the dog's droppings. Okay? And his wife was trimming one of the shrubs. She was trimming one of the shrubs and I thought for a second I could feel what she was thinking. There wasn't anything in her face, but I was so *smart*, like we are, you know, Shannon. I was so smart about it that I knew what she was thinking. I was so *perceptive* about these people we don't even know. These people we're too snobbish to speak to."

"You're the one who makes fun of them," Shannon says.

"Let me finish," he says. "I saw the guy's wife look at him from the other side of the yard, and it was like I could hear the words in her mind: 'My God, he's picking up the dog droppings again. I can't stand it another minute.' You know? But that *wasn't* what she was thinking. Because she walked over in a little while and helped him—actually pointed out a couple of places he'd missed, for God's sake. And then the two of them walked into their house arm in arm with their dog droppings. You see what I'm saying, Shannon? That woman was looking at him with love. She didn't see what I saw—there wasn't any criticism in it."

"I'm not criticizing anyone," his wife tells him. "I'm tired. I need to go home and get some sleep."

"But you *were* criticizing," he says, pulling back out into traffic. "Everything you did was a criticism. Don't you think it shows? You didn't even try to stifle any of it."

"Who's doing the criticizing now?" she says. "Are you the only one who gets to be a critic?"

He turns down the city street that leads home. He's looking at the lights going off in the shining, rainy distances. Beside him, his pregnant wife sits crying. There's not much traffic, but he seems to be traveling at just the speed to arrive at each intersection when the light turns red. At one light they sit for what seems an unusually long time, and she sniffles. And quite abruptly he feels wrong; he thinks of her in the bad days of her growing up and feels sorry for her. "Okay," he says. "Look, I'm sorry."

"Just let's be quiet," she says. "Can we just be quiet? God, if I could just not have the sound of *talk* for a while.'

The car idles roughly, and the light doesn't change. He looks at the green one two blocks away and discovers in himself the feeling that some momentous outcome hinges on that light staying green long enough for him to get through it. With a weird pressure behind his eyes, everything shifts toward some inner region of rage and chance and fright: it's as if his whole life, his happiness, depends on getting through that signal before it, too, turns red. He taps his palm on the steering wheel, guns the engine a little like a man at the starting line of a race.

"Honey," she says. "I didn't mean to hurt your feelings."

He doesn't answer. His own light turns green, and in the next instant he's got the pedal all the way to the floor. They go roaring through the intersection, the tires squealing, the back of the car fishtailing in the wetness. She's at his side, quiet, bracing in the seat, her hands out on the dash, and in the moment of knowing how badly afraid she is he feels strangely reconciled to her, at a kind of peace, speeding through the rain. He almost wishes something would happen, something final, watching the light ahead change to yellow, then to red. It's close, but he makes it through. He makes it through and then realizes she's crying, staring out, the tears streaming down her face. He slows the car, wondering at himself, holding onto the wheel with both hands, and at the next red light he comes to a slow stop. When he sees that her hands are now resting on her abdomen, he thinks of her pregnancy as if for the first time; it goes through him like a bad shock to his nerves. "Christ," he says, feeling sick. "I'm sorry."

The rain beats at the windows and makes gray, moving shadows on the inside of the car. He glances at her, then looks back at the road.

"Honey?" she says. The broken note in her voice almost makes him wince.

He says, "Don't, it's all right." He's sitting there looking through the twin half-circles of water the wipers make.

She sniffles again.

"Shannon," he says. "I didn't mean any of it." But his own voice sounds false to him, a note higher, somehow, and it dawns on him that he's hoarse from shouting. He thinks of the weekend mornings they've lain in bed, happy and warm, luxuriating in each other. It feels like something in the distant past to him. And then he remembers being awakened by the roar of the neighbor's power mower, the feeling of superiority he had entertained about such a man, someone obsessed with a lawn. He's thinking of the man now, that one whose wife sees whatever she sees when she looks at him, and perhaps she looks at him with love.

Shannon is trying to gain control of herself, sobbing and coughing. The light changes, but no one's behind him, and so he moves over in the seat and puts his arms around her. A strand of her hair tickles his jaw, a little discomfort he's faintly aware of. He sits very still, saying nothing, while in the corner of his vision the light turns yellow, then red again. She's holding on to him, and she seems to nestle slightly. When the light turns back to green, she gently pulls away from him.

"We better go," she says, wiping her eyes.

He sits straight, presses the accelerator pedal carefully, like a much older man. He wishes he were someone else, wishes something would change, and then is filled with a shivering sense of the meaning of such thoughts. He's driving on in the rain, and they are silent for a time. They're almost home.

"I'm just so tired," Shannon says finally.

"It's all right," he tells her.

"Sweet," she says.

The fight's over. They've made up. She reaches across and gives his forearm a little affectionate squeeze. He takes her hand and squeezes back. Then he has both hands on the wheel again. Their apartment house is in sight now, down the street to the left. He turns to look at her, his wife, here in the shadowed and watery light, and then he quickly looks back at the road. It comes to him like a kind of fright that in the little idle moment of his gaze some part of him was marking the unpleasant downturn of her mouth, the chiseled, too sharp curve of her jaw—the whole disheveled, vaguely tattered look of her—as though he were a stranger, someone unable to imagine what anyone, another man, other men, someone like himself, could see in her to love.

Letter to the lady of
the house

It's exactly twenty minutes to midnight, on this the eve of
my seventieth birthday, and I've decided to address you, for a
change, in writing—odd as that might seem. I'm perfectly
aware of how many years we've been together, even if I haven't
been very good about remembering to commemorate certain
dates, certain days of the year. I'm also perfectly aware of how
you're going to take the fact that I'm doing this at all, so late
at night, with everybody due to arrive tomorrow, and the
house still unready. I haven't spent almost five decades with
you without learning a few things about you that I can predict
and describe with some accuracy, though I admit that, as you
put it, lately we've been more like strangers than husband and
wife. Well, so if we are like strangers, perhaps there are some
things I can tell you that you won't have already figured out
about the way I feel.

Tonight, we had another one of those long, silent evenings
after an argument (remember?) over pepper. We had been
bickering all day, really, but at dinner I put pepper on my
potatoes and you said that about how I shouldn't have pepper
because it always upsets my stomach. I bothered to remark that
I used to eat chili peppers for breakfast and if I wanted to put
plain old ordinary black pepper on my potatoes, as I had been
doing for more than sixty years, that was my privilege. Writing
this now, it sounds far more testy than I meant it, but that
isn't really the point.

In any case, you chose to overlook my tone. You simply

said, "John, you were up all night the last time you had pepper with your dinner."

I said, "I was up all night because I ate chili peppers. Not black pepper, but chili peppers."

"A pepper is a pepper, isn't it?" you said. And then I started in on you. I got, as you call it, legal with you—pointing out that chili peppers are not black pepper—and from there we moved onto an evening of mutual disregard for each other that ended with your decision to go to bed early. The grandchildren will make you tired, and there's still the house to do; you had every reason to want to get some rest, and yet I felt that you were also making a point of getting yourself out of proximity with me, leaving me to my displeasure, with another ridiculous argument settling between us like a fog.

So, after you went to bed, I got out the whiskey and started pouring drinks, and I had every intention of putting myself into a stupor. It was almost my birthday, after all, and—forgive this, it's the way I felt at the time—you had nagged me into an argument and then gone off to bed; the day had ended as so many of our days end now, and I felt, well, entitled. I had a few drinks, without any appreciable effect (though you might well see this letter as evidence to the contrary), and then I decided to do something to shake you up. I would leave. I'd make a lot of noise going out the door; I'd take a walk around the neighborhood and make you wonder where I could be. Perhaps I'd go check into a motel for the night. The thought even crossed my mind that I might leave you altogether. I admit that I entertained the thought, Marie. I saw our life together now as the day-to-day round of petty quarreling and tension that it's mostly been over the past couple of years or so, and I wanted out as sincerely as I ever wanted anything.

My God, I wanted an end to it, and I got up from my seat in front of the television and walked back down the hall to the entrance of our room to look at you. I suppose I hoped you'd still be awake so I could tell you of this momentous decision I felt I'd reached. And maybe you were awake: one of our oldest areas of contention being the noise I make—the feather-thin membrane of your sleep that I am always disturbing with my restlessness in the nights. All right. Assuming you were asleep and don't know that I stood in the doorway of our room, I will say that I stood there for perhaps five minutes, looking at you in the half-dark, the shape of your body under the blanket— you really did look like one of the girls when they were little and I used to stand in the doorway of their rooms; your illness last year made you so small again—and, as I said, I thought I had decided to leave you, for your peace as well as mine. I know you have gone to sleep crying, Marie. I know you've felt sorry about things and wished we could find some way to stop irritating each other so much.

Well, of course I didn't go anywhere. I came back to this room and drank more of the whiskey and watched television. It was like all the other nights. The shows came on and ended, and the whiskey began to wear off. There was a little rain shower. I had a moment of the shock of knowing I was seventy. After the rain ended, I did go outside for a few minutes. I stood on the sidewalk and looked at the house. The kids, with their kids, were on the road somewhere between their homes and here. I walked up to the end of the block and back, and a pleasant breeze blew and shook the drops out of the trees. My stomach was bothering me some, and maybe it was the pepper I'd put on my potatoes. It could just as well have been the whiskey. Anyway, as I came back to the house, I began to have the eerie feeling that I had reached the last night of my life. There was this small discomfort in my stomach, and no other physical pang or pain, and I am used to the small ills and side effects of my way of eating and drinking; yet I felt the sense of the end of things more strongly than I can describe. When I stood in the entrance of our room and looked at you again, wondering if I would make it through to the morning, I suddenly found myself trying to think what I would say to you if indeed this *were* the last time I would ever be able to speak to you. And I began to know I would write you this letter.

At least words in a letter aren't blurred by tone of voice, by the old aggravating sound of me talking to you. I began with this and with the idea that, after months of thinking about it, I would at last try to say something to you that wasn't colored by our disaffections. What I have to tell you must be explained in a rather roundabout way.

I've been thinking about my cousin Louise and her husband. When he died and she stayed with us last summer, something brought back to me what is really only the memory of a moment; yet it reached me, that moment, across more than fifty years. As you know, Louise is nine years older than I, and more like an older sister than a cousin. I must have told you at one time or another that I spent some weeks with her, back in 1933, when she was first married. The memory I'm talking about comes from that time, and what I have decided I have to tell you comes from that memory.

Father had been dead four years. We were all used to the fact that times were hard and that there was no man in the house, though I suppose I filled that role in some titular way. In any case, when Mother became ill there was the problem of us, her children. Though I was the oldest, I wasn't old enough to stay in the house alone, or to nurse her, either. My grandfather came up with the solution—and everybody went along with it—that I would go to Louise's for a time, and the two girls would go to stay with Grandfather. You'll remember that people did pretty much what that old man wanted them to do.

So we closed up the house, and I got on a train to Virginia. I was a few weeks shy of fourteen years old. I remember that I was not able to believe that anything truly bad would come of Mother's pleurisy, and was consequently glad of the opportunity it afforded me to travel the hundred miles south to Charlottesville, where cousin Louise had moved with her new husband only a month earlier, after her wedding. Because *we* traveled so much at the beginning, you never got to really know Charles when he was young—in 1933 he was a very tall, imposing fellow, with bright red hair and a graceful way of moving that always made me think of athletics, contests of skill. He had worked at the Navy Yard in Washington, and had been laid off in the first months of Roosevelt's New Deal. Louise was teaching in a day school in Charlottesville so they could make ends meet, and Charles was spending most of his time looking for work and fixing up the house. I had only met Charles once or twice before the wedding, but already I admired him and wanted to emulate him. The prospect of spending time in his house, of perhaps going fishing with him in the small streams of central Virginia, was all I thought about on the way down. And I remember that we did go fishing one weekend, that I wound up spending a lot of time with Charles, helping to paint the house and to run water lines under it for indoor plumbing. Oh, I had time with Louise, too—listening to her read from the books she wanted me to be interested in, walking with her around Charlottesville in the evenings and looking at the city as it was then. Or sitting on her small porch and talking about the family, Mother's stubborn illness, the children Louise saw every day at school. But what I want to tell you has to do with the very first day I was there.

I know you think I use far too much energy thinking about and pining away for the past, and I therefore know that I'm taking a risk by talking about this ancient history, and by trying to make you see it. But this all has to do with you and me, my dear, and our late inability to find ourselves in the same room together without bitterness and pain.

That summer, 1933, was unusually warm in Virginia, and the heat, along with my impatience to arrive, made the train almost unbearable. I think it was just past noon when it pulled into the station at Charlottesville, with me hanging out one of the windows, looking for Louise or Charles. It was Charles who had come to meet me. He stood in a crisp-looking seersucker suit, with a straw boater cocked at just the angle you'd expect a young, newly married man to wear a straw boater, even in the middle of economic disaster. I waved at him and he waved back, and I might've jumped out the window if the train had slowed even a little more than it had before it stopped in the shade of the platform. I made my way out, carrying the cloth bag my grandfather had given me for the trip—Mother had said through her rheum that I looked like a carpetbagger—and when I stepped down to shake hands with Charles I noticed that what I thought was a new suit was tattered at the ends of the sleeves.

"Well," he said. "Young John."

I smiled at him. I was perceptive enough to see that his cheerfulness was not entirely effortless. He was a man out of work, after all, and so in spite of himself there was worry in his face, the slightest shadow in an otherwise glad and proud countenance. We walked through the station to the street, and on up the steep hill to the house, which was a small clapboard structure, a cottage, really, with a porch at the end of a short sidewalk lined with flowers—they were marigolds, I think—and here was Louise, coming out of the house, her arms already stretched wide to embrace me. "Lord," she said. "I swear you've grown since the wedding, John." Charles took my bag and went inside.

"Let me look at you, young man," Louise said.

I stood for inspection. And as she looked me over I saw that her hair was pulled back, that a few strands of it had come loose, that it was brilliantly auburn in the sun. I suppose I was a little in love with her. She was grown, and married now. She was a part of what seemed a great mystery to me, even as I was about to enter it, and of course you remember how that feels, Marie, when one is on the verge of things—nearly adult, nearly old enough to fall in love. I looked at Louise's happy, flushed face, and felt a deep ache as she ushered me into her house. I wanted so to be older.

Inside, Charles had poured lemonade for us and was sitting in the easy chair by the fireplace, already sipping his. Louise wanted to show me the house and the back yard—which she had tilled and turned into a small vegetable garden—but she must've sensed how thirsty I was, and so she asked me to sit down and have a cool drink before she showed me the upstairs. Now, of course, looking back on it, I remember that those rooms she was so anxious to show me were meager indeed.

They were not much bigger than closets, really, and the paint was faded and dull; the furniture she'd arranged so artfully was coming apart; the pictures she'd put on the walls were prints she'd cut out—magazine covers mostly—and the curtains over the windows were the same ones that had hung in her childhood bedroom for twenty years. ("Recognize these?" she said with a deprecating smile.) Of course, the quality of her pride had nothing to do with the fineness—or lack of it—in these things, but in the fact that they belonged to her, and that she was a married lady in her own house.

On this day in July, in 1933, she and Charles were waiting for the delivery of a fan they had scrounged enough money to buy from Sears, through the catalogue. There were things they would rather have been doing, especially in this heat, and especially with me there. Monticello wasn't far away, the university was within walking distance, and without too much expense one could ride a taxi to one of the lakes nearby. They had hoped that the fan would arrive before I did, but since it hadn't, and since neither Louise nor Charles was willing to leave the other alone while traipsing off with me that day, there wasn't anything to do but wait around for it. Louise had opened the windows and shut the shades, and we sat in her small living room and drank the lemondade, fanning ourselves with folded parts of Charles's morning newspaper. From time to time an anemic breath of air would move the shades slightly, but then everything grew still again. Louise sat on the arm of Charles's chair, and I sat on the sofa. We talked about pleurisy and, I think, about the fact that Thomas Jefferson had invented the dumbwaiter, how the plumbing at Monticello was at least a century ahead of its time. Charles remarked that it was the spirit of invention that would make a man's career in these days. "That's what I'm aiming for, to be inventive in a job. No matter what it winds up being."

When the lemonade ran out, Louise got up and went into the kitchen to make some more. Charles and I talked about taking a weekend to go fishing. He leaned back in his chair and put his hands behind his head, looking satisfied. In the kitchen, Louise was chipping ice for our glasses, and she began singing something low, for her own pleasure, a barely audible lilting, and Charles and I sat listening. It occurred to me that I was very happy. I had the sense that soon I would be embarked on my own life, as Charles was, and that an attractive woman like Louise would be there with me. Charles yawned and said, "God, listen to that. Doesn't Louise have the loveliest voice?"

And that's all I have from that day. I don't even know if the fan arrived later, and I have no clear memory of how we spent the rest of the afternoon and evening. I remember Louise singing a song, her husband leaning back in his chair, folding his hands behind his head, expressing his pleasure in his young wife's voice. I remember that I felt quite extraordinarily content just then. And that's all I remember.

But there are, of course, the things we both know: we know they moved to Colorado to be near Charles's parents; we know they never had any children; we know that Charles fell down a shaft at a construction site in the fall of 1957 and was hurt so badly that he never walked again. And I know that when she came to stay with us last summer she told me she'd learned to hate him, and not for what she'd had to help him do all those years. No, it started earlier and was deeper than that. She hadn't minded the care of him—the washing and feeding and all the numberless small tasks she had to perform each and every day, all day—she hadn't minded this. In fact, she thought there was something in her makeup that liked being needed so completely. The trouble was simply that whatever she had once loved in him she had stopped loving, and for many, many years before he died, she'd felt only suffocation when he was near enough to touch her, only irritation and anxiety when he spoke. She said all this, and then looked at me, her cousin, who had been fortunate enough to have children, and to be in love over time, and said, "John, how have you and Marie managed it?"

And what I wanted to tell you has to do with this fact—that while you and I had had one of our whispering arguments only moments before, I felt quite certain of the simple truth of the matter, which is that whatever our complications, we *have* managed to be in love over time.

"Louise," I said.

"People start out with such high hopes," she said, as if I wasn't there. She looked at me. "Don't they?"

"Yes," I said.

She seemed to consider this a moment. Then she said, "I wonder how it happens."

I said, "You ought to get some rest." Or something equally pointless and admonitory.

As she moved away from me, I had an image of Charles standing on the station platform in Charlottesville that summer, the straw boater set at its cocky angle. It was an image I would see most of the rest of that night, and on many another night since.

I can almost hear your voice as you point out that once again I've managed to dwell too long on the memory of something that's past and gone. The difference is that I'm not grieving over the past now. I'm merely reporting a memory, so that you might understand what I'm about to say to you.

The fact is, we aren't the people we were even then, just a year ago. I know that. As I know things have been slowly eroding between us for a very long time; we are a little tired of each other, and there are annoyances and old scars that won't be obliterated with a letter—even a long one written in the middle of the night in desperate sincerity, under the influence, admittedly, of a considerable portion of bourbon whiskey, but nevertheless with the best intention and hope: that you may know how, over the course of this night, I came to the end of needing an explanation for our difficulty. We have reached this—place. Everything we say seems rather aggravatingly mindless and automatic, like something one stranger might say to another in any of the thousand circumstances where strangers are thrown together for a time, and the silence begins to grow heavy on their minds, and someone has to say something. Darling, we go so long these days without having anything at all to do with each other, and the children are arriving tomorrow, and once more we'll be in the position of making all the gestures that give them back their parents as they think their parents are, and what I wanted to say to you, what came to me as I thought about Louise and Charles on that day so long ago, when they were young and so obviously glad of each other, and I looked at them and knew it and was happy—what came to me was that even the harsh things that happened to them, even the years of anger and silence, even the disappointment and the bitterness and the wanting not to be in the same room anymore, even all that must have been worth it for such loveliness. At least I am here, at seventy years old, hoping so. Tonight, I went back to our room again and stood gazing at you asleep, dreaming whatever you were dreaming, and I had a moment of thinking how we were always friends, too. Because what I wanted finally to say was that I remember well our own sweet times, our own old loveliness, and I would like to think that even if at the very beginning of our lives together I had somehow been shown that we would end up here, with this longing to be away from each other, this feeling of being trapped together, of being tied to each other in a way that makes us wish for other times, some other place—I would have known enough to accept it all freely for the chance at that love. And if I could, I would do it all again, Marie. All of it, even the sorrow. My sweet, my dear adversary. For everything that I remember.

Fairfax/Broad Run, Virginia
1987–90